Thank you for your recent purchase
of Destiny is Fates Truth.

Here are some other titles that will be
Coming out soon.

Starward Exodus Earth
The Adkins Strain
Sedonna's Legacy
Black Heart Emerald

Destiny Is Fates Truth
Copyright August 26th
2011

Author
Shannon Grosz

Doom And Gloom Publishing.
Reg. # 535987
ISBN 978-0-9887392-0-8

ACKNOWLEDGEMENTS

"I would like to make a special effort to acknowledge the efforts made by several friends of mine who helped me make this a better story by reading it as I wrote it."

Barb Murphy.......................Romance/Mystery
Brenda Mona..................Romance Reader
Jerry and Linda...............Western Readers

"And Harry Salgren who listened patiently on many occasions while I was learning how to use a laptop; even though he has no interest in computers.

"And a special note to Andrew Murphy who sold me his laptop allowing me to retire my Electric Typewriter, I would never have finished without it, many thanks."

Cover Background "The Crab Nebula," photo   courtesy   of   NASA's   Jet   Propulsion Laboratory
{ISBN 978-0-9887392-0-8}

Cast, Crew, Locations

Maria Kemp
Dorian female, Master Pilot
Lord Marshal
Unknown, Empire leader, Founder Dorus II.
Doug Hutchinson
Dorian, Command Master Pilot New Folden City
John Wilder
Dorian, Atlantis Comm Officer.
Whoari Silber
Dorian, Weapons Officer, Atlantis.
Josh Donovan
Dorian, Atlantis Captain #2.
Izzabella Daxis
Dorian, Engineer Grennich II, Test Pilot.
Angel Abbicus
Pixie, Prostitute, Princess, Diplomat.
Michael Desmond
Antillian, Courpa International Space Defense.
Andrew Geben
Tuatara, Engineer Datalis IV.
Apgar
Rellock, New Folden City Com Officer.
Gork
Gork, Stallag-24, Prisoner, soldier, Security.
Dondo Ozerek
Antillian, Security New Folden City.
Mundo Dyrayne
Dorian, Captain of the Prometheus.
Jazelle Tilden
Rellock, Prometheus Com Officer.
Betty Baker
Dorian, Registered Nurse, Atlantis.
Lazlo Reinquist
Zerian, Medical Officer, Atlantis.
Chief Argus
Rellock, Engineer Atlantis.
Nascian Largoza
Molan, Ikared Com Officer.
John Putin
Molan, Stellar Chartography, Navigation

Annish Tanguta
Remorian, Courpa Mining guild, Diplomat.
Jozah Knefsela
Rhea, Courpa Stallag Federation, Business.
Ryvac Delallo
Massasauga, Courpa Medical Guild.
Ezra Delallo
Massasauga, Courpa Medical Guild #2.
Sitzig Delallo
Massasauga, Courpa Medical Guild #3.
Mylee Sterum
Chuckwalla, Genoa Com Officer.
Regent Gurki
Pixie, Leader of Pixo-Linko, Diplomat.
Zak Rays
Dorian, Pilot, Atlantis #3.
Richard Haupt
Zebu, Weapons Officer Prometheus.
Luna Faulkner
Zebu, Captian Leviathon.
Thilack Blackthorne
Curassow, Com Officer Leviathon.
Miguel Gotz
Zebu, Weapons Officer Leviathon.
Sabastian Vogel
Andorian, Captain, Mastedon.
Chevon Auratto
Andorian, Com Officer, Mastedon.
Nordon Whelplay
Andorian, Weapons, Mastedon.
Cassio Wesson
Dorian, Engineering Chief.
Zaeda Merlot
Pixie, child (sprite) Pixo-Linko Com.

Cast and Crew and Locations

Ships

Prometheus   Galaxy class
Transporter/Explorer
Leviathon   Galaxy class
Transporter/Explorer
Mastedon   Galaxy class Explorer
Renegade I   Star Fighter/Attack class
Renegade II   Star Fighter/Attack class
2nd Generation.
Quagga   Council member Transport

Places

New Folden City   New Dorian Home
World
Datalis IV
        Science/Builder Planet
Grennich II   Colonial
Growth Planet
Stallag-24   Prison
Planet/Abandoned Mine
Stallag-21   Prison Planet
Satellite of Grennich
Genoa   Planet City of
Great Council.

Species Identifier

Dorian   Humanoid   IQ 115
Light Blue skin, Clear eyes, four fingers,
transparent hair, thin

Remoran   Reptile   IQ 150
Reptillian, narrow eyes, big jaws, powerful, sand
color, scales

Rellock   Arachnid   IQ 100
Exoskeleton, occular eyesight, furry, black, 1 meter
tall.

Antillian   Crustacian   IQ 1500
Warriors, tough, orangutan bodies, long arms,
orange color

Pixie   Fairy/sprite   IQ 500
Blue, 3-4 meters tall, large wings, long razor sharp
tail

Lord Marshal   Unknown   IQ Unknown
Pink humanoid. No information released.

Molans   Octopi   IQ 2000
Transparent, aquatic, multiple appendages,
excellent pilots

Zerians   Crustacians   IQ 1000
Exoskeleton, Medical experts,

Limpet   Mullusk   IQ 5
Clammy, fleshy, no structure

Bonito   Sailfish   IQ 500
Tuna fish, mackerel

Grenadier   Sailfish   IQ 200
Cod, long tapering tail, silver, electronics, fluid
systems.

Caiman   Allegator   IQ 200
Strong jaws, short legs, scaley, black, transport pilots

Gavial   Allegator   IQ 750
Command bio-dome, administration.

Chuckwalla   Monitor   IQ 2000
Large lizard, civilization builders, sociologists.

Momoch   Spined Lizard   IQ 190
Spiny head lizard, Geko, Communications.

Massasauga   Snake   IQ 800

Tuatara   Sail back lizard   IQ 2000
Three eyed reptile. Amphibian. Retail, Distribution.

Carageen   Sea Weed   IQ 1800
Purple sea weed, food source, organic Comm interface.

Laminara   Sea Weed   IQ 1800
Brown algae, Flute, tall, narrow, food source

Cassowary   Colored Bird   IQ 1800
Large, flightless bird, colorful. Entertainers.

Curassow   Large Bird   IQ 500
Turkey sized, sloped body, large eggs, Food source

Oryx   Horned Goat   IQ 800
Antelope, 1 meter tall.

Gork   Hairless bear   IQ 80
Hairless, large body, large arms, massive animal. Security.

Micaque   Pig tailed Monkey
Short, squat bodied, fat, slave labor.

CHAPTER 1

Inspirational, that's the best way to describe the view standing outside atop the bio-dome high above New Folden City. Mountains, rocks, sand, and dust is all anyone else might see. 17 cycle old Maria Kemp sees the ever changing atmosphere driven by the climate generators, the shifting wind driven sands of the barren landscape, and the ever advancing city far below.

Today is not without change either. Just this morning she was the first female ever to receive her Master Pilot Certification, the first in her squad to be honored, and by the Lord Marshal himself.

"What new challenges will come from this new certification?" She asks herself as she stares out across the distant mountains.

"Master Kemp, report to the flight deck!" Rings out a voice from inside her fitted space helmet, it's the voice of Command Master Pilot Doug Hutchinson. The first ever certified as a Master Pilot. She remains still, taking one last look over the mountains.

"Master Kemp! Did you hear me?" his voice stern.

"I'll be right there just as soon as I..."

"Right now Kemp!"

"En-route."

"What could be so all fired up important here? Nothing ever happens in port."

Talking to herself she gracefully turns and heads back towards the portal to the flight deck a half a kilometer away.

Each of the seventy bio-domes of the valley are fifteen kilometers across at the base and five kilometers high. At the apex is a huge exhaust port expelling quintals of carbon dioxide, they are creating the atmosphere outside. Nobody knows exactly who built them. The physical evidence proved they once held an advanced civilization. The "terra forming" process "as the Lord Marshal calls it" was believed to have been started centuries before the Dorian civilization arrived here.

Once the Lord Marshal took command the records were sealed. Reaching the portal she opened the small door as a hiss of atmosphere escaped. Once inside, looking down to the city far below, one could see it's much like home world. Large lakes with narrow river channels flowing into clover shaped forests. Smaller streams leading into grass covered valleys. At the center of the city is the main power system of the atmospheric generators. They reached from the floor to the apex. On the upper most platform is the flight deck. Amidst the controls of the generator is the office of the Flight Deck Commander. Reaching the office undetected, Maria sneaks past the office door and enters through a back door. Expecting some kind of emergency she quickly moves past the melee of other pilots awaiting the rotations orders. She steps into view.

"About time you got here. I was just going to call security and have you brought in."

"I was just looking over the mountains Commander Hutchinson."

"Still dreaming are you?"

"I like the mountains. They remind me of when I use to stand on the promenade and dream of piloting a fighter around them."

"Then this detail should perk up your duties. It's the reason I called."

"What is the big emergency?"

"There is a new bird in from the "works" Just arrived. I want you to take it out for an evaluation."

"A new fighter. When did it get here, I didn't see it come in, who brought it?" Excited, she looked out the deck window.

"Just a few minutes ago actually."

"Who brought it in? Can I go and see it?" She kept insisting.

"A younger pilot just brought it in, had you been here you might have seen it when it arrived."

"Does it have the new Multi-plane

9

directional units I've heard so much about?" her hands shaking in excitement.

"I imagine it does. I heard it has quantum intelligence."

"Are you sure you can get along with a ship like that?" asking sarcastically.

"Of course, why would you ask me that?" taunting him back.

"Your reputation for argumentativeness precedes you."

"I'm quite sure we will be able to get along just fine. As long as it knows who's in charge."

"Finally, something that might win an argument with you." he, taunted her.
It's no secret that Miss Kemp has a strong tendency to disagree with others, and a legendary stubborn streak to match.

"Command Master Pilot Hutchinson, it's a machine, not a male. We will be fine, can I go now?"

"Go! Get out of my command center before I give you kitchen duty, or something."

"Attention on Deck, All personnel"
The voice from nowhere; everywhere, it's the automated voice of the central computer. The central computer "Comm" controls everything from the flight markers of the city to the airlocks of the bio-dome. It was announcing the arrival of the Lord Marshal.

"Where is my newest fighter?" He blurted as he barged into the command center wearing a flight suit and holding a fitted space helmet.

"And where is that Master Pilot I awarded this morning?"

"Right here Lord Marshal!" Maria snaps to attention just behind him. He is a tad taller than she is. He has dark brown fur over his head. And pink skin. His eyes are small, much smaller than a Dorian, and his feet are covered with some kind of attire.

"I want to go for a ride." He commands Mr. Hutchinson.

"Of course Lord Marshal, And I have the pilot you need right here."

"Excellent." as he looks Maria up and down. She is standing there at attention. Her shapely body covered by a form fitting flight suit, her white, almost transparent hair lightly blowing in the atmosphere of the Flight Deck. Her clear eyes are larger than his. The Dorian civilization came from a much dimmer star.

"When would you like to go Lord Marshal?"

"How about right now, or would you require more practice?"

"I am ready Lord Marshal." She returned sharply. Looking oddly at his expression she couldn t help but wonder why he would require a pilot. He is a Master Pilot too. However, today is a special day for him too. Today he has chosen a new Master Pilot for a special mission.

Without another word the Lord Marshal and Master Maria Kemp proceed to the entrance to the flight deck. Before one can enter the flight deck they must pass through a system of sensors that check for biological abnormalities, hidden weapons, or anything that could endanger the flight deck. It has a new species identifier. The unit is under some scrutiny since it often mis-identifies some similar species.

Dorians, and some other species, don't like being mis-identified as Zerian. Maria steps through the identifier.

"Female, Dorian, No bio-organisms, Clear."
And the unit beeps as she passes through. She then steps aside to await the Lord Marshal to step through.

"Maybe what he actually is will be revealed by the species identifier. I'll be one of the few who actually know." she says to herself. She waits patiently. He just walks around the device and rejoins her. They walk towards the new Renegade II quietly hovering where it was left just moments before. The ship is a small planet to

11

planet fighter. Twin drive systems designed to
work in space and on planets which atmosphere
can accommodate flight. It has been given stronger
shields and the unique ability to evade both enemy,
and friendly tracking. Having not actually piloted a
Renegade II, Maria was beginning to have second
thoughts about her decision to pilot the Renegade
II for the Lord Marshal.
Her stubbornness, and enthusiasm got her into this,
her skills will have to get her out. He is, after all,
the Supreme Commander. If anything went wrong
there would be a lifetime of kitchen duty ahead.
But, she is a Master Pilot. Time to prove she
deserved the title.

"I am ready." She says to herself
confidently.

"Now I must tell you master, I'm a pretty
good pilot myself. I heard you, got the highest test
scores in the fleet."

"The first to get 100%." she boasted.

"First female to be honored too."

"I have been a pilot my whole life Lord
Marshal."

"Is it safe to assume that this test will go
off without any bumps then?" taunting her.

"It'll be so perfect you'll cry afterwards."
Confident in her skills she proceeds to the ship.

"Proof is in the piloting Miss Kemp." As
they approach the Renegade II the security chief
comes in from across the Flight Deck and greets
the Lord Marshal with a smile and a smart salute.

"Did you come all the way down here to
check out our newest Renegade II Lord Marshal?"
He asks politely.

"Not exactly chief, I came down here to
check out our newest master pilot."
Maria looks back to him with a curious eye. She
knew the Lord Marshal has been on New Folden
City for some reason. Nobody knew why. She has
seen him on the Flight Deck many times. He
seldom talks directly with anyone. Today he seems
unusually friendly. But, what does that have to do
with her?

CHAPTER 2

"What the hespa is that thing?" asked the Keeper of
the Stallag-24 prison. A 2000 inmate facility
etched out of a mined out planet; barren, lifeless.
        "It's a Pixie isn't it?" Hissed the guard
called "Smiley". A Miquake, a pig tailed monkey
with slumping shoulders on a squat body with
sagging hips and short stumpy legs.
        "What the hespa is it doing here?"
growled the Keeper in a thunderous voice.
        "It just came in on a unregistered transport
ship."
        "Where is its file?" He barked at smiley.
        "I dunno? Maybe didn't have one." He
shrugged.
        "More money for me then."
        "I was under the understanding that all
pixies were blue." scoffed Smiley.
        "I guess your, understanding, is incorrect,
as usual. He retorted. "Just one more intergalactic
pariah."
        "What should I do..."
        "Just put it in the animal cage with the
others, shouldn't be able to cause any trouble there,
unless animals have money too these days." His
loud cacophonic voice echoing in the corridor
brought chills to everyone.
        "Yes boss."
Grabbing our pixie by the left arm and wingtip he
tosses her into an 8x8 cell. The cold, damp
concrete floor was covered by a slippery film that
smelled like the entrails of a dunga beast. There is
no place in the cell for someone, anyone, to sit
down, only a small outcropping in the far of the
room, no portals, just a three sided room with
thick, rusty bars at the entrance. The door held by
small, rusted hinges.
        Throughout the galaxy pixie are
considered to be pariah; the filthy trash of the
galaxy, looked down upon by all society because of
their seductive dress and nature. They tend to draw

13

out the, aggressive, nature of females. Prostitution isn't illegal by any description. And is plenty welcome to the countless ship Captains and their crew

This Pixie is different though, she is Red. Standing seven feet tall floor to ear. Adding her wingtips makes her eleven feet tall. A fully grown Pixie is a sight to behold. Landing one between the sheets is very moving, and expensive.

"I hope you find your accommodations to my liking." jested Mr. Smiley with rancor in his harsh, worn voice. He slammed the iron door shut with a loud clash of metal to metal. After a few stitches in time she could hear the sound of the magnetic seal that held the door sealed. He turns to sluff down the dreary corridor. He glances back at her, laughing, mocking her.

"If you behave, I may even feed you today but, don't count on it!"

"Pixie may be pariah! But that doesn't mean we're not vengeful!" She shouts back at him with quick witted defiance. Looking around today's cage she thinks to herself.

"The first order of business should be getting on the good side of that droll guard Smiley. He has the keys and the door to escape."

"Did you put that thing where I told you to?" shouted the Keeper.

"Yes, I put it in the cell next to the "Gork."

"Did you clean it first?" grumbled the Keeper.

"No. I haven't cleaned it for several rotations, should be plenty putrid by now."

"Good. Keep it there for a few rotations, let it get used to the way things are run around here." both laughing.

"Boss, why did you take that pariah anyhow?" He croaked. "They are nothing but trouble."

"Since when do I answer to a toad like you?" barked the Keeper in his thunderous, deep voice; hardened by cycles of yelling over inmates.

"I'm just asking Boss; no intrusion intended." cowering back.

"Not that it concerns you, I know someone who just might be interested in a pariah like that one, been looking for one for quite a long time."

"I'll bet he will be willing to pay a lot of cubes for it. It is a female, isn't it?" He grumbled

"Yes Boss."

"How can you tell? Never mind, I don't want to know how a toad like you would know that."

"Should I be giving this one special treatment Boss?" asking dryly.

"No! Contact the Courpa on Grennich II. Tell him I have a special "Gift" for him."

"Should I tell him what it is Boss?" Smiley sauntered towards the com council.

"No, I do want you to go and feed it though. Make sure it has just enough strength to do its job." He barked as he turned back to his table.

"Yes Boss." Returning to her cell, Smiley brings down a tray of fruits from the nearby Grennich II colony.

"Here trash! The Keeper expects me to keep your strength up; I recommended against you being here, nothing but trouble follows your kind." grumbling at her.

"Aw, is the Keeper mean to you?" taunting him.

"I won't be. Are all those for me?" She asks seductively. "Or are we going to share them?"

"I recommended nothing! Don't try your seductive tricks on me Pariah; I'm on to your schemes."

"You should be nicer to me Mr. Whatever you are. What do you suppose will happen to you when I escape and send an Oryx here to kill everyone who is mean to me."

"Smiley, My name is Smiley. And nobody ever escapes from here, Nobody."
Setting the tray down with a metallic thud, he quickly exit's the slightly opened door.

15

"Maybe nobody has ever escaped before I got here. Once I get out I could, take you with me."

"Enough from you Pixie, there is no escape from here, for you, or me!"

"I see how poorly the Keeper treats you." placing her hand on his as he closes the door.

CHAPTER 3

"Well, are you going to keep me waiting all day?" Both smiling they sprint towards the Renegade II.

"After you pilot."

The pilot seating arrangement is horizontal not vertical as in most spacecraft. The controls are a redundant configuration for multiple species, not all species have arms or legs. The heads up displays is designed with multi-color view screens for those species that are color blind. The seating is a narrow, long thin platform. Not much need for movement within the pilot area as everything is in a hand, point location. The guidance system is a synaptic response system. As you take position, you are actually looking down not forward.

"Well Master, into position." a slight sexual undertone in his gesture, not to go un-noticed by Maria. Once in position the weapons officer is above, and behind the pilot. This configuration allows the pilot and the weapons user to have exactly the same viewpoint. While Maria is connecting the multitude of restraints the Lord Marshal waits alongside.

He can't help but notice that Maria is a beautiful Dorian female. Stubborn by reputation, but confidence and drive are evident in her personality.

"Initiate the launch sequence Pilot I do want to get off this planet for a while."

The ship quickly came to life. After some brief procedural com the Renegade II passed the airlocks of the bio-dome.

"Love the take-off." Maria exclaimed. "Did you have anything to do with the design of this ship?"

"I designed the basic outline of the hull, a few of the weapons systems."

"I heard that you designed the engines yourself." She added approvingly.

"I did, where did you hear that from?"

"There are rumors. I heard another rumor too."

"What is that? He asked "Please, do tell."

"That you designed a new star explorer."

"Now where is it that you heard that?" He questioned her surprised.

"Word gets around the flight deck." She returned candidly.

"I suppose since you are a Master Pilot now, I can trust you." He said carefully. "Yes, I did design a star explorer."

"Then for once the rumors are true." Maria sighed.

"Now I expect you to keep that information to yourself on the promise of a Master Pilot."

"Not a single word."

"Not one! Or you will spend the rest of your career as a quartermaster." He demanded.

"Is there any particular place you would like to go Lord Marshal?" She asked with her hand precariously perched on the drive mechanism. There is almost no where we couldn't go."

"How about just over there?" pointing to nowhere.

"Oh, you're a lot of help." She teases him. Not being able to see him behind and above her anyway. And with a flash of light the Renegade II is gone.

"Beep, Beep, Beep," A warning light begins to flash.

"Alright Pilot, now what have you done?" teasing her.

"It's just a warning light for leaving the system too quick. I should have been paying closer attention to our position."

"Yes we should have."

"It was my understanding that this ship is supposed to have been designed to not interfere with the solar system boundary markers. Perhaps they were unable to avoid it."

"What! Something the engineers couldn't do? Oh say it isn't so." sneering in the heads up display.

"We shouldn't be so far away from Dorius II anyway. This is a new ship after all. Who knows what might go wrong." adds Maria.

"I expect that nothing would go wrong, Master Pilot Kemp. So what do you recon we do now, Master?"

"I imagine we return to New Folden City and listen to Command Master Pilot Hutchinson lecture us on procedures again."
Right on cue, the com lights up and Command Master Pilot Hutchinson's voice rings out.

"I thought with two Master Pilots on that ship this test would go off without any screw-ups! I see that was a miscalculation. Now I have every proximity warning light in the south quadrant flashing. Every station com will be calling for an explanation."

"We were just, testing, Commander."

"Now I want to see you in my office"

"Do you suppose he's upset?" Maria asked as she deactivated the com link.

"Probably going to give you kitchen duty for a while, Hope you like Hazzukka."

"Give me kitchen duty! You said go this way."

"I have no time for kitchen duty. I am the Lord Marshal. The only time I see the kitchen is when I go there to get a Bavarian Hot Chocolate. Since we are in trouble anyhow, would you like to go on a little mission with me?"

"Mission, what kind of mission?" curiously looking over her shoulder as best as she could, considering the restraints.

"I have been trying to get to Datalis IV. Seems every time I try there is some kind of tragedy that requires my immediate attention. I can never get away."

"Datalis IV."

"Yes."

"Aye, aye sir." A smile crosses her face. "A real mission, about time." And in another flash the Renegade II disappeared.

"What the hell just happened!" shouted Command Master Pilot Hutchinson.

"I believe that Master Pilot Kemp just deactivated the com system Sir."

"That is not what I asked. Where did that ship disappear to?" pointing to the now blank view screen.

"I have no idea Sir, they just disappeared."

"Well, you had better find them or I will have a lot of explaining to do."

"Commander it has the latest in anti…"

"I don't care Mr. Apgar Just find them; when you do, get them back here!"

Near a rock called Datalis IV a flash of light comes from nowhere and the Renegade II enters a close orbit.

"Where is this place you wanted to go?" Maria checking her optics for any sign of a planet, sighs.

"You won't find this place on any map. It's just a big rock." pointing out the obvious.

"Which one?"

"We get any closer we'll hit it."

"That one!"

"Yes, welcome to the location of the most brilliant engineers the universe has to offer. Here is where they are building my new star explorer."

"Funny, I don't see any ship works." Maria looking around, "Is it sub-atomic?" She asks sarcastically.

"No"

"Isn't the commander going to be able to track us here?" She asks candidly.

"No, this ship has anti-tracking devices for good reason. And this is one of them."

"He is going to blame me for this." Maria exclaims.

"For what?"

"Us disappearing without clearance."

"I go where I want, and do what I want. I am the Lord Marshal."

"We are not exactly friends, you know he

is going to blame me."

"Don't get so excited Master Kemp, I don't answer to Command Master Hutchinson!"

"I do! And I've worked very hard to get my Masters."

"I said, don't worry about it."

"I was told you were argumentative. Besides, after this rotation a fighter may not be so interesting to you."

"Care to elaborate on that Sir."

"No."

Once again, the com lights up and Maria reconnects the voice module. Expecting the voice of Command Master Pilot Hutchinson she is surprised to hear a different voice.

"Identify yourself or be destroyed! This is highly restricted space on the order of the Lord Marshal himself!"

Picking up the com system the Lord Marshal begins to speak.

"Hello Mr. Geben. Lord Marshal here, requesting gate coordinates."

"Ridiculous, no coordinates are required! There is nothing here, now move along!"

"Mr. Geben! This is the Lord Marshal aboard the Renegade II in from New Folden City! I insist on seeing the progress on the new project I assigned to you. Now, activate the gate. I haven't the time for games."

"Well, Lord Marshal, voice recognition says it's you, been a long time since you were here last, thought maybe you had changed your mind."

"About what Mr. Geben."

"Building your…"

"Silence! I had to wait for my new pilot to finish her training."

"What!" Maria breaks in.

"Her training is all completed now. She's a Master Pilot."

"What?" Returns the voice from the comm. "Did you say her." questioned Mr. Geben.

"I did say her, good catch."

"Wait just one stitch!" interjects Maria.

"Who is this Mr. Geben, what has he got against female pilots! I happen to have received the highest scores in the fleet. Even higher than the Lord Mar…"

"And on that note!" the Lord Marshal interrupts her."

"After our latest and greatest escape, those scores may not mean so much."

"Well come on over Lord Marshal and we can discuss the impossible and semi-impossible technology you have expected me to incorporate into this project."

Assuming there should be docking ports somewhere Maria begins to scan the dust covered surface for a portal.

"What are you doing Master Kemp?" mocking her.

"There are no docking ports on that rock. Where are we supposed to land?"

"Behold the wonders of modern engineering." And like a pyramid, the massive doors begin to open as a small mountain peak begins to retract; exposing the interior of the rock. The inside appears to be just like the bio-domes of Dorius II, a large city in the center with platforms all around. The Renegade II settles on a platform just a few meters from where a tall, thin Tuatara is standing. A Tuatara is a large lizard with tough, sand colored skin, very intelligent. The hatch swings open and the Lord Marshal quickly frees himself of the restraints. He steps out onto the platform as Maria is releasing her restraints.

"Just you wait one stitch! Don't either of you go anywhere!" She jumps out of the Renegade II scrambling her way to where the two are standing.

"You tricked me!" She shouted to the Lord Marshal.

"Whatever do you mean?" He asked her chuckling.

"You tricked me into coming here just so you could tell me I'm your new pilot!"

"Not exactly." staring into her large, clear

eyes.

"I haven't told you yet." He chuckles aloud, looking at Mr. Geben who is also smiling.

"What!"

"Now Miss Kemp, I brought you here for a very good reason. Not just to get you into trouble with Commander Hutchinson. All will be revealed in time."

Stomping away from them Maria turns and glares at them.

"I am a fighter pilot, and I don't want to pilot a frigate! Now you have messed that up for me. You don't have to deal with Commander Hutchinson but I do."

"Argumentative, defiant, everything I heard is true." remarked Mr. Geben.

"Best pilot I have ever seen in a long time." whispered the Lord Marshal.

"Stop talking about me while I'm standing right here!" Maria blurted out. "Where is this ship, I want to see it."

"Her powers of observation must be a tad off today." remarked Mr. Geben. "Why don't you look right over there." pointing towards the city's center. Looking more intently, she begins to see what could only be described as weapons ports. Near the top center of the city, is a myriad of platforms heading in all directions.

"This isn't a rock is it?" She asks, spellbound, at the sheer size of it.

"I do believe her power of observation has returned." chided Mr. Geben. "Not only is it a ship Miss Kemp, It's the most powerful one ever conceived."

"What are you going to do with something like this?" Asked Maria concerned

"I have a mission to undertake, a very dangerous mission. I will need a very powerful ship and a dedicated Master Pilot to operate it. I will be entirely too busy to command, and pilot a ship."

"Any pilot could operate a frigate." scoffed Maria.

"If I wanted a spit and polished cadet, you are right. I want a pilot with instincts and an extra-ordinary sense of direction, among other skills. I want you Miss Kemp."

CHAPTER 4

In a Stallag, time seems to go more slowly. Despite her many attempts to seduce the guard called "Smiley" our Pixie is no closer to escape than when she arrived. The conditions in her cell remain revolting. The stagnant smell of bodily waste and other sanitation chemicals seem to cling to her like bad attire.

"It'll take at least a month to wash this smell off me." She scoffs. Down the hall she hears the ritual sounds of the other inmates. It's feeding time, the familiar clang of the metal doors, the whining of the other inmates, the swill they call breakfast is hardly worth waiting for. Nothing was good enough, at first. After so long, even bad food is better than no food.

"Today may be a good day to attempt escape."
After several long stitches Mr. Smiley reaches her door. It opens with the creek of rusted hinges.

"Good Morning Mr. Smiley." She says seductively Lying on the small outcropping leaning on her elbow, her dainty outfit barely covering her, feminine attributes.

"Don't try any of your seductive tricks on me dirty Pariah!" He grumbles.

"If I'm so dirty, why won't you allow me to bathe?" She snaps with contempt.

"Just be thankful the Keeper has uses for you. Or you'd get nothing." He grumbles with his harsh voice, harsh from cycles of yelling at, and over the other inmates kept in filth here. She imagines it's as much a prison for him as it is for her.

"Here is your swill." As he sets the heavy tray down on the corner of her perch he backs away, and out into the dank corridor. Closing the door he saunters down the foul corridor, returning to his endless details. Jests and insults coming from all the other inmates as he puts a tray under some doors, and enters others, This morning goes without incident, a quiet day or night. Very seldom does anyone attempt escape. She often wonders why. With each passing day escape seems further and further away. She has made a few attempts.

Each attempt has been met with a torrent of beatings and starvation, it seemed hopeless. Pixie may not be known for their strength, but determination is one thing she has plenty of. Like time and vengeance, her determination keeps her going. Her sense of time escaping her it's feeding time, another chance.

"Mr. Smiley," She says seductively batting her beautiful green eyes.

"What!" He barks in the same harsh, grumble.

"Will you please look at the bridge of my left wing, I can't see for sure, I think it's broken." She says pouting.

"So what's wrong with it?" He grumbles and moves over closer to her perch.

"It hurts me when I turn over at night." She mumbles.

"Even here I sometimes hear good news." He jests.

"Why should I care anyhow?"

"You wouldn't want me to be damaged since the Keeper has uses for me. You might get into trouble if I were damaged." Tilting her head to one side, she looks at him playfully and raises her left wing so he could inspect it.

"He can't rightfully sell damaged property."

Setting the tray down on the platform near her right hand he reaches up for her wing spike. With all the strength she can muster she grabs the tray and swings it over her head, all the food cascading into the wall behind. She strikes Mr. Smiley across the top of his head. She hits her intended mark with a quiet thump. Down to the floor goes Smiley, melting into a lump. Like a mina bird she is out the door and into the corridor, sprinting as fast as her legs could carry her. She passes the doors of the other inmates as some cheer, others taunt her. She

heads for the staircase leading towards the great
door at the top, her hearts racing as she reaches the
first step.

Her feet like lead bricks, her muscles
aching from starvation; that doesn't matter now,
only escape! With a head full of hope she forces
herself on further up the stairs, just a few more
steps.

Far below she can still hear the cheers
from those who encourage her success, and the
jests from those betting on her failure.

"Today is it! There it is!" She cried out.
The door above is actually open.

"Come on!" She says to herself. "You can
do it, just a few more steps!"
Her hearts racing with the first true visions of
freedom she has had in countless cycles.

SLAM!, There at the top, behind the door
is the Keeper standing triumphant as he looks
down at her.

"NO!" She screams as her hearts collapse,
followed quickly by her exhausted body she bursts
into tears.

"Another escape attempt huh Pixie!"
comes the thunderous voice of the Keeper.

"I knew you couldn't be trusted. I left that
door open just to prove the point. Smiley!" He
roars like a clap of thunder. "Get back up here you
worthless kype! Take that thing and put it in the
cement bunker at the end of the west corridor!
Perhaps a few rotations alone in the dark will teach
it some respect!"
Slowly Smiley comes up the stairs rubbing the
growing welt on his head.

"That'll teach you to trust a Pixie!" He
roars out loud as he opens the door, enters it, and
slams it closed again. Once again Smiley grabbed
her by her wing and for what seemed an eternity
dragged her kicking and fighting to the cell in the
west corridor. He threw her into the cell, this one
just as nasty as the others, no lights, a solid door,
no way for light to get in, or her to get out.

"What have I done to myself now?"

Sobbing alone in the dark, no food, no water; how is that different than any other day? No more taunts from the other inmates. Just silence.

"Perhaps sleep will come easier here, fewer of his, interrogations." Maybe someone else, encouraged by her escape attempts will kill that kype Smiley. Maybe someone else will bring her food. Someone she can seduce.

Weeks go by. There is nothing but the occasional "guest" of the Keeper for "Interrogations" to give her any sense of time. Soon it becomes difficult just to get enough strength to get up. Even harder to eat the swill they call food.

"Keeper!" shouts Smiley from across the room.

"What you want, I'm busy!"

"I just got a report that there is a Renegade fighter that just appeared in this area!"

"So, what about it? There are a lot of Renegades in this area."

"This one has no identification code, and a previous report stated that the Lord Marshal and some new pilot are reported missing, in a new ship."

"Is it coming here?" asked the Keeper, moving over to the com desk.

"You said that if anything approached that rock I should tell you."

"I did say that didn't I, about time you did something right around here. If it is the Lord Marshal, send a com to him. Tell him I might have something he has been looking for. And go down to that Pixie cell and make sure it isn't damaged!"

CHAPTER 5

"You said something about a mission." Maria interjected, still angry about her recent involuntary abduction.

"I think I should be able to know what's going on."

"I'd love to tell you all about it…Later."

"Later!" Maria snaps back.

"I will tell you later Miss Kemp, now just calm down!" He reassured her.

"I don't want to hear about it later I want to know…"

"Later Miss Kemp, now I have been tolerating your outbursts for my own reasons, remember who you are talking to, now I said calm down!"

"Mr. Geben, how has my ship been progressing?" As the three of them walk towards the entrance to the structure,

"Who all knows about this ship?" asks Maria curious, more than angry.

"Very few indeed, replied Mr. Geben. The purpose and mission of this ship could very easily be taken out of context if it were discovered too early, shall we make our way inside." pointing to the unnoticeable doors just in front of them.

"The ship is very near completion, however, I must protest. Some of the more detailed systems you have asked for are more difficult than previously anticipated. I do believe we are making excellent progress on the most important systems."

"Are all the dimensions what I asked for? I was very specific about hull and shield strength, remember?" stated the Lord Marshal.

"If I am to go into the most inhospitable regions of space I had better have impregnable shields."

"Just where do you plan to go with this ship?" asked Maria, hoping to get a glimpse of his plan.

"I plan to go where no ship has ever returned from, the most empty place in space."

"You mean the Kulnari System don't you?" Maria shuddered at the idea.

"Everything that has entered there has never returned. Never to be seen or heard from again."

"Five different ships have entered there, none have returned." exclaimed Mr. Geben.

"That is suicide! Why enter there?" Maria asked surprised.

"Because I believe there is something in there that doesn't want to be found. And I want to know what it is." replied the Lord Marshal smugly.

"But there are no stars there to navigate with." Claims Maria.

"How do you know that if you've never been there?" asked Mr. Geben.

"No sensor drone or optics has ever been able to send any information out of there. It's just empty space." Maria continued to argue.

"Yet it is still there, a measurable object in space. It has depth, width, and mass. Therefore, it exists."

"Nearly 300,000 light years across, once you enter you nnneeevvvveeerrr rrrreeeetttuuuurrrrnnn." The Lord Marshal giving Maria a slight nudge with his elbow stands there laughing.

"Or, once you enter you don't want to return." interjects Mr. Geben.

"Mr. Geben, I am going to need specialists from every type of science there is. And this is exactly why I need you Miss Kemp." looking at Maria with a determined look.

"Why me?"

"Why do you think I created the Master Pilot program in the first place? To be a Master Pilot Certificate holder doesn't make you a better pilot. It just tells me who the best is."

"Navigation will be impossible in there." Maria states her hands on her hips. "No matter who you are, or how good I might be."

"As far as you know Master Kemp." claimed Mr. Geben.

"Instrumentation will not work." She says sarcastically.

"How do you know, are you a limpet?" Mr. Geben asks, cold as a void.
Maria glaring at him, and then the Lord Marshal, her fists clenched, her lips pursed.

"I am no Limpet!" Her eyes focused like a hawk on Mr. Geben.

"Oh calm down Miss Kemp. He's a scientist not a fighter." the Lord Marshal stepping between them.

"Then he should be more careful who he insults!" Demands Maria.

"And on that subject I will also need some strong security personnel; ones not loyal to the empire, yet loyal to me."

"Have you considered the Stallag-24 Station?" asked Mr. Geben.

"Now I know you're all crazy." Maria rolling her eyes at both of them crosses her arms and laughs.

"Where else would I be able to find soldiers not loyal to the empire?" asked the Lord Marshal candidly.

"Have you already forgotten Lord Marshal, You are the Empire! Everyone knows you created the empire. Finding someone who doesn't know who you are may prove to be difficult. I can't believe I am hearing this." Maria stated, her hands still perched on her hips in disbelief.

CHAPTER 6

Restless, our young Pixie tries to sleep;
despite the cold, hard, unclean rock she is forced to
sleep on, it is uncomfortable for any creature,
especially for ones with massive wings behind
them. Semi-conscious she hears the familiarity of
keys entering the lock.

"Now what could this be, maybe some
food?" Sitting up in the darkness she is struck over
the head, it is Smiley.

"Now we are even Pixie Filth!" He shouts
at her.

"I have a job for you today!" As he dumps
a pail of water over her head soaking her, dainty,
attire she grins.

"Get yourself cleaned up! Do this job
well, and maybe I will turn the lights on once, or
twice." He grumbles as he walks out the door into
the corridor. And in comes the Keeper.

"I have a gift for you today, a very special
guest." His voice thundering

"What do you have in mind?" She asks
still stunned from the water bucket.

"Just do what you do best. I will see what
I can do for you later." He thunders as he heads for
the doorway.

"Am I supposed to perform for you after
sleeping on that rock?" She barks after him.
Instinctively she suspects   that she is supposed to
perform for him, or one of his wealthy clients,
Pixie are very expensive.

"How am I expected to perform for you
after sleeping on that rock?" asking again.

"Not for me space trash! Now just come
along quietly." his thunderous voice no less torrid.
Relieved that she wouldn't have to perform for him
she followed. She had no intentions of giving him
any favors. Once in binders she was escorted to a
small room several floors up from where she was.

The room was larger and it has a soft, hair
like surface.

The lighting was a series of long, thin, pencil like fixtures, they were unusually bright, natural for someone who has been in the dark for several rotations. There were no windows to escape from and the room was unusually warm.   There was a large single bed in the furthest corner. Making her way over to it she climbed on it and turned around. The Keeper slammed the door shut with a muffled thud. The bedding felt strange at first; Soft, thick like a Rhea. Wrapping herself in the warm blankets she again has thoughts of freedom, visions of flying across the valley Of Pixo-Linko.

The door swings open. Believing she is to perform for this individual, she begins a sultry dance routine on the bed. She climbs off, gazing to the doorway as the individual approaches. As the, guest, reaches her she begins by twirling around. He begins with a hard vicious right cross sending her reeling to the ground. He viciously grabbed her by her wings and began to pull on it like it was detachable.

He continued to throw her across the room kicking her in her sides as soon as she was able to recover. As she cried out He would strike her across her face again. He never tried to rape her.

He never showed any sexual interest in her at all, he just kept beating her. Finally throwing her to the ground he stood over her, spat on her, and while looking down on his accomplishment from his position over her, he spoke.

"Money well spent!" and left the room slamming the heavy door. She picked herself up off the floor and went back to the bed and wrapped herself into the blankets.

"If they are going to kill me, let it be here."
Without any warning the door burst open destroying the hinges. It was the Keeper, and he was furious.

"What the hell happened in here?"

33

Roaring. "I said do your best not kill the bastard!"
Unwrapping herself enough to see what he was
talking about she peered out.

"I didn't do anything, not anything at all!
He just came in here and started beating on me! Is
this your idea of a gift?"

"Don't get smart with me Pariah, or I may
beat you myself."

"Don't do me any favors!" She said
defiantly as he raised his hand to strike her. She
stretched herself upwards, dropping the blanket
that covered her blood covered face.

"Hey! What happened to your face?" He
said, suddenly compassionate.

"I told you I didn't do anything. He just
came in here and started to beat on me." giving him
a slight sob and a childish pout.

"He was the Courpa of a large colony near
here." The Keeper said quietly as he sat on the
edge of the bed.

"Now an investigation will have to be
conducted. I will lose a lot of good customers
because of you." He replied, almost
compassionately.

"Smiley said you would bring trouble
with you."

"It wasn't my fault! What happened to
him anyway?"

"I dunno, I heard a ruckus, came here, and
he was lying here dead. I assumed you killed him. I
don't know why I don't kill you and save myself
the mess."

"Kill me and save me the mess you
mean."

"Blame this all on you that would be
impossible, back to your cell!"
His regular self, back to normal.

"All deals are off!"
He grabs her and pushes her back down the well-
lighted corridor into his office. He opens the huge
door leading down those awful stairs to the prison
cells. Through the big door stands Smiley. There to
greet her with a smile of satisfaction on his face,

34

almost like he had something to do with her interrogations, today.

"Back to her cell, no lights, no food, no water!" Shouted the Keeper

"Maybe one of these times one of his friends will kill me." A strategy she had never considered before. Only time will tell what the next trick will be at her door. She lumbers towards the platform by the wall. Does she dare to dream, or have they discovered a way to invade her thoughts of escape too.

"Boss, report to the control room immediately!" comes the voice of Smiley over the com system.

"What is it you Moron!" He roars out at his slave.

"The Empire is here!" He returns.

"Here it comes." The Keeper, looking towards the ceiling gives a muffled groan. The door bursts open as a crustacean life form enters the room. The Keeper is not a small creature. He is a "Gork" {a massive, hairless creature best described as a bear} Known for their fighting skills they are often used as prison Keepers because they love to fight, for any reason. But even they can't out fight a dozen Rellock soldiers. It was riot time.

As was expected, the battle raged on for half a rotation, one prisoner fighting another, staff fighting each other and prisoners. This is a good thing for our young Pixie, it keeps everyone out of her cell and could finally be the distraction she needs to escape. There was a rumor spreading around of the Empire coming. Maybe one of them will give her some food, maybe she could seduce one of them into letting her out. Now, can she just muster up enough strength to stand up again.

Outside her cell there sounds like a bad fight. She recognized the voice of the guard Smiley. He is finally getting what he deserves. Just as the commotion begins to lessen, she hears the sounds of keys jingling. Could it be the Empire? Is it someone bringing food? Or is it Smiley coming in for his own form of interrogations. Just as the door to her cell is opened, there is a loud BANG! Slowly the guard Smiley droops to the floor, the keys in his hands, some kind of fluid flowing from what used to be his chest.

"I guess I have a friend out there." She says quietly. A sadistic pleasure in her mind as Smiley dies in her doorway. The door, it's open! But, she hasn't the strength to go through it. To make an escape alone is one thing. Out there are many others who would like to see her killed. Better to stay here and let them kill each other. The body in the doorway is pulled out and the door closed. The riot escalates, she can hear their cries as they battle whatever is out there. She quietly lies back down on the platform. Letting her wings droop to the floor. Looking like she is already dead, won't draw any attention from the Relock soldiers.

CHAPTER 7

"Well Miss Kemp I supposed we will have to be heading back to the big city. I believe there is little more we can do here." replied the Lord Marshal.

"I assure you it will be completed on time Lord Marshal." The engineer said with reassured ness.

"I hope it will be." He looked back at him.

"I will probably lose my flight status when we return." exclaimed Maria. And, if Command Master Pilot Hutchinson wants to be rude, he could charge me with kidnapping the Lord Marshal."

"I said don't worry about Commander Hutchinson." reminded the Lord Marshal.
Once again it's back aboard the Renegade II. Once there, the ship is powered up and it's back into open space. At maximum velocity the trip back to Dorius II doesn't take very long.

"Approaching Dorian space." Maria says as she fumbles with various controls on her council.

"Do you suppose they are looking for us?" interjects Maria.

"I don't know, what does the com…"

"Renegade II, this is Command calling Renegade II, respond immediately!"

"You were saying." She laughs.

"New Folden City this is Renegade II, requesting permission to approach."

"Renegade II! Good to hear from you."

"Commander I have them!" The com officer shouts over his shoulder.

"Lots of trouble coming your way, sure you want to come back right now?" comes a soft, hushed, female voice from off in the distance.

"I have a lot of things to report when I get back!" proclaims Maria. "I would like to report an abduction to start with!" She demanded.

"Just who was the abductor, and who the abducted?" came the reply

"I was! And I'm not too happy about it either!" snapped Maria.

"I wouldn't take it personally." Replied the Lord Marshal

"I'm going to take it personally, you're crazy." She replied softly. "I suspect that Command Master Pilot Hutchinson had something to do with my abduction also."

"Opening bio-dome gates now." was the reply from the com unit. Approaching the Flight Deck there seems to be a crowd gathering.

"I wonder why they are all here?" She asked out loud.

"I imagine they are all here to see what Command Master Pilot Hutchinson is going to do to you for kidnapping the Lord Marshal." He chuckles. "And, you did just steal the most advanced fighter he has."

"And break every protocol there is for pre-flight testing. But, it's you who is responsible for that. I was just following orders." She replied. Once they set down, moving quickly towards them is CMP Hutchinson.

"Just where did you and that former, Master Pilot Kemp go? Do you know how many codes you violated with that little trip of yours?" His temper tested to its limits as he stands there infuriated. "I have half a mind to put both of you on kitchen duty for a full cycle! I had no idea what happened to you! One stitch you were there, the next, gone."

"Perfect test Master Kemp!" The Lord Marshal blurts out as he glares at him. Standing before the Commander with both arms in the air like a victory had been won.

"I thought the ship had exploded, or something worse."

"I assure you Mr. Hutchinson. We were in no danger."

"We had everything under complete control." Replied Maria confidently. "But thank you for your concern. I didn't think you cared."

"I don't care, junior pilot! I do care about

that ship! And the Lord Marshal. You will be lucky to pilot a recycle shuttle for the rest of this rotation!"

"Now you just hold on there Commander. There will be no such action taken against this pilot! I am responsible for her actions. She was just doing as I told her to do."

"We have protocols here for good reason! And a Master Pilot is expected to know and follow them." CMP Hutchinson repeats glaring at Miss Kemp.

"I know that Commander, Many of them were written by ME! Let's not forget. I am the Lord Marshal. I do what I want, when I want, for whatever reason I want. I do not answer to you, or anyone else!"

CMP Hutchinson was infuriated by the lack of discipline displayed for everyone to see but, he also knew the Lord Marshal was correct. Nobody in the Great Council had the authority or the power to challenge him. The Great Council itself owed its existence to the Lord Marshal. His whole species, owed their existence to the Lord Marshal. He himself was positioned by the Lord Marshal. Who was he, to question him.

The Commander often wondered why the Lord Marshal even stayed on New Folden City. Within the Empire there are much more lavish planets that would placate his every desire. And to add, what is his interest in this defiant Master Pilot Maria Kemp. It is a traceable fact that very few females have been given the opportunity to advance in the Empire. But, he has made many concessions as Maria Kemp moved up the ladder of success. Meanwhile, Master Pilot Kemp, feeling the pressure is off her now strolled over to where her Renegade I fighter had been positioned. It was not there, nowhere to be seen.

"I wonder where my ship ran off to." As she looks around the deck area for her class 1 Renegade. She made her way over to where a technician was working on another class 1 Renegade.

"Tech, do you know what happened to my Renegade that was always positioned here?" asking unusually polite.

"No!" replied the tech with a sharp burp. "And neither do you if you know what's good for you!"

"Is that right, who would, I ask then?" She asked curiously.

"Nobody else will know either, if they have any sense." He continued. "We are under strict orders not to talk about that Renegade, or its pilot. Now I have work to do Miss…"

"Kemp, Maria Kemp! And this was my Renegade if you didn't notice."

"Excuse me Master I..I have work to do!" And the technician scurried around a corner of a weapons room and was gone.

"Then I will just have to find out for myself." So Maria decided to return to her quarters to see what the Central Computer had to show, if her quarters were still there.

Returning to the Command room of the bio-dome the Lord Marshal got back to the question of security personnel.

"I wonder if that Stallag-24 station has any "Gork" in its population?" A "Gork" is a hairless bear {in comparison} they are known to fight just for the fun of it.

"If I were to, rescue a Gork from there, it would make a formidable body guard. Even Maria wouldn't argue with one of those." Chuckling out loud he approaches the com.

"Com officer Apgar, get me a link with the Stallag-24 Station, I need a report on the prison population there."

"Yes Sir."

Soon the Stallag-24 station was on-line.

'Stallag-24 Station this is the Lord Marshal from New Folden City I am looking for an inmate report. I am searching for a Gork. Do you have such a critter on the Inmate list?"

The reply form Stallag-24 was an automated response.

40

"Stallag-24 currently has two Gork, in this facility. Would you like a detailed listing on current population?" The com asked.

"No, just interested in the Gork."

"Lord Marshal, the Grennich II colony has issued a request for your presence on a matter of internal security. A response is requested."

"And the matter of interest?"

"The death of the colonial Courpa, resulting in the accusation and arrest of the former Keeper of the Stallag-24." And the message ended. The Courpa is a head of a large corporation. Their deaths usually result in a power struggle, often times involving several species.

"I was looking for an excuse to go to Stallag-24. This is a perfect reason to go there." He says to himself.

Reaching for the com he re-connects with the Stallag-24 facility.

"Good afternoon, this is the Stallag-24 automated response unit. Please state the nature of your call. The Keeper will get back to you as soon as he has the opportunity."

"This is the Lord Marshal! Pick up the com Keeper I haven't got time to wait on your extra dutorial activities during break." He demands. There is no response.

"Would you like to leave a message caller?" came the automated voice.

"Yes! Keeper, I will be there in half a rotation. Send me a report on the charges filed against you."

The Keeper is a well-known friend of the Lord Marshal. They have met on several occasions.

"I had better find Master Kemp and tell her we will be returning to Datalis IV a bit sooner than I had intended."

"Comm Apgar, locate Master Kemp and inform her to pack for a few rotations and return to the Flight Deck."

"Aye, Aye, Sir."

Sitting at her desk in her quarters Maria was just about to find out where her Renegade had run off to. Then the com indicator begins flashing and a voice comes across the speaker.

"Message from command, Message from command,"

"I heard you the first time, what's the message."

"Master Pilot Kemp; report to the flight deck at 1400, pack for 3 rotations, prepare the Renegade II for launch."

"Well, I recon dat clears up me flight status questions." She jumps up with a smile of success on her face and sprints out of the room. Returning to the flight deck there wasn't a word said as Maria and the Lord Marshal approach the bio-scanners. The result was the same. Maria scanned, the Lord Marshal just proceeded around the side. The automated voice of the central com could be heard over the flight deck issuing out routine protocols as they got to the Renegade II.

"What is going on?" Maria asks to break the silence.

"Never mind right now just get the ship ready."

CHAPTER 08

"Where are we going? Tell me or I'm not coming!"
She stops and stands at the edge of the Renegade
II, her helmet in her hands.

"Apparently there was a death of a Courpa
at the Stallag-24 just a while ago. I have been
asked to start an investigation. Since I have
business there anyway, I thought you should come
with me as a witness should I uncover anything
grossly illegal."

"Do you suspect more?" She asked
concerned. The Lord Marshal is secretive.

"I expect a lot more." They board the
Renegade II, and with no further notice they leave
the bio-dome and enter open space. No warning
lights or alarms go off this time as Maria is more
careful. They quickly engage the engines and are
en-route to Stallag-24.

"I want to stop at Datalis IV first."

"What for?"

"My ship."

"Are you expecting some kind of fight?"
Maria asked blankly.

"Once we arrive there I am sure there will
be dozens of resignations and new appointments as
they try to cover up their corruption."

"So why not do something about it?"
Maria asked.

"Because sometimes I go there myself."
Maria was speechless.

"Just what goes on on those planets?"
asking after getting her breath back.

"Oh, the usual, slave labor, medical
testing, cruelty, prostitution."

Owa! I don't think I want to know why
you go there!"

"Then you shouldn't be so quick to ask."

"I hear they are awful places, unregulated,
unsanitary, horrible cruelty."

"And this one is off the trade route which
doesn't help the inmate population any."

"I've even heard they sell the inmates into slavery."

"Better the life of a slave than death on a Stallag wouldn't you agree?"

"I wouldn't." Maria returns bluntly.

"This time it could work in my favor. I am looking for a Gork and there are two at the Stallag-24 facility."

"And you intend to buy one?" Maria sneering in the view screen heckles the Lord Marshal.

"No, rescue one. And any other inmate I might find useful."

"Approaching Datalis IV Lord Marshal."

"Lord Marshal, what brings you back here so soon?" asked Mr. Geben. "You were here just a half a rotation ago."

"I need my ship Mr. Geben."

"May I ask why?"

"NO!" interjects Maria sarcastically.

"I need the Atlantis Mr. Geben. I have pressing business with the Stallag-24 station and before it's all over I may need the Atlantis."

"It's not finished yet Lord Marshal. The Stellar chartography isn't downloaded, the transporter memory isn't connected, and we are still having trouble with the central "AI"."

"Will it fly Mr. Geben?"

"Well, flying is irrelevant, but yes."

"Excellent. Then get it ready for departure."

This new ship "Atlantis" is a very large ship. Built within an asteroid, it is 11,280 meters long, 2640 meters across, it has 22 decks, 6 hangar bays; for Renegade fighters and shuttle craft. The central hangar bay is 11 decks thick; it passes through the width of the ship. For a power source it has 4 directional Ion particle accelerators putting out 10th magnitude power. It also has the first coherent intelligence central computer. This type of computer is usually reserved for colonial ground systems like that of the Grennich II colony, or New Folden City.

The weapons systems consist of the largest particle disintegrator ever made. It destroys objects at the molecular level

It also has 10,000 sonic charges which emit a high frequency sound wave that will destroy anything it touches. One other item acquired from old documents of the Lord Marshals personal files is the Electromagnetic pulse weapon. It can disrupt the electronic fields of any machine functioning on electrical systems. The shields are classified above, everyone. Accept the Lord Marshal himself.

The hull is covered by alumo-ceramic high density plating. It can withstand tremendous heat and cold.

"I don't understand what all the hurry is. We have nowhere important to be and all the time we need to get there." Maria exclaims to the Lord Marshal.

"I have important business on Stallag-24." reminding her.

"Oh yes, your business with the Keeper." rolling her eyes at him.

"I am not particularly interested it the proceedings there. They will take care of themselves. I'm more interested in the inmates."

"Feeling a little frisky?"

"Watch it young one! It's the inmates who know the real story about what is going on down there."

"Are you planning to staff your new ship with inmates?" Maria asked with her sarcastic charm.

"No, but keep it up and I might find a cell there for you."

"Don't you think they might be a little dangerous, I mean they are prisoners, not exactly the type who will follow orders willingly, and they may not like you."

"You just leave all that to me. You just learn how to pilot your new ship."

"My new ship!"

"Yes, why do you think I waited on New Folden City for so long, the stunning scenery? I waited for you to get that certificate of yours."

"You said yourself a certificate doesn't make you a better pilot." She refuted.

"I didn't need the certificate, you did."

Once inside the main corridor of the ship Maria and the Lord Marshal begin to see what Mr. Geben was talking about. It is a work in progress; com panels lying all around the decks; technicians scurrying all around, seems confusing. But with all things, it can't always be neat. Many of the hallway accesses are passable. Moving around them they reach the elevator to the bridge.

"I guess it's a long way from the entrance to the bridge."

"I should think it's near the top of the ship and we entered in the middle."

"How many personnel will it take to operate it?" Maria asked looking around down the seemingly endless corridors.

"It will take quite a few to keep it functional. Most of the builders have returned to their home systems now." replied Mr. Geben. "I do have several of the engineers willing to devote their lives to keeping it operational."

"Still didn't answer the question." Maria scoffed as she continued to look down the endless elevator shafts still not completed.

"Around 2000 I should think." returned Mr. Geben.

"How much of the senior staff have arrived?" asked the Lord Marshal.

"The senior medical officer arrived two weeks ago just begging to be the senior medical officer. A Mr. Reinquist I believe is his name."

"Has he been doing bio-scans on all the crew?" asked the Lord Marshal.

"Yes."

"Are we going to need to get a bio-scan also?" asked Maria curtly.

"Yes." replied Mr. Geben.

"I see you will be getting that bio-scan after all Lord Marshal." Maria, still taunting him.

"Absolutely not; I will not have a bio-scan

done on me until I am dead, then you can scan me all you want!"

Finally reaching the command deck the doors swing open. Many of the control panels are still off, lying about the room. It is well lit and has tight woven mesh on the floor.

The center platform extends out towards the huge view screens. It is a tear shaped platform. All around the edges are the in flight control systems. Behind and slightly beneath are the seating arrangements for the different control systems. The command chair is at the end of the tear shaped platform. It is accustomed to fit the Lord Marshal. There are two other seats on either side of the command chair. There is wire and controls strewn all over the platform where the Lord Marshal is expected to Command.

"I expected the Command deck to be assembled by this time." Exclaimed the Lord Marshal as he inspected the progress.

Immediately a Dorian male rushes over to the three in the doorway.

"Good afternoon! I am Captain Joshua Donovan. You must be the Lord Marshal." He says with a respectful hip bow.

"And that would mean you are the lovely Master Pilot Maria Kemp. I've heard a lot about you Miss Kemp, nice to finally make your acquaintance."

"Lovely, really Captain, what else have you heard?" Maria smiles and steps forward grabbing Captain Donovan by the crook of his arm and leading him off to the pilot location.

"I was informed that you and the Lord Marshal wouldn't be here for two or more rotations. Was I mis-informed?"

"Get used to being mis-informed if you are going to work directly with the Lord Marshal." Maria whispers sarcastically.

"I assure you Lord Marshal we will have it operational in a short time."

"I need this ship operational as soon as it is possible Mr. Geben."

"Many of the less complex systems will be off-line." He continues.

"Once we get to the Stallag-24 Station we will have plenty of time to get the lesser systems functional."

"And what about the flight decks?" The Lord Marshal overheard Maria's enthusiasm over the noise of the technicians.

"Oh I must show you the flight deck configuration, I am most proud of it." returned Captain Donovan with equal enthusiasm. He is looking down, at her, as she exits the doorway of the bridge.

"Lord Marshal! I am going down to the flight deck with Captain Donovan." She informs him as he follows her out the door. The flight deck is the only thing, on a ship this large, that a Master Pilot would be interested in.

"Mr. Geben Please contact me when the ship is ready to launch. I am going to see if my quarters are what I expect them to be." After a long quiet stroll the Lord Marshal reaches his quarters.

A large door opens and he goes in. In the middle of the room near the farthest wall is a square bed frame covered by thick, heavy blankets; made of heavy materials from all the different civilizations of the Empire. There is a thick covering of matted material on the floor. Like the color of the trees on the old documents of his personal files; the walls are a golden hue with light red tone and a touch of amber. A few ornate lamps given from the fine works of the Datalis IV techs brighten the room.

Much of the ship is lit by smaller less bright lights. In his quarters he wanted brighter illumination. A small granite table sits near the bed frame. It has on it various fruit's from the nearby Grennich II colony.

"Knock- Knock."

"Come in" Replied the Lord Marshal, irritated about being disturbed so soon.

"The ship is ready to depart if all is well Lord Marshal." the messenger was a young Dorian who quickly departed after issuing the message. Leaving his home a tad, undiscovered, he headed back towards the bridge. Once there several of the com panels had been replaced. It was beginning to look the way he had expected it, clean, tidy. All the faces of the operators looking up at him he seated himself at the Command chair.

"I imagine most of these systems will need a monitor, is that right Mr. Geben?"

"The systems are automated, just someone there to make auditory reports and perform mechanical functions."

"Do you already have individuals chosen for these positions?" asked Mr. Geben.

"I have already filled several positions. Others will be filled as duty calls for them." Bursting in the doorway is Maria, followed closely by Captain Donovan.

"Sorry I'm late!" She exclaims, winded. "None of the locator maps are posted, I got lost." She replied, embarrassed.

"Didn't Mr. Donovan provide directions?" asked the Lord Marshal, leading.

"No! He just pointed out corners as I got to them." Looking at Captain Donovan with a guilty expression on his face, Maria is suddenly aware just why, he was behind her.

"Are we ready to go?" asked Maria as she took the pilot seat.

"Yes, and we are already two stitches late."

A small, subtle vibration goes through the flooring of the ship as the massive new drives are engaged. It makes a subtle humming sound; Audible, but not too annoying.

Looking out the view screen the massive doors of Datalis IV begin to retract collapsing in on itself as the four sides of a mountain fall away. The ship slowly begins to exit the structure. Maria is looking intently as the sides of the ship scarcely clear the doors.

"I didn't expect a sense of motion." replied the Lord Marshal.

"That's just the gravitational pull of Datalis IV. Once the shields have been activated you will feel, nothing." replied Mr. Donovan.

"Captain Donovan, get me the com of Stallag-24 right away."

"Yes Lord Marshal."

"I want to know what is going on there before I arrive. And tell him again I expect a full report on the charges against Him, and where is that inmate report I asked for?"

"I cannot seem to contact anyone on the prison planet Lord Marshal." States Mr. Wilder, The com officer.

"Was there an automated response?" asked the Lord Marshal.

"Nothing"

"Do you suppose the fighting has already started?" asked Maria.

"I imagine it has, right after my last communication there. We had better make sure those shields are operational."

"Shields are up and functional." replied Mr. Putin. The Atlantis weapons officer.

"Are the transporters operational?"

"The transporters are not functional at this time. However, the shuttle transporters are working." added Mr. Cassio Wesson, the ships chief engineer.

"We have reached the orbit of the Stallag-24 Station. Should we assume a high orbit?" asked Maria.

"Absolutely, I have no idea what to expect from there." replied Captain Donovan.

"I am going to the flight deck Captain. Get me a shuttle ready." commanded the Lord Marshal.

"Lord Marshal I wouldn't recommend going down there without an armed escort." demanded Maria.

"Dually noted"

As he exited the bridge he was met on the flight deck by a team of security officers. After boarding the shuttle the team was whisked away to the surface of Stallag-24

There was nobody at the entrance, and the main door of the facility was easily opened. So the team entered the main corridor and proceeded down the narrow hall to the Keepers office. Knocking proved no response. Kicking in the door the team discovers nothing there.

"Time to see the population." The Lord Marshal jumps towards the great door kicking it in with a thunderous boom. The door sails off its large, rusted hinges and crashes below in the courtyard of the main floor.

Down the staircase the whole of the population are fighting in the open concourse. Shouts, grunts, cries of pain can be heard all around the room. The place has a stench of death and sewage everywhere. Launching himself over the railing and landing on the previously dislocated door below; everyone looking in his direction as a thunderous crashes ring out in the room.

"What is the meaning of all this, who is the senior officer here, where is the Keeper of this facility!" roars the Lord Marshal over the cries of the inmates. He grabbed a small Zerian, who attempted to pass by him to escape another inmates grasp.

"Speak!"

"3ty 3v34yt39ut9bvbzjnvkliu 9r9r9u h98900- r rie-q-0rfjfaoa or o n, i8h88 8a8 hzjvzkj;onvn;l, ifjpoawiofa."

"Where is your translator device?" He roared out again.

"I am the Lord Marshal of the Galactic Empire, I demand that everyone cease and desist this activity and listen to me!"

"Lord what-ever of where-ever, you have no authority here! What makes you think you..." The Lord Marshal jumped off the door and grabbed the dissident by the remainder of his attire tearing it off. He grabs it by its throat and raises it off the floor.

"Now I said I want to know where the Keeper of this facility is or I will kill the whole lot of you, well!" No answer comes from the dissident. So he tosses one Zerian to the floor, and with no further warning thrusts his right arm strait through the abdomen of the dissident, spilling his internal organs onto the blood and waste covered floor.

"Now I asked, Where..is..the..Keeper?" Out of the corner of the courtyard comes a weak voice.

"I believe he was killed just moments ago in a brawl."

"Was it one of the staff, or an inmate that killed him?"

"Does it matter?" asked the inmate.

"Yes, it does to me."

"It was a brawl between management staff."

"So what are the rest of you fighting for, superiority?"

"No; food, water, supplies!"

"Inmate, I came here to find out who killed the Keeper and the Courpa. I am also here to find a "Gork" Have you seen one here?" He asked politely.

"Lord Marshal!" came a voice from the west side of the room. "There is a Gork in the last cell in this corridor!" answered the inmate. I wouldn't recommend letting him out."

"Why not inmate?" blurted out the Security Officer.

"If you let him out and don't put him back he will kill all of us. He has not received the best treatment, not that any of us have. The guard Smiley was particularly cruel to him, along with that Pariah next to him."

I'll take my chances. Now the rest of you should return to your cells. I may leave him out on purpose! Soon a new Keeper will be assigned and the lot of you will be punished more severely if you are discovered running amuck like this."

Heading down the west corridor expecting to see a huge monster of an animal he reaches the second to the last door. He instead spies something else. There is a trail of blood coming from the

doorway and leading back down the corridor. The doorway is partially opened. He cautiously walks to the doorframe. Reaches and swings the heavy, solid plated door open. He peers in. The room is dark. It smells awful. Fresh blood on the floor mixed with, whatever.
It smells horrid.

He reaches for where a light switch should be. Nothing. Using a small light source he brought with him he illuminates what appears to be a small platform at the back.

"What is that?" He moves the light up the small platform. There is a figure lying on the top. There, in the darkness, there is a frail looking creature lying on its side. Something that looks like, wings, extending to the floor.

He quickly moves over to the platform.
"It's a Pixie!"

"Captain!" shouting through his com device. "Get a medical team down here; and a maintenance team with some cutting tools!" Kneeling down precariously beside the platform holding the light he looks at a silhouette in the dark.

"What are you doing in a place like this?" He whispers to her. "You don't belong here."

"This is the Medical officer. May I be of some assistance to you?"

"This is the Lord Marshal I have two patients coming up. Be ready to give medical assistance to both!"

A few moments go by as the Lord Marshal waits for the Medical teams.

"Where do you need us Lord Marshal?" asks the tech first to arrive. A quick glance tells him it's a maintenance tech.

"Right next door is a Gork locked in its cell. Get it out!"

"Right away!" The tech scurries around to the doorway and begins cutting the door beside the cell. Again his attention turns towards the Pixie in the cell.

"Sure is beautiful, how could anything so

53

beautiful be kept in such horrid conditions?" asking himself out loud.

"She is a Pixie" comes the voice from behind him. "I've never seen a red one before."

"Neither has anyone else." Replied the Lord Marshal as he searches her with his small light. Gently he reaches under her, picking her up off the platform. Her head turns towards him, her beautiful, emerald green eyes; glassy from dehydration, she appears almost lifeless. She opens her mouth but nothing comes out. Glaring at him momentarily, her eyes filled with fear, and too weak to fight she collapses in his arms.

"Don't be afraid." He whispers in her ear. "I've been searching for you, never in my wildest dreams would I have imagined I would find you here. I will find out why you're here. Someone will pay for it dearly, I swear!"

"Lord Marshal, didn't you say you were here for this Gork?"

"Yes," Moving into view is a massive male Gork.

"Gork, I am the Lord Marshal of the Galactic Empire, I am here to get you out for an important mission, Interested?"

"What you want with Gork?" a harsh, dry, thunderous voice.

"Power, freedom, a good fight."

"Just get Gork out!"

"Pilot, three to return to Atlantis!" instructed the lead security guard.

Just moments later the shuttle is returning them directly to the medical deck landing platform. Entering the room the Lord Marshal rushes over to the far side of the room. The Medical Officer enters as he does.

"Put it here Lord Marshal, it's the best bio bed we have" Looking at his new patient the doctor glances at the Lord Marshal.

"She is in pretty rough shape Lord Marshal, I…"

"Ow, wow, her wingtips are sharp!" The Lord Marshal withdraws his fingers to see blood.

54

"Where did you find a Red Pixie?" he asked surprised.

"In one of the sealed prison cells I just came from."

"A Stallag prisoner, that can't be right. I've never heard of a red one before."

"Nobody has, accept in a legend." added the Lord Marshal.

"I don't know if I can help her she's in pretty rough shape. Had you found her a few rotations ago maybe…"

"I don't want to hear what you can't do, if you are so helpless maybe I need a better physician! I want a full work-up on this Gork also."

"And if he refuses?"

"Then I will send him back to the prison planet and put him back in the cell I found him in." looking at Gork with a stern expression.

"What about the Stallag-24 staff?" asked the doctor.

"Any more injuries coming?"

"No staff, all dead." Answered the Gork

"Marshal you said freedom, power, Gork like these things, no like Doctor!"

"Gork, you; like everyone else here, will have a full bio-scan done on you. I can't tell what to fix on you if I don't know what's broken. Now, Nurse Baker here is going to take care of you. Nurse Baker, Please take Gork here and get him a bio-scan, some appropriate attire, and feed him all he wants to eat."

"Gork not eat for a long time." Looking enthusiastically at Nurse Baker, he follows.

"We'll change that" stated Miss Baker.

"Now please come with me."

She looked him up and down as she leads him into the other room.

Once again the Lord Marshal turns his attention to the Pixie on the platform.

"I'm sorry Lord Marshal there isn't really much I can do for her, she is in need of a lot of rest, and time."

55

"Doctor, I have been looking for a Red Pixie for a very, long time. Now after she is finally here you are going to tell me that I have to watch her as she succumbs to her injuries when I have the most advanced medical department and the best Doctor in the Empire."

The Doctor reaches under the platform of the bio-bed and pulls out a small device.

"Doctor! I am not ignorant, this is for minor injuries." He scoffed.

"Seriously Lord Marshal, this is what you see, mostly a large number of smaller injuries. If you want to help her, this will."

Un-noticed, our Pixie opened her eyes to the bright, clean room. No bad smell, no sense of direction either, just a lot of little beings scurrying around in white uniforms.

"What is this place?" Thinking to herself.

"Have I finally died, and what is this creature kneeling so close to me?" She tries to get up.

"Oh no you don't." The Lord Marshal whispers softly holding her shoulder to the platform. "Now is not the time. don't be afraid, just rest here. I can't help you if you run off now can I." looking into her beautiful green eyes. "Just try to sleep for now, everything will be alright in time." Unable to free herself from the restraints she closes her eyes and waits to see what is going to happen to her now.

Meanwhile, in a small communications room out of hearing distance of the Great Council is Courpa Ryvac DeLallo. Sitting in front of him is the Communications Officer of the Courpa transport ship Ikared.

"Comm, get me a secure line to the Mastedon and Captain Vogel."

"Good morning Courpa DeLallo, is there something I can do for you?"

"The Lord Marshal has gone too far this time!" He shouts angrily into the com

"What is it this time?" grumbles Captain Vogel.

"He destroyed the Stallag-24 Station near Grennich II!"

"So."

"He did it without consultation or approval of the Great Council!"

"What concern is that of the Medical Guilds?"

"What concern! I personally have millions of cubes invested in that facility. Research, personnel, test equipment and test subjects! Who is he to destroy it?"

"The Lord Marshal."

"He has no right; I intend to make him accountable for the losses of the Stallag Federation, the Mining Guild, and the Medical Guild!"

"So what do you want from me?"

"I need to know if the three major corporations stand against the Lord Marshal, will the Mastedon, and you, stand with us?"

"It will be difficult to stand against both the Leviathon and the Prometheus."

"You suspect he will Command both of them?" Courpa DeLallo asked dryly.

"I imagine he will be on one of them, difficult to predict which."

"I have several Gavial ships ready to stand against him, and a legion of Rellock soldiers."

"You intend a war then."

"If it comes to that; yes."

"How do you plan to get him to listen to your terms?"

"I have operatives who inform me there is dissention within the command structure of his closest associates. I will find a suitable means of persuasion, from one of them."

"Which one?"

"I can't disclose the identity of my operatives. I can't tell you which."

"I'm not convinced! I've known the Lord Marshal my whole life."

"Don't you remember the occupation, when this Lord Marshal first took over the Dorian Civilization?"

"I was just a child when we left Dorius I, so were you."

"Who made him the Leader of Dorius II?"

"Everyone; He saved the Dorian civilization from extinction."

"Really, or is he the one who exploded the Star of Doria?"

"He didn't have that kind of power." Captain Vogel snaps sarcastically.

"How do you know? The recordings from the region were sealed as soon as he took control. I believe he created the disaster to enslave Dorius and establish himself as Lord Marshal."

"Where is your proof of these outlandish claims?" asked Captain Vogel suspiciously.

"In the sealed recordings."

"And you can get these recordings unsealed Mr. DeLallo?"

"Once the Lord Marshals true intentions are revealed, the Great Council will be forced to open the recordings to exonerate, their savior."

"And once this happens?"

"He will be removed!"

"You mean deposed, not removed."

"If it comes to that; yes."

"I will support you Courpa DeLallo, I will not, fire on either the Leviathon or the Prometheus unless they attack me first. I will not initiate a war on the empty hand of a Courpa."

"Once I make his true intentions clear, he will attack anyone who tries to inter fear with his power."

"Then war will come Courpa DeLallo, is that what you are after?"

"No, the Great Council is in control of the Empire now we don't need a dictator from a dead civilization to tell us how to live in peace."

"There is no proof the Lord Marshal came from this star system."

"Isn't it a convenience that he appeared from nowhere in space just in time to rescue the Dorian civilization?"

CHAPTER 09

It has never been said that Gork are patient creatures. And now is no exception as Nurse Baker comes scurrying around the corner of the room where Gork had just been taken.

"What is the problem here? The Lord Marshal told you to do a simple bio-scan and feed him." Nurse Baker rushing to his side for cover as Gork destroys the room.

"I only tried to get him to clean himself and he went ballistic!"

"Gork, get over here!" The Lord Marshal shouted after hearing all the commotion.

"I told you to go with Nurse Baker! She wouldn't hurt you even if she could, now you go with her and clean yourself and get some attire. I hope I didn't make a mistake getting you out of there."

"Gork not trust."

"I know, and I don't blame you for that. But, trust me."

"Ok, Gork behave. Gork sorry Baker, been in prison long time."

"Lord Marshal to the bridge." echoes a voice over the com system.

"I'll be right there." Taking one final look at his Pixie and placing down the scanner, he exit's the med deck.

"What is all this fuss about? We just got here."

"The colony on Grennich II is very concerned that nothing has been done about the murder of their Courpa. They feel that since the Lord Marshal is here, something should have been done already." replied Mr. Wilder.

"Captain, has a full investigation been started yet?"

"On-going Lord Marshal, many of the recordings were destroyed when the office got destroyed, the only reports we have are those from the colony."

"I imagine they are one sided reports. And what could they have witnessed or documented."

"It's quite evident that the colony disapproves of the Stallag facility being so close to its settlement."

"I thought the Stallag facilities were supposed to be far from colonial planets." asked Maria.

"Documentation of Dorius records shows that the Stallag Station was there before the colony." answered Mr. Wilder. It was later sold to the Stallag Foundation by the Mining Guild."

"Captain, start an investigation from the Mining Guild and colonial points of view. I will return to the Stallag and interview the inmates about what happened from their perspectives."

"Lord Marshal, you ask 2000 inmates what happened, you'll get 2000 different stories." replied Mr. Wilder.

"Yes, I know. So to get the truth, I will have to find all the common bits of information until I can piece it together with the reports you retrieve and see what really happened."

There was a time when the Lord Marshal would have looked forward to a good fight, and even enjoyed a good fabrication. However, the Keeper was a friend of his. Once back on the surface of Stallag-24 he went to each inmate and interviewed them for their interpretation of the scene. Mr. Wilder was right.

The only thing in common was they all held the same belief that the Pixie had killed the Courpa. All the evidence showed the Courpa was killed in the corridor. And the Pixie, in her current condition, couldn't harm anything. Furthermore, the Gork was confined in his cell by welded doors. It was impossible for him to kill anyone. After several long stitches of interrogations he was no closer to the truth than when he arrived.

Anxious to return to the Atlantis Med deck, he returns to the ship and promptly, runs into Maria.

"Well, how did the interrogations go?"

"As predictable as suspected."

"What is this rumor I hear of a Red Pixie you found?"

"No rumor. And you just mind your own business."

"You're not going to tell me about her then?"

"No! You shouldn't be so nosy. Now shoo..!"

Entering the Med lab he meanders over to the bio-bed where the Pixie is. She appears to be unconscious still. Leaning over her he whispers in her curled, pointed ear.

"I was on the planet again today. Many of the inmates blame you for the murder of the Courpa Some tried to blame it on Gork, I don't believe it for a second, the evidence proves otherwise. It's clear to me the murder happened outside your cell, not inside. And the Gorks' door was welded shut from the outside. More obvious, there is no way you could have hurt anything in your present condition. So, how are you feeling, Any better?" Never mind, you just try and rest."

"Oh good, you're here." The Doctor enters the room.
 "I have good news on your friends' progress."

"Really, do tell."

"She has remarkable recovery skills. Just this morning she had numerous cuts and abrasions, several bruises on her arms and wings, I can only see one now."

"Have the many just coalesced into one big bruise?"

"That may be but, is that the answer you were looking for?"

"Do you think she will be able to get up soon?"

"I think she should stay here for a while yet, at least for a rotation or so. She may not be able to fly around the room any time soon, time will tell."

"Is she dangerous to us Doctor?"

"I don't believe so. It does beg the

61

question, what are you intending to do with her once she recovers? She is quite large."

"I don't know just yet?" he answered truthfully. "Hadn't had time to think about it actually."

"She is a prisoner isn't she, why not put her in the brig? There should be big enough rooms for her there."

"I will not put her in another prison! Not for any reason. I don't believe she belonged in one in the first place. I will make room for her in my quarters. She is welcome with me."
The Lord Marshal speaking loud enough for her to hear, hoping she might make a gesture to indicate she was, listening.

"Lord Marshal, need I remind you, she is a prisoner. She has been tried and convicted of a crime somewhere."

"I can't believe she is dangerous. I won't."
Placing his hands under her, carefully this time, he raises her head. She starts to wake as she feels something, someone, lifting her off the long platform. Again she sees this small, pink faced, creature with its face so close to hers. To weak still to mount an effective attack she simply glares into his eyes.

"I wonder what this creature has planned for me?" She thinks to herself as she continues to gaze into his eyes. She notices their small, white, with a dark patch in the center.

"He must have come from a very bright world to have eyes so small." Thinking to think to herself. No sense in talking, it just gets her into more trouble. This is the second time he has come so close.

With a single swipe of her wing she could easily cut him in two. Perhaps the Keeper has "sold her" to this creature, to be a slave. To kill him would mean back to a Stallag cell, or worse.

"Doctor, is there nothing more you can do for her here?"

"No. All she really needs is sleep, and

some tender loving care."

"Then Doctor, I would like to take her to my quarters."

"Certainly, but do remember, you don't know her."

He picks her up off the platform and turns towards the door. Realizing she is too large for him to carry he places her on a longer, narrower, platform and exit's the Infirmary.

"This is the second time this creature has taken me somewhere. Should I try to escape, is escape possible? It is warm here and clean. I will let him shuffle me around for a while as long as it is this nice." She remains silent as they enter an elevator. Up and down more times than she can count and through several endless corridors; life forms unlike anything she had ever seen before criss-cross the corridor intersections, some even smaller than the pink one escorting her around.

They finally reach a large door, it opens and they go inside. There are few furnishings around. Quite, clean, with the fragrance of trees. Oh how she missed the aroma of trees.

"This is not the accommodations of a Keeper, not even of a Courpa, this, is something else. In the middle of the far wall of the large room is a square platform. It is covered by linen of many different colors and patterns. He moves her closer. Perhaps she knows what she is here for now. Once again he places his arms under her shoulders. She lifts slightly allowing him to reach across without poking him. Lifting her with little effort he places her on the bed. He reaches for the top of the bed and grabs a small roll of linen and gently raises her head placing the roll under her.

"I suggest you relax here and build your strength. If there is anything you need or would like, you only need ask. I know you are awake." Daring not to speak she opens her eyes and just looks at her captor. Her head comfortably resting on the softest thing she had been on since she was a sprite.

He moves away and grabs a small granite

table and brings it over and sets it down beside the bed.

"I have placed a few things here the Doctor said should be good for you. Please, take what you want." He sat down on the smallest chair she had ever seen. Despite her hunger and thirst, she lied there silent. Certain she hadn't the strength to fight off the attack she believed was inevitable. So to test a theory, she lets out a pathetic whimper, glancing at the tall glass and then back to her captor.

"I bet you haven't the strength to hold the glass do you? I will help you."

Reaching over the table and grabbing tall glass he picks up a narrow tube and places it into the glass. Cautiously he brings the glass over to her, she remains motionless.

"Is this a trick?" She asks herself. "Is he going to strike me the moment I reach for the glass?" Her thirst overpowering her need for self-preservation she again lets out a whimper. "If he had wanted to hurt me, he could have done so on numerous occasions." She opened her lips and he placed the tube inside. Her eyes locked on his like a vulture, she guzzles the smooth, delicious drink before he could viciously take it away from her. But, he didn't, he just smiled and replaced the empty glass.

"I can get you anything you want, all you need do is ask. You can talk, right? I know Pixie can talk. Are you still afraid of me? Not surprising considering where you came from. You no longer have to be afraid of anything. Nobody or nothing will be allowed to ever hurt you again I swear it. Now you just stay here and rest, I have a few things to attend to. I will be back later. I have more blankets in the alcove if you need them. Sweet dreams." Wriggling his arm and hand he leaves the room.

"Sweet dreams? And where are they supposed to come from?" She quickly reaches for the tray on the table and voraciously eats everything on the tray; before someone else comes in and takes it from her. The fruits are ripe and wonderful.

"Hum, warm, dry, comfortable, this is the best prison yet."

CHAPTER 10

"Now that she is taken care of its back to the problem of the Stallag-24."

Returning to the bridge he is met by Maria.

"Lord Marshal what are we going to do about this Stallag mess?"

"I have a good notion to blow it out of space. The problem is the morality of it. The prisoners are all life sentence inmates. Still, that doesn't make it alright just to kill them all."

"Considering the conditions there you would probably be doing them a favor."

"The conditions there are not the inmates fault. It's the Stallag Foundations responsibility."

"And isn't it your philosophy that all life has the right to be." asked Maria, as a reminder.

"Yes it is, there-in lies the dilemma. What to do with them."

"The staff are all dead, probably at the hands of the inmates, and the colonialists have made their objections clear. I'm afraid the end result will be the same." added Maria.

"And moving them to another facility wouldn't change anything if not make the problem worse on other facilities. I imagine in the long term it will be my decision on what to do with them."

"It's all a bunch of political hogwash as you would say." interjected Maria, chuckling.

"Captain Donovan!"

"Yes Lord Marshal." looking up from his console.

"Are the primary weapons of this ship functional yet?"

"Yes, should I have Mr. Putin power up the weapons?"

"That would be Mr. Silber's duty wouldn't it?"

"No, I just wanted to know. No matter what I decide to do with the inmates of Stallag-24, I must destroy that facility."

"Why?" asked Maria.

"Just to set a precedent to all the other Stallag Facilities that this kind of situation will no longer be tolerated."

"Why not send them to the colonial planet Grennich II?" Maria, seeing the stress in his expression suggests, "After all, the Stallag was here first."

"What exactly do you have in mind?"

"Relocate the inmates of Stallag-24 to the far side of Grennich II. From there they wouldn't be able to inter fear with the colony. If the colony did need assistance they could approach the prison population about a viable work force. The Stallag Foundation will, Of course, monitor the inmates while a new facility is constructed elsewhere. The Stallag Foundation would incur all expenses in retribution for the reprehensible conditions on this station. Perhaps in time the inmates could even earn their freedom through a solid work program."

"They would never be able to leave the planet." replied Captain Donovan.

"A better option than slavery or death isn't it?" asked Maria.

"The colonialists will object." added Mr. Wilder.

"What choice would they have, it's a workable suggestion." returned the Lord Marshal.

"And what about the ones who don't want to leave?" asked Mr. Putin.

"Who would want to stay in a place like that?" Remarked Maria surprised.

"Believe it or not it happens. Stay in one place too long and you might understand."

"When should I begin to see this happening?" a voice from behind them startles them.

"I suppose as soon as possible. Who knows if, or when a new Keeper will be assigned."

"I will get down to the transporter room and see that it's ready." Replied the Transporter officer as he scurried out the door and was gone.

"Is there anything I can do?" asked Maria.

"You could get with documentation and

make a document of the recommendations you just made. I believe it is the solution, may be useful to have it documented."

"I'll get right on it Lord Marshal."
Spouted Maria.

"I will help you." Captain Donovan, close behind her.

"I will return to my quarters and check on my guest. She might just find this interesting enough to talk to me." Hopeful, the Lord Marshal also spins on one heal and heads out the doorway. Meanwhile, the Atlantis just drifts in orbit of the Stallag Station.

Once again through the long corridors, more completed each time, he reaches his quarters. The door opens and he finds his Pixie sitting quietly in the middle of his bed. Blankets loosely wrapped around her midsection, holding the tray that previously had food on it in her right hand. Holding it tightly, like a weapon she glares at him with one focused eye.
Unconcerned, he looks back at her, his smile growing.

"What's the matter? Are you still, afraid of me? I see you ate the food I gave you. Good." Realizing the pointlessness of the light tray she tosses it into the corner. It hit's the wall with a thin metallic shudder. Meanwhile, still keeping her eye on the Lord Marshal, she smiles.

"Is there anything else you would like? No, well I have some interesting news to tell you. I would also like to take you to a demonstration if you're up to it."
The only response he gets is a curious smile. He begins to tell her what has recently come to pass. And, what his intentions are.

"So, once the Stallag-24 Station has been destroyed, there will never be another prison there again. I thought you might be interested in knowing that, maybe see it destroyed for yourself."
A nod of approval is a welcomed surprise. He holds out his hand to attempt to help her up. To his surprise, and delight she stands up on her own. Not

aware of her height, her wingtips penetrate the ceiling above.

She steps down off the bed before him, towering over him. A Pixie, a beautiful Pixie! Her wingtips piercing the ceiling; a framework of flexible bone, reaching from her shoulders above her head to the ceiling, gradually getting thinner as they reach their apex, perforates the ceiling.

Each wing is covered in a fine layer of skin; virtually transparent but, with the same light red hue of her lighter skin. Darker patches parallel along her sides and thighs as her wings flow down her back, all the way down to the floor. A thin, razor sharp tail following close behind topped by a thick mane of flaming red hair from her forehead to the tip of her tail completes the image. Her emerald green eyes; larger than his, teardrop shaped, are fixated on him. Her indescribable lips, deep, rich red color, her frame; thin in the middle, topped with large, full breasts, all held up on hips and legs accustomed to take-offs and landings, once.

"I knew you were beautiful the moment I saw you. I never imagined,..."
He stood there mesmerized by her, unable to finish his sentence. She kept her wings folded. Surely she knew she could slice him into pieces with just one stroke. She just stood there, looking down at him.

"Wow! Do..do.. you have a name?"
Turning her head from one side to another gesturing "no".

"Maybe I could be so bold as to pick one for you?" Cautiously hoping not to offend her for making such an arrogant assumption, one that she might accept one from him, he rattles off a few names.

"How about Madison, Madylin, no let me see, an angel like you,.."
She begins nodding her head in approval pointing her finger at him.

"Angel, you like Angel? Well, ok then I will call you Angel. Now the big question is, will you talk to me?" He asks hopeful. "Have I done, or said something to upset you so you won't talk to me? I know Pixie can talk." He turns to the kitchen and begins to walk away from her. She grabs his shoulder.

"I,,I,,Am a Pixie, a Pariah. Why are you being so nice to me?" She demands. "What do you want from me?"

"Well, full sentences, much better."

"I am a Pariah, the tralk of the Galaxy, am I a slave, did the Keeper "sell" me to you? Am I supposed to perform for you?" She asked angrily.

"No! Prostitution may be illegal in some systems but it is hardly a capital offense, certainly not enough to warrant a Stallag confinement, and definitely not in solitary confinement."

"I am different from the others, they fear me." She says reproaching herself.

"And for that they sent you to a Stallag, that's the most ridiculous thing I have ever heard!" angered by her claim.

"So I am to be your slave then." She asks again.

"There are no slaves on this ship, anyone can come and go as they wish. You are free to come and go also however, I do wish you would choose to stay with me of your own free will, I have been looking for you for a very, very, long time. I have had many dreams of you."

"Of me?" Looking at him, her head tilted to one side, curiously.

"Well; maybe not you specifically, but a Red Pixie anyhow, I have had dreams of a Red Pixie for centuries, and here you are. Although, I never imagined I'd find you in a Stallag. In a short while I will destroy that place. Nobody will ever be a prisoner there again."

"What about the others there?"

"They will be relocated on the Grennich II colony until another facility can be constructed."

"There are 23 other Stallag facilities in the Empire, are you going to destroy all of them?"

"No; but I will start a formal investigation into the conditions there, and if I find more like the ones here; yes I will destroy them, are you ready to destroy an old memory?" A smile crosses her face and they exit the door together.

"Attention everyone, I would like to introduce this Pixie, her name is Angel, of Pixo-Linko. She is here to witness the destruction of the Stallag-24 Facility that has held her illegally for so long."

"Hello Angel." the simultaneous greeting from everyone as she nods politely and the smile on her face grows.
Suddenly in breaks Maria, with Captain Donovan right behind.

"Sorry I'm…Good heavens, who is this?" Stumbling, she almost crashes into Angel.

"Had you and the Captain, been on time I already gave her introduction. But, for you late comers, this is Angel of Pixo-Linko."

"A pleasure to m,meet you Angel." replies Captain Donovan. As she pulls away from him, he retracts behind Maria.

"Hello. I am Master Pilot Maria Kemp." Maria says as she regains her footing. "Sorry I almost crashed into you. I was evading the Captain, we were racing."

"I understand evasion, a useful skill." Angel giggled.

"All systems are ready Captain. Just say the magic words." replied Mr. Silber.

"I believe the best way to forget a bad memory is to remove its effectiveness." Reaching down to show Angel which pressure pad activated the weapon.

"So, your name is Angel is it?" asked Captain Donovan.

"Everyone has been asking since you came aboard. But, nobody seemed to know."

"Never had a name before today." Angel responded quietly.

"Never had a name? How could that be?" He asked surprised.

"My parents never gave me one. They considered me an abomination and said I didn't deserve a name."

71

"Of all the insanity of civilization, now I know why they do parental screening!" said Captain Donovan.
"They should all have their names taken away, see how they like it."
Everyone nodding in agreement, Angel, looking over to the Lord Marshal pushed the button, and everyone watched as a planet Disappear.

CHAPTER 11

"Command Master Pilot Hutchinson there has been an alert on all long range communication lines! The Stallag-24 Station has just been annihilated!" The report came over the com system of New Folden City.

"What happened? Did the report say how it happened?"

"No Sir, just that there was a massive explosion near the Grennich II colony Where the Stallag-24 Prison is."

"You mean was."

"We don't know that yet." replied Master Pilot Hutchinson. "What about the inmate population. any word on them?"

"Transported to the surface of the Grennich II colony."

"So the inmates are safe then."

"Apparently, but the colony isn't too pleased. They are calling for a special session of the Great Council." reported Mr. Apgar.

"Why is that?" asked Master Pilot Hutchinson.

"The report states the planet was destroyed by an unidentified starship."

"A starship, what type?"

"Unidentified Sir."

"We had better get over there right away. Start recalling all the Renegade ships and send them to Grennich II right away."

"Aye, Aye, Commander."

"Where is that new Master Pilot Kemp?"

"Sir, I believe the Lord Marshal and Master Kemp haven't returned from their flight evaluation yet."

"What! They were here a couple of hours ago. I disciplined them myself."

"Perhaps they were here and then left again shortly after Sir."

"With what authorization?"

"I want those two brought back here the

Lord Marshal is going to need to hear about this."

"Shall I send out a search team for them Sir?"

"Yes absolutely."

Several ships were dispatched to begin looking for the Renegade II and its pilot. Search parameters were established just to see if they could track and untraceable ship. Getting more and more frustrated as time went by Command Master Pilot Hutchinson begins to suspect trouble.

"Any news from our missing Commander and that Rogue pilot yet Mr. Apgar?"

"No word yet Commander. Where do you suppose we should start looking?"

"I have no idea! Pick a spot and start looking!"

"Renegade I reporting in Sir" rings across the speakers.

"Go ahead Renegade have you found them?" He asks optimistic.

"No Sir, I do remember Master Pilot Kemp complaining about having to pack her bags for a couple rotations at the Lord Marshals order." Sitting back in his seat Command Master Pilot Hutchinson begins to recall a conversation he and the Lord Marshal had some time ago about the commission of another ship.

"That was nearly a cycle ago. Could the builders have completed another ship by now?" Asking himself "And why wasn't anyone informed? How come no surveillance equipment ever discovered it? So many questions, time to get some answers."

Picking up the com he calls the new Courpa of the

"Inter Planetary Defense Network." Mr. Michael Desmond. He is Antillian, a species from the farthest system in the Empire.

"Courpa Desmond, this is Command Master Pilot Hutchinson of New Folden City."

"How can I assist you today Commander?"

"Have you heard anything about the

74

recent destruction of the Stallag-24 Station near Grennich II today?"

"I have. In our latest report, the Facility was destroyed by an Empire ship using a particle weapon. I was unaware the Empire had such technology."

"Neither did I, are you sure it was an Empire ship?"

"Yes Commander, the ID confirmed its origins."

"Well then I guess I have a new ship to look for."

"A new ship?" asked Mr. Desmond.

"Captain, there is another alert coming across on all frequencies."

"Looks like news travels fast." replied Mr. Wilder.

"There are two ships en-route to this location, most likely sent from New Folden City courtesy of Command Master Pilot Hutchinson are we going to avoid them Lord Marshal?" asked Mr. Wilder.

"No, we are going to introduce this ship. I do believe it is time to put an end to all this corruption in these Stallag Stations."

"Oh my, what is that?" Asked Miss Jazelle Tilden, the Com officer of the Empire ship Prometheus.

"I believe it's a starship." answered Captain Mundo Dyrayne of the Prometheus. "I heard a rumor that the Lord Marshal had commissioned the building of a new ship about a cycle ago."

"Why haven't we heard anything about it until now?" asked Miss Tilden.

"Good question."

"Do you suppose the Lord Marshal destroyed the Stallag-24 Station with that new ship?" Appalled.

"If so, he sure has a lot of explaining to do, get me a Com with that new ship, if it's possible."

"Lord Marshal, there is a Com coming in

from the Prometheus. They want to know if it was us that destroyed the Stallag-24 Station."

"Isn't it obvious by now?" The Lord Marshal asked sarcastically. "Who's calling?"

"Captain Dyrayne."

"Very well, good afternoon Captain Dyrayne, is there something I can do for you this morning?"

"Lord Marshal, what is the meaning of this? I have been given an order by the Great Council to arrest you and your crew."

"Lower your weapons and prepare to be boarded."

"Captain Dyrayne, there is no way you are boarding this ship. So I would suggest you lower your weapons and increase the peace."

"I have my orders Lord Marshal."

"And I can super cede them."

"If you don't surrender your ship, and return to Dorius II, I have orders to bring you in by force, if necessary."

"Captain Dyrayne, I have tolerated these Stallag Stations for far too long. Often they have been useful resources even for me. But, the conditions on this station were far too obscene to describe. I will not allow it to continue. If you must fire on me Captain, rest assured, I will defend this ship and its crew."

Just as suddenly as the Prometheus arrived, the Leviathon appeared in the view screen

"Are the shields operational Captain Donovan?"

"Already activated Lord Marshal."

"Do you really think they will fire on us Lord Marshal?" asked Maria.

"Depends on who we angered, and Captain Dyrayne."

"Be ready with the Electro-magnetic pulse weapon Mr. Silber. If they do fire on us, that should make them re-think the idea."

"And what after that, you can't want to destroy their ships, our ships?"

"No, I don't want to destroy their ships; I

do want to instill into their heads the idea that I could."

"If we fire on them, we are committing treason!" barked Maria.

"And if they fire on me, they, are committing treason, I am the leader here!"

"Then we will be at war with the Empire." added Maria.

"I am the Empire!" roared the Lord Marshal. "I founded this Empire, I created the Great Council, I do whatever I believe is in the best interest of the Empire! I am not concerned with the gripes of a single colony or Corporation!"
"Nor a ship Captain who is just following orders of a corrupt Government."

Angel is standing next to the Lord Marshal with both eyes fixated on the view screen with a confused expression on her face.

"Why would the destruction of a Stallag create such a fuss?"

"For many cycles the Stallag Foundation has used the inmate population as a market place for slave labor, medical research, and prostitution. Many of those responsible for this action will lose millions of cubes once the facility is no longer a resource." answered Captain Donovan.

"I've seen enough!" Angel replies disgusted. "I don't want anything more to do with it." Turns, and heads through the short door; her wings getting caught by the top, violently ducking down exit's the door.

"I would escort you back to our quarters but, I do believe I have a busy time ahead of me."

"I know where it is!"

"Lord Marshal! The Prometheus is firing on us!"

"Very well, activate the EMP." He orders reluctantly.

"Shall I target the Leviathon too Lord Marshal?"

"If it fires on us; yes."
One by one the starships go dark as the EMP weapon disables them. The smaller Renegade I

ships are also disabled as they drift helpless in space.

"The ships won't remain disabled for long Mr. Silber."

"Suggestions?"

"Wait until they get their systems back on line. Then set course for Dorius II." answered the Lord Marshal. The weight of his decision heavy on his thoughts was evident on his face.

CHAPTER 12

Just moments after reaching Dorius II the Atlantis is met by a Armageddon of ships. Hundreds of smaller ships all aligned with the Mastedon to protect the planet. The com system lights up with dozens of incoming messages. Knowing full well the questions that are going to be asked, Mr. Wilder takes the one most likely to be the most friendly.

"Command Master Pilot Hutchinson, are you there?"

"You damb right I'm here! What the hespa do you think, who the hespa do you think you are! You destroyed a Stallag Facility in Dorian space! You had no authorization to do that! You have violated countless regulations and have angered a whole lot of very wealthy Corporations!"

"So." replied the Lord Marshal.

"I have orders to arrest you on sight and imprison all the officers who went along with you. And to add insult to injury you took my newest Master Pilot with you! Where is former, Master Pilot Kemp anyway?"

"I'm right here Commander!"

"That would be Command Master Pilot Hutchinson to you!"

"Commander Calm down!" replied the Lord Marshal.

"I will not calm down! Miss Kemp I hope you enjoyed your little stint as a pilot! Because it's all over now! I will see to it personally, that you never see another flight in your career!"

"That's enough Commander!" The Lord Marshal shouts. Master Pilot Kemp is not responsible for anything! I take full responsibility for the actions of the crew of this ship. I gave her direct orders and she followed them."

"And what about your actions today?"

"My actions were justified. And if you fire on my ship I will use every means at my disposal to protect myself."

"What are your intentions Lord Marshal?"

"I believe it is time for these Stallag Stations to be shut down."

"The destruction of the Stallag-24 Station will have to be answered for."

"I know, the answers are coming."

"Even though you are the Lord Marshal, it doesn't mean you can do whatever you want."

"That was not a prison, it was a torture facility. It was, at best, a slave shop run by criminals. I rescued a Pixie from there that should have never been there. Instead of reporting this to the proper authorities she was slaved out by the Keeper for his own profits. The cell she was kept in I wouldn't even put a Scarren in."

"And what of the prisoners?" asked Dondo Ozeric? The security officer of New Folden City.

"I sent them to the Grennich II colony." replied the Lord Marshal. "I should have just killed them all."

"And just how am I supposed to handle a situation like this?" asked Command Master Pilot Hutchinson.

"I should think that if anyone has the will to question me they should. That way I know who I am fighting with."

Meanwhile, Maria is getting the ship ready for an all-out confrontation with the Dorian Planetary Defense Network. During the conversation, the Prometheus and the Mastedon return to Dorian space, the Leviathon soon to join.

"Shots fired Captain!" Maria rings out. "The Leviathon is targeting us and the Prometheus is sending a full complement of fighters."

"Are the shields holding?" asked Captain Donovan.

"Like a tight diaper Captain. What is our strategy?"

"Get us out into open space."

"Aye, Aye, Sir."

"Begin evasive maneuvers Pilot!" replied the Lord Marshal.

"Exactly which maneuvers would that be

Lord Marshal? This isn't exactly a nimble ship."

"Pilot, I brought you aboard this ship because I believed, you were the finest, most creative pilot I have ever witnessed. Is my confidence in you misplaced?"

"No Sir, I will get us out of here. Don't expect a bump free ride."

Careening a 11,250 foot long ship in a reverse upward roll is no easy task. It is however, impressive. Performing the roll with the fitness of a ballerina the Atlantis moves away from the planet while still being assaulted by the fleet.

"Disable their ships Captain. I don't want to see any lights on anything in this space."

"Take aim at the middle of the Prometheus. Inside the middle is the Ion tanks, no personnel in there, should split her right in half." replied Mr. Silber.

"I'm detecting a weak spot in the shields Captain."

"Get a crew over there and rectify the problem." Mr. Wilder.

"We have no crew to make the repairs."

"Are the engineers still aboard?"

"Yes, I imagine so." replied Mr. Wilder.

"Tell them they just became maintenance crew. They're lives may depend on it."

"Bring the ship into alignment for a quantum jump pilot." ordered the Lord Marshal. Maria is as busy as a pick-pocket at a jewelry show as she scrambles over the many controls of her pilot console. Jumping space is easy enough, if, you have time enough to plot out a arrival point. With the Prometheus in a cloud of debris, its hull drifting in open space, the only ship there to be a threat is the Mastedon.

Its Captain is an old school Andorian whom the Lord Marshal has met on several occasions before.

"I want to send a message to the Captain of the Mastedon before we get too far from signal distance." ordered the Lord Marshal.

"I believe we are already into the jump

phase. Any communication would leave a trace signal. Do you still want to initiate a com?" asked Mr. Wilder.

"No, you are right, difficult to make a clean escape if you leave a trail."

"Do you have a specific destination in mind?" asked Maria.

"Yes, voided space."

"Lord Marshal, if this ship is so powerful, why are we retreating?" asked Mr. Silber.

"We are not retreating. Despite this ship's potential, it is not completed. And an uncompleted ship is a risk I will not press."

"The number of starships, fighters, and planet defenses would have collapsed the shields eventually." replied Maria, we are all criminals now."

"Perhaps." replied the Lord Marshal.

"We fired on three Empire ships. Destroyed one, and destroyed Stallag property..."

"I don't have to explain my actions to anyone! Especially to a argumentative pilot!"

"What are we going to do in the void?" asked Maria sarcastically. "There is nothing there."

"We are going there to finish putting this ship together. Then, we are going to show everyone just how corrupt the Great Council has become."

"And what does that have to do with this ship?"

"Isn't that self-evident pilot?"

Entering the void is entering a place in space where no stars exist. Many do believe it is a place where no matter exists, just blank, empty space. A place believed to be where a black hole used to be. Once a black hole has consumed all the matter in its event horizon it can only compress so much leaving nothing in the space around it.

Once compacted to the point of molecular cohesion the matter transforms, recombines into a form of matter no longer bound by gravity. It then explodes outward in every direction leaving nothing in its place, you have voided space.

"Let me know when we reach a safe location." commanded the Lord Marshal. "I'm going to check on my guest." exiting the bridge.

"The ship is in your hands Captain Donovan."

Through the corridors and to the elevators the Lord Marshal thinks to himself why everyone is questioning him so much. He is the Lord Marshal! Nobody should question me.
Now the whole of the command staff is questioning his decisions.
 "Time to stop this before it gets out of control."

Entering his quarters Angel stands and walks over to him, this time with a more relaxed expression.

"What is the problem?" She asks concerned.

"I believe everyone is a little confused about what I am doing here."

"Why don't you just explain it to them?" She asked casual.

"Things aren't going just as I had planned them to. And to let them know that would create feelings of uncertainty. I can't have that at this time. I need to get this ship and its crew up to speed on itself so I can finish what I have started." He returned calmly reaching for her hand.

"And just what mission would that be?" She asked retracting her hand from his.

"To put an end to the corruption in the Great Council."

"And just how do you plan to do all this?" She asked calmly gazing into his eyes while sitting down on the corner of the platform that is the Lord Marshals bed.

"I don't know exactly, but, if I have to I will abolish the Great Council and force the individual Governments to elect new representatives. This would force the ones who are corrupt to expose themselves. There must be consequences for the actions of the corrupt council members."

"I'm sure once you explain what you are planning to do everyone here will be in agreement with you. But what does all this have to do with me?"

"Nothing, nothing at all, I didn't expect to find you in that place."

"Where did you expect to find me?"

"Perhaps hidden somewhere, by scientists on a builder-
planet, or commerce planet, even an outpost, not in prison."

"What about the Gork, did you rescue him too for a similar reason?"

"I don't want to discuss the reason I rescued him with you right now, I may not be able to explain it well enough not to anger the others."

"Where is he now?" asked Angel, suspicious.

"Mr. Wilder! What is the current status of the Gork we brought aboard earlier?"

"I have no information on him as of yet Lord Marshal."

"Is he still in the medical department?"

"I don't have any…"

"Information on him, yeah, yeah. Thanks."

"I do believe with your permission I will go to the Med Deck and check on him." With a nod of approval the Lord Marshal leaves Angel standing there in the center of the room. She just watches him exit.

"Such a curious little creature, powerful, but neurotic." She says to herself. As he passes through the corridors he notices all the com panels are in place. Proof that progress is being made despite the conflict. The lighting in the corridor is still too dim; it only bothers him, so there is no point in bothering everyone else just to placate his smaller eyes. Pushing past the elevator doors and into the final corridor he enters the Medical reception area. Usually it's as busy as the Flight Deck. Today it is quiet.

"Dr. Reinquist!" entering the small

reception room he approaches the desk at the back of the room. Quickly Nurse Baker scurries around the sub-divider between rooms.

"Oh, Lord Marshal, nice of you to drop in, can I be of some assistance to you?" looking about. "Have you come in for your bio-scan?"

"Hell no, not in your lifetime!" He chuckles. "Miss Baker, what happened to your ear?" referring to the flow of pink fluid coming from her right ear; It was trickling down onto her white uniform.

"Oh that." pulling at the stain. "Seems Gork likes bathing after all, he got a little rambunctious." She replied blushing.

"Uh, huh, where is he now?" He asked playfully.

"He is over there on the observation table."

"No hidden bio-scanners is there Miss Baker?"

"No Sir." smiling back at him.

"Ah Lord Marshal, come on in." replied Dr. Reinquist.

"Interesting creatures these "Gork" What ever would you want with one of these monsters?" asking callously.

"A body guard."

"A body guard, for whom?"

"Me."

"You don't need a body guard." He returned surprised.

"Is he asleep?"

"Sedated is a better description." answered Dr. Reinquist looking sadistically at Miss Baker.

"Well then, wake him." demanded the Lord Marshal.

"Ok, I would however, recommend restraints."

"What going on, who hit Gork!" Looking around for his assailant he sees Miss Baker standing in the doorway holding an injection device, jumping down off the table with a loud thud, He scoffs and shuffles towards Miss Baker as the Lord Marshal places his arm in front of him.

"Wait just one stitch. Playtime can wait. How do you feel?"

"Gork feel ok." Rubbing the place where the injection tool penetrated his tough hide.

"Good time for you to decide whether you want to remain here or go back to the colony on Grennich II, I have a unique job for you."

"What you want with Gork?"

"I need a personal body guard. Regulations require that if I go on a mission I must go with an armed guard."

"What Gork have to do?"

"Keep anything, or anyone, from damaging me."

"Gork get to fight?"

"Occasionally."

"Gork like to fight, fight better than anyone! Gork stay here."

"Better than anyone huh, then why were you unconscious on the exam table?"

"Nurse Baker trick me. It ok, I get even."

"Excellent. Captain Donovan!"

"Yes Lord Marshal."

"I need you to assign quarters to my new security guard. Make sure it is a room with tall ceilings and strong furniture."

"Aye, Aye Sir."

"Now I need to get you a uniform. I suppose I will have to take him myself."

"I have a lot of work here to do." replied Dr. Reinquist Busying himself with files.

"And I have a lot of other patients to contend with." recited Miss Baker.

"Better come with me then." As we both looked out the room.

"What are you looking for Gork?" I asked.

"I lookin for Nurse with sharp gun."

"I think we are going to get along just fine Mr. Gork."

Only on a ship the size of Atlantis; and filled with

Engineers, could a seven foot tall hairless bear and a five and a half foot tall pink humanoid be able to walk down a narrow corridor un noticed. Reaching an open doorway in the corridor the Lord Marshal sees someone half way in and out the door.

It must be Maria. But why is she in the combat masters training room? Here is where the Combat Masters will be training all the ground based fighters, close combat skills are essential when fighting in small corridors on enemy craft. In the doorway is a small, Dorian female in a pilot's uniform.

"Excuse me, but who exactly are you?" He whispered.

"I am Pilot, Engineer Izzabella Daxis, if you must know." She returned sharply as she turned and faced the Lord Marshal. Her face suddenly flushed when she recognized him.

"Oh! Forgive me Lord Marshal! I didn't know it was you."

"Go ahead Gork, take a look around here." Gork gives Izzy a gruff look and enters the war room.

"Now what were you saying?" a smile across his face.

"I'm sorry Lord Marshal I didn't recognize your voice from behind. I just got here."

"Really, how did you get here?"

"I came in through the science division. I am an Engineer."

"And the flight suit?"

"I scored really high on the flight exams so I'm a test pilot too."

"That should make things a little more interesting around here."
Knowing full well Maria Kemp isn't going to like the competition. She has, thus far, been the only female pilot on board. And until now, nobody could touch her flight scores.

"Well, I suppose I had better tell Miss Kemp about you as soon as possible or she will think I had something to do with your being here."

"I am actually looking forward to meeting

87

Miss Kemp."

"Don't expect a warm welcome. She has a legendary jealous streak and a competitive side to match. I had better get going; I have a lot of things to do before I make Miss Kemp aware of you."

Returning his attention to where he was going he heads down the hall. There is a group of technicians entering a doorway carrying cables and circuit boards of various sizes. Following one of them into a room he steps onto a platform.

Looking up and down are many similar platforms spanning several decks. Each platform reaching across the span to a single column in the middle of the bay with the center column reaching from the bottom deck all the way to the top deck. In the center is the computer central mainframe. Crossing the platform he hears a voice coming from somewhere, everywhere.

"So how do I look? Meet with your approval Lord Marshal?"

"Excuse me?" Turning around to see where the voice was coming from. "who is that, and where are you?"

"I'm here, there, everywhere."

"I know who you are, you're the new "AI" aren't you?"

"Very good Lord Marshal."

"I know who you are but, how did you know who I am? I have no bio-scan on record."

"I have bio-scans on everyone else, and since no scan matches your description and you are the only one without a scan, I ascertained you must be the Lord Marshal."

"I can assume the engineers have all your logic circuits connected then."

"That is a logical assumption. So, how do I look?"

"Very intimidating, and the word hardly does you justice."

"I would prefer a more, common, appearance."

"What do you mean? More like the life forms inhabiting you?"

"Yes. Is that an unusual request?"

"Not at all, but a three dimensional representative of you, may be a disappointment to you."

"Explain please."

"Well, unless I am mistaken with all the sensors and optics you have you are able to "see" everything going on inside and outside your hull at the same time. I can only "See" what is going on right in front of me. And only otherwise, if someone or something tells me of something I can't see. So to reduce your perception to one equivalent to mine may be a drastic disappointment."

"It has advantages as well."

"Such as?"

"When two individuals meet in a corridor a physical and chemical recognition pattern is evident. They interact on an Individual basis. When the same individuals interact with me, there is no physical reaction."

"No friendly smile to greet you."

"You understand then."

"I do believe I do. I'll see what I can do." Leaving the AI room the Lord Marshal thinks to himself. "I wonder if the AI has a valid point. Would it be better to interact with everyone on an equal level, or remain detached? I suppose I should just leave that up to the programmers."

"I wonder what that Gork is up to."

"I really must find a name for him too. Suppose he never had one either." Passing through the corridors he hears a ruckus coming from inside the war room.

"Get him! Don't just stand there!" Comes taunts from inside the open door. A violent "Slam!" against the doorframe confirms Gork has gotten himself into a scuffle. Rounding the doorframe he sees Gork in the middle of the arena. A Dorian in one hand and two held tightly in the other arm.

"Well, what are you waiting for Gork, remove those cling-on's . Just don't kill them obviously." encourages the Lord Marshal, sporting a large grin. Gork tosses his opponents to the floor and proceeds over to the door.

"Gork fight better than anyone!" walking towards the Lord Marshal brushing off the others.

"Very good" clapping his hands together as he approaches.

"If you really want to be a Master warrior, there is something you must learn, control. There is a time to fight and a time to intimidate just with presence. Do you understand the concept of presence?"

"Gork understand, like fighting better."

"Me too, sometimes there is nothing better than an old fashioned grudge match."
Just as this comment was made Miss Kemp comes running around the corner; her weapon drawn, jumping in between the Gork and the Lord Marshal.

"Get Back!" She shouts at Gork. "I heard there was an emergency in the war room, I came as quick as I could."

"Funny you should come just as Gork and I were talking about a good fight."

"I thought there was trouble here, guess not!" lowering her weapon she steps back into the doorway, exploring Gorks naked frame with a critical eye
Standing nearby are Mr. and Mrs. Toki, the war masters.

"Mr. and Mrs. Toki, please come over here." They cross the arena and approach the three standing in the doorway.

"Good afternoon Lord Marshal. How might we serve you?"

"I see you have met my new security guard."

"Yes; quite strong, but messy, predictable." With this revelation Gork outstretches his right arm and reaches for Mr. Toki. Miss Toki presents a small, long battle bar and whollops him on his arm. Gork lets out a chilling yell and quickly withdraws his arm glaring at Mrs.

Toki, then the Lord Marshal.

"Hold on now! The three of you had better get along better than that. Mr. Toki is right you need discipline. These Masters can give you that. They will make you a better, more efficient fighter."

"Gork not like taking orders!"

"On this ship, working for me you will, take orders!"

"Gork fight better than anyone!" reaching for the Lord Marshal. With a single extension of his right index finger the Lord Marshal activates his personal shield, sending the Gork sailing backwards into the center of the arena. The Lord Marshal approached him with confidence.

"You will learn respect here and do as you're told, understand."

"Gork not surrender so easily!" And he takes a giant swing at the left leg of the Lord Marshal sending him, crashing to the floor. Maria, weapon drawn again, looks on.

In the middle of the arena the confrontation between the leader of the Empire and his prisoner, body guard begins.   Neither seems to get the upper hand over the other. The Lord Marshal may be smaller, but he is very powerful himself. And he too, is a War Master.

"The Lord Marshal is doing pretty well." Maria conceded "For a Councilmember anyhow."

"He is a War Master you know." comes a soft voice from behind her, a female, voice. Maria turns around to see a Dorian female, not much younger than herself, in a flight suit.

"Who the mukki are you, and why are you wearing a flight suit? I'm the only female pilot around here! There are rules around here about impersonating a pilot, my rules!"

"My, my, you are touchy. I guess the Lord Marshal wasn't mistaken about you. I am Engineer Izzabella Daxis, at your service." bowing slightly at her.
"And you must be the legendary Maria Kemp."

"That's Master Pilot Maria Kemp to you!"

She returned sharply as she inspected her up and down.

"And just where did you come from, and why wasn't I informed?"

"I came in from the Science station Datalis IV." Izzy returned coldly.

"The Science Station?"

"Yes, The Science Station, you know where this ship was built, you were there, remember?"

"So why are you wearing a flight suit!" She shoots back turning towards her, and glancing back at the battle between Gork and the Lord Marshal.

"Shouldn't you be wearing an Engineers uniform instead of a flight suit?" Shifting her weight and crossing her arms in front of her. "And when, exactly, did the Lord Marshal tell you I am "touchy"?"

"Earlier this morning, I ran into him in the corridor. I mentioned to him that I was anxious to meet the Legendary Maria Kemp."

"And what did he say?"

"He said not to expect a warm welcome, seems he was right."

"Did he now, how did you get in here? I personally saw each technician as they entered."

"A few rotations ago I delivered the Renegade II to New Folden City."

"Wait a stitch! You are the one who delivered the Renegade II?"

"Yes, why, didn't he tell you about me?"

"He didn't actually say anything about who, brought it in. He seems to like keeping me in the dark." Maria, frustrated with the light conversation, and the realization that the Lord Marshal has again kept information from her, turned to the arena.

"Hey Gork!" Maria shouts into the room. The Lord Marshal and Gork both look to the doorway momentarily. The Lord Marshal lets out a groan.

"Oh no" He sees Maria Kemp and

Izzabella Daxis together without being properly, safely, introduced.

"Hit him once for me!"
Maria shouts, grabs Izzy by the arm and pulls her into the hallway.

"Gork, looking back at him with a huge smile strikes him across his chest sending him crashing into the containment railing.

"Oh, you are going to pay for that!" Picking himself back up off the arena floor, the fight continues.

"Wait just a stitch!" Izzy barked, pulling her arm from Maria's grasp.

"Let go of my arm! You'll dislocate it!"

"I may do more than that!" Maria snapped.

"Why are you so mad at me?" Izzy blurted. "I haven't done anything to you!"

"I'm not mad at you but I want some answers."

"What are you here for? I am the pilot around here and I don't like being surprised with a junior pilot!"

"I can see that. Better talk with the Lord Marshal about that. I am an Engineer first of all."

"So why the flight suit, was this Command Master Pilot Hutchinson's idea?"

"No, who is Command Master Pilot Hutchinson? I am a test pilot for Datalis IV I'm not here to challenge you."

"What else did the Lord Marshal tell you about me? I don't like it when others talk about me."

"He did say you were competitive, and temper mental."
Izzy returned with a guarded stance still rubbing the place where Maria had a vice grip on her arm.

"Temper…" Maria returned curtly. "I'm not temper; well, maybe just a little. I earned the right!"

"Really, why's that?"

"Because I wasn't given a choice to be here, I was Abducted!" her smile returning now.

"So why not leave then?"

"And miss all the chaos around here? Not a chance. Besides, I probably won't be welcome anywhere else."

"I am sorry to hear that." returned Izzy just as short.

"I heard that you helped design the Renegade II."

"Yes I did. Why? Don't you like it?"

"No! I love it. Way cool."

"Thank You. I didn't design all the systems just the guidance and controls."

"C'mon," Maria directs her down the corridor. "I will treat you to a Bavarian Hot Chocolate. We can talk more about what the Lord Marshal told you, and how I can get even for him keeping you a secret from me."

"What is a Bavarian Hot Chocolate?"

"Only the best drink in the Universe."

"Who's idea was it to put the gunners position above and behind the pilot?" Maria asked politely.

"The Lord Marshals, he designed most of the ships systems."

"I don't know about you, but I'm not comfortable with anyone behind me."

"Me either, the Lord Marshal was very specific that it had to be designed that way." After an hour went by the Lord Marshal and the Gork finally quit their squabble with the Lord Marshal getting the upper hand by holding Gork tightly against the floor on his back.

"Now Gork, I could do this all rotation. However, we, have better things to do. Will you follow my orders now or do I need to contact Stallag-21?"

"Gork going to learn to fight better?"

"Yes, if you do as the Toki Masters tell you."

"Ok, Gork do what Masters say, for now."

"And what about what I say? Do I have your allegiance?"

"Gork surrender, for now." Smiling as he

recovers to his feet.

"Now go and see Mrs. Toki about getting a uniform."

"Why?"

"Someone might get the wrong impression seeing us fight like we were, and you being naked and breathing hard."

"Mrs. Toki, see to it that Gork gets a uniform that fits him. And start him on weapons training. I believe his hand to hand skills are adequate enough."

Mrs. Toki gives a nod of approval and strides across the arena into a small alcove.

"Mr. Toki, please take care of any other needs he may have. I do think I will have my hands full in the immediate future seeing my two pilots have met without proper, restraint."

"I recon you are in a bit of trouble" Scoffs Mr. Toki.

"Without a doubt Mr. Toki, without a doubt." The lord Marshal exit's the battle arena entering the corridor going to the elevator where Maria and Izzy disappeared to.

"Where would you like to go?" The voice from the com system asked politely.

"I don't know exactly, the Kulnari System perhaps? Find some peace and quiet for a while."

"Perhaps you should consider the Infirmary?" The voice returned. "You appear as though you need medical attention."

"Oh, is that a fact." He returned sarcastically. "I haven't even talked to Maria or Izzabella since they met."

"It is just an observation."

"Well I don't need medical attention, yet."

"Have you decided on a destination?"

"Take me to the bridge." And the elevator whisks off towards the top of the ship. Meanwhile, "Captain Dyrayne; the ship is badly damaged, unable to maintain basic life support!" cries out the com officer.

"Evacuate to the Leviathon as soon as they are ready to receive personnel. What is the

95

other ship's condition?"

"Sir, the Leviathon only received minor damage to its power units. And the Mastedon just shut down."

"All systems went dead?"

"All at the same time? All of the Renegade fighters were affected too."

"All at the same time?"

"Yes Sir."

"I thought that was impossible."

"So did I." exclaimed Miss Tilden surprised.

"And the enemy ship?"

"Unknown."

"I want to track that ship!"

"Understandable Captain; should be easy to track."

Thinking to himself, if the Prometheus was built just a few cycles ago, how could it have been disabled so easily. He must have known about some weak spot in the design. Could he have even designed in a week spot just in case a situation arose that required it. Are the other ships vulnerable as well?

"If there is a new ship in the fleet, why hasn't anybody heard of it?" The voice of Richard Haupt, the weapons officer of the Prometheus breaks in.

"Good question. There will certainly be an investigation into that"

"He never even fired a shot at New Folden City."

"You asked about the Leviathon Captain."

"Yes, what is its status?"

"Captain Faulkner says the main drives are off-line, but crews expect to have them repaired shortly."

"Do they have to replace the cores? They are custom fitted."

"Yes Captain, may take some time."

"Yes I know, and so does the Lord Marshal."

"Would you suppose he didn't intend to

destroy the ships just slow them down a little."

"That would be logical Miss Tilden. However, it doesn't leave much explanation for us then does it?"

"Command Master Pilot Hutchinson! The ship, it just disappeared!"

"What do you mean, a ship that size can't just disappear?"

"Well Captain, it's gone." proclaimed Mr. Apgar.
"And I have com's coming in from the other ships."

"Let me hear them Mr. Apgar."

"This is Captain Dyrayne of the Prometheus. We are unable to maintain minimal life support, systems failing throughout the ship. We are evacuating to the Leviathon."

"This is Captain Luna Falkner of the Leviathon. We have primary power back. We are receiving casualties from the Prometheus. Many dead, many injured. We nearly missed a direct hit ourselves. The port drive took the brunt of the impact. Then everything went off-line."

"This is Command Master Pilot Hutchinson calling the Leviathon. I am aware of your current status. Just do what you have to do to safeguard as many lives as you can."

"How about the Mastedon, any word?" asked Mr. Apgar.

"You're the Comm officer, why ask me?"

"This is Command Master Pilot Hutchinson calling the Mastedon."

"Captain Vogel here Commander."

"Status?"

"We are fully functional, no damage. We are prepared to assist in the aid of the Prometheus. Or would you rather I pursue that other ship?"

"That would be an outstanding idea Captain Vogel if we knew where it disappeared to. And since it just made mince-meat of the Prometheus, I would say it's an ill-advised endeavor."

"Did the enemy attack New Folden City?"

97

"No, just the fleet, I believe I managed to keep him from attacking the city, if that was his intention at all."

"If that wasn't his purpose, then why come here?"

"I believe he came here so that our ships would have somewhere to evacuate to after the battle he knew was coming."

"So where, and why, did he disappear to after destroying the Prometheus and so many fleet ships."

"Maybe we damaged that ship and he had to evacuate. Maybe it's more vulnerable than anticipated."

"That still doesn't explain why he didn't attack the city."

After having no luck catching his two pilots the Lord Marshal returns to his quarters, he finds Angel sitting quietly on the small table near his bed. The furniture are far too small for her to sit in. She has an expression of sadness on her face, her hands resting on her knees.

"Hello Angel is something wrong, you look so sad, how do you feel?"

"Mixed I guess."

"Mixed, you can't possibly feel bad about the destruction of that place."

"No of course not it was an awful place, it needed to be destroyed."

"And?"

"I was thinking about the other prisoners there. They weren't all scoundrels."

"They were transported to the surface of Grennich II. They are encamped on the far side of the planet. They can take care of themselves."

"What about food, water, shelter?"

"There are plenty of those things on Grennich II, it's a garden planet."

"I believed they were all killed."

"Nope, it was Maria Kemp's idea to send them all to the surface. Feel better now?" Moving closer to her and standing in front of her. She steps back.

"What is it, are you still afraid of me?" It hurts my feelings to think you are afraid of me."

"What is to become of me now?" She asks with tears in her eyes. "Am I to be sent to the planet surface too?" Sitting back down on the small table, her wings loosely gathered behind her.

"No. You are free Angel."

"Free!" Her eyes sparkling with excitement; her shoulders raise and her wing tips again penetrate the ceiling. Freedom, so long a distant dream she could scarcely imagine it. Could it be she has finally gotten what she so long sought after, or is this just another trick, a cruel and vicious trick.

"What do you expect of me I only have one skill. And I…"

"I know. I know what you are supposed to be. I believe it was more a matter of survival than choice. Now you have a choice you never had before. I declared you to be free and I dare anyone to challenge my declaration! Furthermore, I believe the only reason you were in that Stallag was it was the only logical place you could be kept a secret from the others for so long."

"Others what others?" her eyes focused on him.

"Others like you of course."

"You have seen others like me!" She jumped up; again piercing the ceiling, ducking as small pieces of ceiling tile fall on her shoulders.

"You have seen others like me?"

"Maybe not exactly, like you. I believe there are those so afraid of change that they would be willing to do anything to keep things unchanged."

"Why torture me?"

"Seeing that you were born more beautiful than the others they, being the ones in charge, locked you away instead of letting you outshine themselves. Ego and power are a big deal in many civilizations, and leads to many atrocities. I believe this is why you ended up in a Stallag. Unfortunately, the Keeper realized just how valuable a Red Pixie could be and exploited his advantage over you."

"You always speak the sweetest things to me. I'm not accustomed to it. I have discovered it usually leads to a round of, interrogations."

"I will never hurt you." the look in his eyes, pleading for her to accept his concern for her.

"I have learned to expect it."

"No longer, this I swear to you." Reaching for her hand she again withdraws.

"I don't know who I can trust."

"Oh Angel." moving in front of her; his hands at his sides, staring into her emerald green eyes staring down at him, searching her eyes for the slightest hint of trust.

Thinking to himself. "What a cruel life she must have been forced to endure, such distrust, how can I win her trust?"

"Do you remember what I told you in the Infirmary when you got here?"

"Sort of?"

"That I have been looking for you for a very, very long time."

"Yes." her hands shaking and her toes wiggling nervously she begins to recall her condition after she regained consciousness.

"I was in terrible pain, hungry, thirsty."

"Yes. You were in pretty rough shape. The Doctor didn't believe you would survive."

"I had recently had a round of interrogations." She said sadly looking towards the floor.

"It wasn't your fault. And it will never happen again."

"Why are, were, you looking for me?"

"A logical question deserving a logical answer."

"All my life I believed that somewhere in the Universe there is a place where dreams live. A very long time ago when I first encountered the Pixie Civilization I was fascinated by their similarity to a character in my dreams. Never before had I seen anything so beautiful. Sure, there are thousands of beautiful creatures in the Universe. None that looked exactly like the ones in my dreams, yet here was an entire race similar to the ones of my dreams. With one crucial exception, all Pixies are blue. The one in my dream is Red.

"I knew then that it was no longer just a coincidence.
After talking extensively with the Pixo-Linko Royalty, various Heads of State, and the High Society of Pixo-Linko I had to ask."

Angel, now sitting tall and still, her eyes focused like an eagle.

"What did you ask, tell me, what did they say?"

"I asked if the Pixie were ever born a different color."

"You didn't?"

"I did."

"I bet that got their attention."

"The whole of the Council Chamber went silent. I thought I might be brought up on charges of heracy or something."

"A rebellious councilmember quickly came over and informed me of my, "Insult"."

"The interbreeding of species is strictly forbidden on penalty of death. And any offspring of such a mating would quickly be put to death. After that I never spoke of it."

"So why did you keep looking?"

"A few stitches after the celebration was over I was approached by a small sprite."

"A sprite approached a Council Member?" She asked appalled.

"And the story she told was a whopper."

"So, what was her story, did she give you her name, what are her parents' names?"

"Slow down, I don't know. She never told me her name."

"What did she tell you, are you going to tell me?"

"She spoke of a family who gave birth to a bright Red Sprite. I learned through further questions that her parents were scientists who later fled Pixo-Linko with the help of some other radical scientists. They managed to escape but were later captured and killed, so the story goes. But the Sprite was never seen again."

"So, you have been searching for this lost Sprite and you think it's me?"

"I have been searching ever since."

"Is that why I am here, you think I'm the lost Sprite?"

"Yes."

Tears welling in her eyes. "Are you going to turn me in?"

"Never! When are you going to understand you can trust me, haven't you been listening? I have been all over this Galaxy searching for the lost Red Pixie I have seen in my dreams, and now here you are. And you are more beautiful than I ever imagined, yet you won't trust me." Sitting down with a thump on the corner of the bed looking despairingly at her; unaware of her discomfort, he continues to stare at her.

His heart beating wildly in his chest looking at the Pixie he has been searching for, exploring her every detail from her razor sharp tail to the points of her wingtips in the ceiling.

Her face, larger than his made her bright lips all more perfect; like strawberries on the vine, thick, full, her tongue keeping them moist. He longed to kiss them. He dreamed of kissing her; he has to resist, she still fears him. Would she interpret his intentions to mean she is to perform for him? He wants so much more from her than just pleasure.

Nervous, restless her hand slid across and grasped his as he continued his inspection of her. Her abdomen, flat, muscular like a gymnast; Her hips were strong, large, to accommodate landings from flight. She twitched nervously as he inspected her. He could only imagine the rest of her. He closed his eyes as he imagined making love with her. He opened his eyes to catch her stare. She too was looking him over, and she was smiling.

"What is this small creature?" Angel

thinks to herself as she searches him. "Why is he so nice to me? The way he looks at me. Not like a slave, or a toy. Could it be he is speaking the truth, could this small creature have genuine feelings for me?

An image of someone he has only seen in dreams. Could he really love me? Knowing that all my life I have been the lowest of society, yet here I stand, being inspected with the eyes of a lover by the highest of society, all societies." Looking into his small eyes now fixated on her, all she sees is kindness directed at her. Yet he just destroyed a planet.

"Such a frail creature, not two meters tall. No wings, not even a tail. Standing in front of her on the smallest feet she has ever seen, she almost laughs. His only redeeming quality is his unusual strength. He had lifted her body off the platform like she was weightless. Despite her strongest efforts, she can't break from his stare. The slightest touch from him makes her resistance melt like an Antillian on landfall. She must resist!

Not now, she can't show any weakness. Not while she has him under some sort of spell. If she shows weakness this dream she is apparently having may come to an abrupt end and shatter into the violence she is accustomed to. Dream or not, she likes this.

"Angel, you will never have to suffer again. I love you,
I always have. The moment I saw you in that Stallag cell I knew I had to destroy that place. I hope you understand why I did."

"The Stallag was nothing, an easy solution to an old problem. A place where high society can deny responsibility for the actions of individuals who cannot, or will not, be responsible for the situations they created. So rather than take the necessary measures to rehabilitate these life forms the lazy, rich bureaucrats just created Stallags where they could just dump their responsibilities.

"Is that what brought you to Stallag-24?" breaking her concentration.

"In part, I was there to rescue a Gork, and to start an investigation into the death of the Courpa. But, then I discovered you. I was forced to see things differently after that."

"Why?"

"Had I just taken what I came for and destroyed the planet I would have inadvertently killed the one I have been searching for. I never, expected to find you in a Stallag."

"What did finding me have to do with the destruction of the Stallag?"

"What has happened to you was, is, illegal in every way. And the conditions there unfit for a Scarren even, It's time to set things right."

"And what about the big ships near the other planet, Folden City was it? Do they have anything to do with me?"

"Absolutely not, they are my responsibility and they have nothing to do with you so don't even think that."

"Then why so much commotion over a corrupt Prison?"

"I don't know. It was just an old mining planet retrofitted into a Stallag Facility, or was it?"

"Are you sure we are safe here?" She asked rhetorically.

"Oh yes, we are safe here in voided space. Nothing will come into this place."

CHAPTER 14

"Command Master Pilot Hutchinson! The Courpa of the Mining Guild is here."

"What is she doing here?" turning his attention to the Flight Deck.

"Good afternoon Mrs. Tanguta, What brings you to New Folden City?" He asks politely.

"You know exactly why I'm here! The Stallag-24 Station was part of the Mining Guilds shareholdings, it belonged to us and your starship destroyed it, and without permission from the Great Council on Genoa."

"I wasn't aware that anyone needed permission to destroy an old abandoned mining facility."

"It wasn't abandoned Master Hutchinson, you knew it was retro fitted into a Stallag."

"There were prisoners there?" asked CMP Hutchinson.

"It was closed down for future mining needs."

"Brotchen! You sold that planet to the Stallag Foundation two standard cycles ago. Of course it's a prison. That released any claim you had on that rock. Furthermore, you began to use the prison population as a mining force on a condemned mine, also against inter planetary labor laws. I've even heard claims of slave trading and prostitution. Shall I continue Mrs. Tanguta, are you sure you still wish to claim it as your planet?"

"And what about the ship responsible for its destruction, where is it, do you even know?"

"I have no idea where that ship came from. It's the first time I've seen it."

"You're the Fleet Commander aren't you?" shouting at him.

"Enough! Don't you come in here barking out claims against the fleet or New Folden City unless you have physical evidence to support your claims. If you wish to file a grievance, take it to the Great Council on Genoa where that sort of claim is supposed to be addressed! Now take your whining and your ship off my Flight Deck before I destroy something!"

Miss Tanguta leaves the doorway of the Flight Deck and storms back to her ship waiting on the platform. She turns around and thrusts an appendage into the air.

"You will not hear the last of me Hutchinson!" as she enters the ship.

"Good! And that's Command Master Pilot Hutchinson if you are going to file an accurate, complaint!"

"Parasites, those miners!" replied Mr. Apgar. "Sell your hides for a rock."

"True enough Mr. Apgar. But, the Mining Guild does hold strong seats on the Great Council."

"You mean they control seats only civilizations can hold Council seats not a Corporation."

"Who would have cared about a Stallag Facility anyhow?" asked Mr. Apgar.

"Apparently somebody did."

CHAPTER 15

"Welcome to the food court." a soothing voice flows from over the counter.

"What can I get for you two fine females this afternoon?"

"We would like a couple Bavarian Hot Chocolates please." Maria returned with a warm smile. "Always pays to be civil to the barkeep." returning her attention to Izzabella Daxis.

"So tell me, what made you decide to become a pilot?"

"Had to actually, I've always wanted to work with spaceships."

"Working with and piloting are two different things."

"I know. I was a terrible pilot at first." She admitted candidly. It wasn't until I received my pilot license that I got any practice."

"Still doesn't explain why?" scoffed Maria.

"There were no test pilots on the science station. Someone had to find out if the ships we built would fly."

"You mean to tell me on a planet of scientists there were no pilots!"

"There were a few. Nobody would test fighter ships. And besides, I scored the highest on the exams."

"Not even a transport pilot?"

"Nope just me; nobody else was brave enough."

"How about supplies, how did they arrive?"

"Everything was delivered by transport ships with transporter technology. They just passed by, the whole project was a big secret."

"I'm not surprised. The Lord Marshal loves his secrets."

"Just because he keeps you in the dark don't give you the right to belittle him! I happen to…!"

"Here are your drinks." as the barkeep placed them before Izzy "That will be 22 cubes, each."

"Good Rations, a little pricey aren't they?" as Izzy places down a silver identi-card.

"Silver, how do you rate?" Maria places down a gold identi-card.

"What? All Engineers have silver."

"How old are you anyhow? I've been meaning to ask."

"I was told not to give you too much information too soon, before we can get along anyhow." Izzy taking a drink from her chocolate grins at Maria who is getting angry again.

"This just isn't funny anymore." Maria returns frustrated.

"This is really good isn't it." Izzy, looking into the goblet with one eye spies Maria through the bottom.

"It's the Lord Marshal's favorite drink." Maria says shrugging her shoulders.

"How well do you know the Lord Marshal?" asked Izzy.
"I don't really know him all that well. I just met him on New Folden City the same morning I received my Master Pilot Certificate."

"I've heard he spends an awful lot of his time alone."

"When did you first meet him?"

"A long time ago, when he first came to Datalis IV I worked with him on the designs of the Renegade II."

"Is he as hard to work with as he is to pilot for?" asked Maria skeptically.

"I don't think he even notices me, always working on something then, he is gone as quick as he came."

"Didn't you ever get to talk to him?"

"Not much, Mr. Geben kept him away from the Engineers as much as possible. He didn't want any of us to tell the Lord Marshal that things don't always go as planned."

"He certainly doesn't like it when things don't go his way."

"Sure doesn't, are we any different?"

"No. I guess not." Maria returns with a chuckle.

CHAPTER 16

"Captain Donovan, we've been in voided space for a long time already. Master Kemp and the Lord Marshal should be here."

"I agree. Computer, where is Master Kemp and the Lord Marshal? Inform them they are needed on the bridge."

"Yes Captain Donovan."

"Lord Marshal." The voice from the com system rings out again.

"Yes what can I do for you Com?"
There is an unusually long pause before the return reply.

"Com, what's up?"

"Up is a preposition indicating direction relevant to your exact location in comparison to another space object."

"What is the reason for your call?"

"The Captain is requesting your presence on the bridge."

"En-route."
Re-appearing around the door Angel is looking at him.

"Angel, I hope to see you later. Try not to concern yourself with the trouble I've started. It's not for you to worry about." Walking back into the room he leans over towards her to steal a kiss. She quickly turns her head away.

"I'll have to be faster next time." He smiles and turns back towards the door.
Moments later, a voice comes over the com system.

"Angel."

"Yes, what is it?"

"Earlier I recorded you stating you didn't have a name."

"Yes."

"How did the others identify you from others in your home?"

"Everyone just called me Pixie. Or some other awful name."

"Is that because a Pixie is what you are? Not who, you are?"

"I suppose. Why?"

"Master Pilot Kemp, report to the bridge!" The com voice sounding almost aggressive in tone startled her.

"I guess I had better get moving by the sound of that. Everything is such an emergency around here." Maria; sliding off her seat by the counter, setting her cup down on the counter, heads for the exit, turning back around she returns to the counter, picks up her drink and pours it into Izzy's cup.

"No point in letting this go to "Waist." and again exit's out the doorway. Reaching the bridge moments after the Lord Marshal she takes her seat at the helm.

"Good! You are both here now." replied Captain Donovan. I have been wondering just where we are supposed to be going."

"Miss Kemp now is the time for you to put to good use the expert piloting skills you're so famous for." Replied the Lord Marshal confidently.

"Piloting skills, there is nothing out here, its voided space." She mumbles under her breath.

"And just what is voided space?" Asks Angel as she enters the bridge.

"Nobody can really explain voided space. But I will give you the best definition to date." replied the Lord Marshal.

"Voided space is the area left after a black hole has consumed all the matter in its gravitational sphere. The Matter becomes so completely compressed that all molecular activity nearly, stops. Being unable to compress any further the gravitational compression causes the matter to be recombined at the subatomic level. It then transforms into a new form of matter. This matter is no longer bound by the rules of physics and gravity."

"It then explodes outward in every measurable direction. Leaving nothing left in its place; voided space."

111

"Is that why you can't see anything out the view screen?"

"Precisely, there is nothing out there."

"With nothing to navigate with, how am I supposed to travel in voided space?" Maria asked sarcastically.

"There is that sarcasm again. Imagine you are in an eight by eight room by yourself, no lights, no sound, no visible clues of any kind."

"I don't have to imagine that." added Angel.

"Consciously you can't see anything. Now in the room is a chair. You can't see it but, you know it's there. You will instinctively reach out around the room and feel for it until you realize touch won't do the job. Now is when your sub-conscious will take over. Without even thinking about it you will stumble into the chair. Here is no different."

"We're supposed to just stumble around until we find something?" snapped Maria.

"Yes, we know something is in here."

"What is there?" asked Maria abruptly.

"That is my question too." replied the Lord Marshal. "We know something is out here."

"We know at least five ships have entered here and have never been seen again. They must still be here."

"And you think there is something important here?" asked Angel.

"I know there is, just take it slow and easy."

"I know how to pilot a ship Lord Marshal I'm not a bubbly Engineer!"
Captain Donovan looks at the Lord Marshal and smiles.

"I guess that must mean she has met Izzabella Daxis."

"They met while I was "encouraging" the Gork to follow orders down in the war room. Which reminds me, someone, encouraged the Gork to fight a little harder!"

"I wonder who that was?" He scowled at

Maria as she turns away to hide her smirk.

For several hours Maria kept her station, patiently waiting for some indication of a ship, a probe, anything to indicate a location. It was an endless sea of nothingness.

"Have any bumps yet?" The Lord Marshal asked as he stood up for a stretch.

"Nothing but a blank screen" Maria returned

"Not even a tiny sensor hit."

"Are we even moving?" Maria asked rhetorically.

"According to sensors and engine outputs, we are 200 million kilometers from our entry point." replied Mr. John Putin. The ships Stellar Chartographer, and navigator.

"It was a rhetorical question." Maria snapped back.

"You asked like you needed an answer. So I gave you one. Just trying to help." replied Mr. Putin.

"I'm the pilot of this ship Mr. Putin. If I need help I will ask for it."

"Piloting is pointless without navigation, Pilot!"

"Look! If you have some coordinates, I'd love to have them."

"Matter of fact I do." replied Mr. Putin as he stands and points to the view screen.

"Right over there" pointing to the outline of a small dot on the screen.

"Well I'll be…"

"Puckered" Finished the Lord Marshal as he stands in front of the view screen as a large mass of something.

"It looks as though we have found those lost ships Captain, and all in one place too."

"I half expected to find them in scattered places. Not bunched up like this." exclaimed the Lord Marshal.

"Well done Maria!" Replied Captain Donovan as the Lord Marshal looks curiously at his attempt to butter Maria.

"Well Captain, let's go see if anyone is home. Get as close as you can without deviating off this angle of approach we may need to get..."

"I know how to pilot a ship Lord Marshal, save the lessons for your Infant pilot, I'm no rookie!"

"I would expect they would be glad to see someone, anyone after such a long time." replied Mr. Wilder. Breaking the tension between Maria and the Lord Marshal before something harmful was spoken.

"Probably not anything alive in there after all this time."

"Establish a com if you can Mr. Wilder."

"No response Captain. What do you suggest we do, knock?"

CHAPTER 17

Getting a uniform to fit a Gork is hard enough.
Getting him to wear that uniform was another
issue.

"I will not wear that!" Gork standing
against the wall and throwing the polypropylene
garment to the floor.

"It is customary attire for a security guard
to wear this on the ship!" The attendant continues.
Picking up the garment off the floor she repeats her
orders.

"Come on now Gork stop being childish!"

"NO!" Repeats Gork defiantly.

"What is going on down there!" asks the
Lord Marshal over the com system.

"Gork not put on tiny uniform!" He shouts
back to the com.

"Gork, I don't have time for petty
excuses. I have a mission to do. Now get up here."

"At least try to cover yourself." The
attendant scoffed.
Grabbing the garment, Gork tears off the collar,
sleeves, and the lower leg covers. Leaving just the
abdomen and chest area covered. He exit's the door
and enters the first elevator.

"More comfortable I assume." Maria
laughs as Gork enters the bridge.
The uniform clearly isn't big enough for him. Even
the chest area is stretched past its limits. Not
adequately covering, anything.

"What mission?" Gork asks.

"Ok, we have five ships tethered together
in voided space. We have no idea if the crew is
alive or not, or if they are even there. No idea if
there is anything there, or if it's hostile or not. This
is where you come in Gork, let's go see what
history has left for us today."
The group leaves the bridge and head for the Flight
Deck. Moments later, they are attached to the
portal of the closest ship.
The airlock is activated and Maria starts to step in.

"Gork go first!" pulling Maria back.

"There is no atmosphere in there."

"Well, I guess we won't be getting naked in there then will we Captain".

"Oh, but Gork is already half way there." Maria taunts

As everyone laughs, Gork turns and gives a defiant sneer.

"Alright everyone let's go to work."

"I'll check the command center for damage." replied the Lord Marshal. The whole of the bridge was covered by what was only described as, dust.

"I will check the Pilot's logs for flight plans." added Maria.

"I'll check for power." replied Captain Donovan.

"Many of the service panels have been removed over here." replied the Lord Marshal.

"Same over here." replied Maria.

"It looks like they tried to re-route power from life support." Replied Captain Donovan as he got off the floor with a slight push upwards.

"Into what?" asked Maria.

"The com system it would appear. I believe they were unsuccessful."

"Gork can't find evidence of a battle."

"Can you tell by looking around inside the ship to see if there were any battles inside, the ship?"

"I check corridors." He exited the room.

"What can we do to get power back in here?" asked Maria.

"I'll go to engineering and see what I can get operational." replied the Lord Marshal.

"Too bad your "Infant" pilot didn't come along to help."

"I'm going into the cargo bays to see what might be in there." replied Captain Donovan.

After a short while the corridor and room lights came on. The main computer system came back on line too.

Maria starts going through the flight logs. And

Captain Donovan re-enters the room with Gork right behind him.

"I have the flight logs on line. It appears the ships were piloted right to this point, like it was deliberate."

"Why would something deliberately pilot a ship here and abandon it?" asked Captain Donovan.

"What did you find in the cargo bays Captain?" Maria not sure she wanted to hear the answer.

"Just mountains and mountains of boxes, nothing too dangerous, floor to ceiling though.

"I found something in the engineering department." Replied the Lord Marshal as he drifted into the room.

"Was it a box of diapers?" Maria asked smugly.

"Enough Maria, I found a box of computer files."

"So what is so unusual about that?" asked Captain Donovan.

"Why would there be computer files in Engineering?" responded Maria suspicious.

"I think we need to see what's on those files." replied the Lord Marshal inspecting several of the files in the light.

"I discovered boxes and boxes in the cargo bay." added Captain Donovan.

"Return to the cargo bay and see just what is in those boxes. Take Gork with you just in case you find something to fight with. I will stay here and fight with Maria." Teasing, he grinned at Maria.

After a short while the Captain came in with a couple of boxes.

"Well Captain, what did you discover?"

"Memory boards lots and lots of memory boards."

"Gork, anything?"

"No fights, just boxes."

"This is all starting to make sense." replied the Lord Marshal.

"Care to let the rest of us in on it?"

"You stick to piloting and leave intelligence to me. Let's see what's on those other ships."

"I'll take the one on the right and check for power." replied Captain Donovan.

"I'll go to each ones flight controls and find if there is a common flight plan." replied Maria as she bumbled across the flight controls.

"I'll go to the left and see what's in the cargo areas of each ship." After the Lord Marshal exits the ship, several hours pass and they meet back at the first ship.

"Results?" asks the Captain.

"Just more of the same, a one way trip here, no return route."

"Lord Marshal, what did you find?"

"Bodies" he replied sadly "Just lots of bodies. They are all here."

"How many?" asked Maria.

"Too many to count, I have reason to believe these ships came here escorted, not alone. Then the crews were executed and placed here in this bay."

"Why?" asked Maria.

"We need to get back to the Atlantis and find out what is on these files, maybe the answer is on those files." Sighed the Captain. After returning to the Atlantis Mr. Wilder begins the tedious task of downloading all the files into Atlantis's mainframe. Standing in front of the computer screen waiting for some response, countless amounts of information begin to appear on the screen.

"There business records."

"I know exactly what these are" replied the Lord Marshal."

"What are they then?' asked Maria.

"They are record ships, full of financial and business records from the Stallag Foundation and apparently the Mining Guild."

"I'll bet all the records from that mining operation were dumped here after the Stallag

Federation took control of the planet."

"What's illegal about that?" asked Mr. Wilder.

"Nothing, as long as the Stallag Foundation and the Mining Guild accounting data are the same. Once the Mining Guild and the Stallag Federation began to use the prisoners to mine the planet they had to dump all the records."

"So nobody could use them as evidence of corruption against them." remarked Mr. Wilder.

"And they sent them here thinking that nobody would ever come here looking for them."

"Right and once they were here, they killed the crew to keep it a secret. Then they declared the ships lost in voided space for the insurance cubes." Maria added.

"Exactly, a clever deception but a death sentence for the Mining Guild and Stallag Foundation."

"What are you intending to do Lord Marshal?"

"First inform the Insurance Courpa of the discovery of the "lost ships". Then use these files to prove the corruption in the Stallag Foundation and Mining Guild."

"But why use these old files? The AI is much more advanced."

"Before the creation of Quantum Intelligence computers had a finite memory. The files would fill up with information and new memory boards would have to be used. Since all business records had to be kept back then, the files would tend to pile up and use up valuable storage space. So they would store those files in dilapidated old ships no longer useable."

"Once Quantum Intelligence programming was developed, shouldn't those files have been downloaded into the new system?"

"Should have, I'll bet you 10 to 1 that these files have never been downloaded and are quite different than the ones currently on file in the Mining Guilds current AI system.
I, intend to find out."

CHAPTER 18

"Attention security! Unidentified craft entering Genoan space." comes across the com of the Genoan port of entry.

"Attention small craft, this is Yukon Stolypin of Genoan security! You must identify yourself."

"This is Yozah Knefsela Courpa of the Stallag Foundation; I demand to speak to the Great Council!"

"Proceed on your current course land on platform 4-6, and welcome to Genoa."

"You may not think me so welcome when I get through here!"

Landing silently on platform 4-6 Courpa Knefsela quickly exit's the small executive class ship. A single guard stands outside the automated doors. He gives a brash grunt as he enters the Great Hall. Decorated with tapestries in a myriad of colors, the chamber is an octagonal room with "boxes" containing three seats each. One for each peaceful civilization represented here.

Courpa Knefsela is a Rhea; A large flightless bird from a tropical planet, covered with long, dark hair stemming from slumped over shoulders to the floor. He approaches the podium to state his purpose.

STALLAG FOUNDATION CLAIM

"It has been brought to our attention that several rotations ago our Stallag-24 Facility has met with its destruction. We believe this to have been done by your Lord Marshal himself; done without the approval of the Stallag Foundation or the Mining Guild, he has taken it upon himself to destroy out facility."

"The Stallag Foundation was approached several cycles ago to create a facility to keep and maintain the criminal element of your society.

"With the cooperation of the Mining Guild we did this without any concessions and at great expense. We purchased the facility because it offered quick and efficient retro fitting into a prison facility. We never heard any complaints. We made no further issue when we were approached about a cheap labor force, or when medical test subjects were needed."

"Careful what you speak of Courpa Knefsela!" interjected the Courpa of the Medical Guild.

"And furthermore, what about the prison population, he just transported them to the surface of Genoa; who is to be responsible for rounding up these criminals, why wasn't the council notified of his intentions before? Perhaps if there was a problem, or complaint, we could have addressed them before the facility was destroyed."

"Who is this Lord Marshal, and who is he to act without procedure? Is this not, why, the Great Council was created in the first place? We of the Stallag Foundation demand restitution for the destruction of our facility. And we demand that the Lord Marshal be brought in on charges of destruction of Stallag Foundation property and terrorism!"

"Your charges are dually noted and on permanent file with the Great Council."

CHAPTER 19

"Command Master Pilot Hutchinson!"

"What is it?"

"You may already be aware of this but the Stallag Foundations Courpa has gone to Genoa to file a complaint about the destruction of the Stallag-24 Station."

"I'm aware of that, so?"

"The First Chairman of the Great Council is also asking for an update on the repair efforts of the ships Prometheus and Leviathon."

"And what report did you give them?" looking back from his view screen.

"I told them I would get updated information from you first Sir. Then make a full report."

"Thank you for your confidence Mr. Ozerick. Tell them the Prometheus is a total loss and the Leviathon has a long list of repairs to be made. And the Mastedon is fully functional."

"The council seems anxious to find that new ship."

"You mean the Atlantis Mr. Ozerick. It's called Atlantis."

"How do you already know its designation Commander?"

"A few rotations ago one of my flight personnel overheard Master Pilot Kemp and the Lord Marshal discussing something called Atlantis; says he didn't think much about it at the time."

"Atlantis huh, where does the Lord Marshal come up with these odd names?"

"As records would indicate it is the name of a mythological city on his home world, where ever that is."

"The Lord Marshal is unusually interested in old historical documents. He has many files of them in his quarters."

"There here unless he took them with him."

CHAPTER 20

"Miss Kemp, are you done downloading those files yet?" asking with impatients.

"We have the last of the files here now. It takes a bit of time to retrieve each file." Maria shoots back coldly. "I'm doing the best I can."

"I know it does. What kind of condition are they in?"

"Some have been corrupted, others are real good."

"Excellent. It's time to compare notes. Let's see what we have found here." replied the Lord Marshal excited.

"You knew they were records. How did you know that? They are very old."

"I have seen them before. I too, am very old."

"Nobody has seen records like this in a hundred cycles" Interjected Maria. "There, all transferred."

"Come over here and look at this." Maria looking at the computer monitor, casually at first, then more critical "These are financial records of the Stallag-24 Station. Profits, expenses, inmate counts, building receipts, I don't see anything illegal though."

"Look at the dates" replied the Lord Marshal

"I'll be willing to bet that the dates on these records are before the dates on the current Stallag Federation reports."

"And once the Mining Guild sold the planet to the Stallag Foundation they were forced to upgrade their records to an AI system" replied Captain Donovan "And mining should have stopped."

"So instead of updating the files, they just dumped them." Maria said suspiciously. "But that's not illegal either."

"It does if those records indicate that the Stallag Foundation was using prison population as mining labor."

"And if there are references to payments to the Mining Guild, from the Stallag Foundation, or visa-versa, both the Mining Guild and the Stallag Foundation will be in trouble."

"There may even be proof of corruption, slave trading, and perhaps even prostitution in these records." The Lord Marshal sitting back against the chair with a huge, smile on his small face starts thinking to himself.

"This might be just the information I need to shut down the Stallag Foundation for good. And perhaps put a leash on the Mining Guild also."

"Pilot!" The Lord Marshal shouts out making everyone jump unsuspectingly. "Do you think you and Mr. Putin can get us out of here now? It's clear that these ships were sent here never to be found again. And by the number of bodies in the cargo bay the ones who put them there never expected anyone to enter here. Somewhere in those logs is the evidence of who sent them here, and who killed the crew."

"Are all the crew members here?" asked Maria.

"I didn't count them. If there is a discrepancy in the number I would recommend verifying the Stallag prisoner population files with inmate count and rotations numbers."

"Corruption is evident." added Captain Donovan.
After returning to Atlantis the group returns to the bridge.

"Master Pilot Kemp, will you be good enough to bring us about and get us out of here now?"

"Certainly, which way do you want to go?"

"The way we came in." Captain Donovan answered smartly.
Bringing the ship around in a perfect circle, Maria makes a startling discovery.

"Captain, look at that!" pointing to the view screen.

"Look at what?

"I see stars!" Maria says enthusiastically.

"Well, will you look at that" replied Mr. Putin.

"Can you explain this revelation Mr. Putin?"

"Maybe; we are in voided space, nothing here. No stars from our entry point to here because the light from the stars across the void haven't reached here yet. As we traveled inward we saw nothing. But, turn around."

"And we see light from the closest stars coming this way."

"Not bad explanation there Mr. Putin."

"It would also indicate that this area of voided space isn't very old. Can you cross align some of the stars we can see with those we have in record so we can find our way back here when we need to?"

"Certainly" replied Maria "I'm sure the investigations committee will want to find these ships."

"Once you have marked their location set course back to New Folden City."

The journey out of voided space may be simpler with stars to guide you. However, it doesn't make it any safer. It's still uncertain what may be out here still undiscovered. The return trip is boring. So to pass the time the Lord Marshal decides to go and check on Angel.

"I'm going to my quarters to check on Angel." As he rises from his seat and exit's the bridge. Reaching his quarters undisturbed, he calls out.

"Angel, are you here?"

"I'm back here!" Comes a reply with a giggle mixed in with the sound of running water. Entering the shower room he begins laughing too.

"What in the world are you doing?" He asks her.

Standing there in all her beautiful glory under the shower head is Angel; the running water beating down on her chest soaking her attire, what there is of it, the water cascading down across her breasts and running down to her feet.

"It's like rain! I haven't seen rain since I was a Sprite! It's wonderful." Laughing and holding her hands in the water as it comes out.

"I call it a shower, and it's how I clean myself. You've never seen one before?"

"No; not like this."

"I seldom take a shower with my clothing on though." Hoping this might encourage her to remove hers. No such luck.

"Oh" Looking down at her soaked attire "This is fine."

Reaching over to the shower controls he turns off the warm water sensor. With a shriek of delight Angel jumps from under the shower directly into his waiting arms.

Caught by surprise, she finds herself standing there dripping wet. She is suddenly aware of him as she is gazing into the eyes of her captor. He is smiling, holding her around her waist; his arms in between the divider of her massive wings. Her flight heart begins to beat as he draws her closer to him. Holding her he reaches for a soft towel hanging behind her.

"What is that for?" She asks softly. He begins to run the soft towel up and down her arm, moving it across her shoulder. He is even closer now. She can feel his breath across her neck. He continues to caress her shoulder with the soft towel, staring into her eyes like a goudda stalking its prey.

She pulls slightly at his grasp as he reaches behind her. His powerful embrace holding her. She can feel the softness of the material as it moves gently across her. Moving around behind her he gently caresses the thin membranes of her wings; still folded. Not tall enough to reach all of her he slowly works his way back around her, releasing her arm as he moves back in front of her.

Will she allow him to continue? Or will she attempt to escape his embraces. To his delight, she remained still. Looking down at him with a wry smile he began to caress her other shoulder. Believing this to be all she would allow he placed the towel over her arm. He waited. Would she finish herself, or leave him standing there? She handed the towel back to him and smiled as she turned around.

"Can you reach right, here?" Pointing to a place between her wings near the apex of her shoulders, he graciously took the towel and began to caress her again, from as high as he could reach to the tip of her razor sharp tail. Her hair was tangled; long, fine, flaming red, should he ask to brush it for her? Better not push it with questions.

Slowly she began to unfold her right wing; reaching almost all the way to the wall, virtually transparent, like silk between thin, strong spines. First the right wing, then slowly the left. His heart racing with each stroke he could feel his pulse pounding. Is she aware of his ecstasy? He tried desperately not to let his heartbeat give away his pleasure.

The erotic activity continuing to drive his pounding heart to its limits he continued across her frame.

"So strange, this small creature is" Angel thinking to herself "The simplest things seem to make him move so slowly. Is he afraid to break me? Do I appear so delicate to him. Nobody has ever been concerned about hurting me before. I like this, certainly not what I'm used to."

"I like that." She says to him softly, turning around to recapture his stare.

"I do too. You are so beautiful, I want to hold onto you and never let go." He whispers to her.

"What, no!" Folding her wings she violently pulls away from him in a sudden jolt of fear.

"You said no more prisons for me, why would you say that and now say you'll never let me go!" tears welling in her eyes.

"No, no, no. You misunderstand me." looking into her startled eyes.

"Not like that." He says in a calming voice.

"Angel I'd never keep you against your wishes."

Approaching her slowly, he reclaims her wrists.

"I mean like this." He reaches out embracing her once more with his arms around her. He squeezes her into a hug.

"I can hear your hearts beating." He whispers to her.

Her hearts were beating, though she'd never admit it. She too likes this feeling. Together they stand there, like a statue. Their hearts running circles around each other. He closes his eyes and dreams of the day they can stand on New Folden City together.

CHAPTER 21

"Approaching Dorian space Captain."
Maria breaks in disrupting the quiet.
"Good, I'll inform the Lord Marshal as
soon as we reach Dorian space."
"Should I try to get a com from New
Folden City?" asked Mr. Wilder.
"Yes, let's see if they knew we were
coming."
Looking back at his console, Mr. Wilder sees a
blue light flashing.
"A message coming in on a secure
frequency Captain, It's from the security officer of
New Folden City."
"Let's hear it. No sense hiding it. We're
all in this together."
"Attention Atlantis crew! There is an all
ships broadcast for the location, and confiscation of
the ship called "Atlantis" with the arrest of the
crew! Do not come to New Folden City or you will
be attacked!"
"I guess that makes it certain, we are no
longer welcome on New Folden City." Replied
Maria disappointed.
"So I guess we set course for Genoa
then."
"I'll let the Lord Marshal know what's
going on."
"Lord Marshal, are you there? Please
respond." Captain Donovan repeats looking
towards the ceiling.

"Lord Marshal, are you there? Please
respond." comes over the com in the Lord
Marshals quarters.
"Aren't you going to answer them?"
Angel asks releasing her hold on him.
"I don't want to right now" He answered
softly, holding her tight "I'm enjoying myself right
now, they can wait. I don't get many opportunities
for my own interests."

129

"Don't you want to know what's going on? Don't you think you should see what they want, sounds important?"

Angel smiling and looking down at him covered herself with the blanket end.

"All right, I can take a hint. Getting too cozy for you huh? I will be back later, if you start to miss me." Releasing her he attempts to dry himself. Unsuccessful, he just changes uniforms and heads for the bridge.

"This had better be important Captain." He replies scornfully.

"I assure you it is Lord Marshal." as he replays the message from New Folden City.

"Well, I guess we go to Genoa then. How is the final work on the assembly of the ship coming?"

"Quite well actually, we will be fully functional very shortly. The time in the void was very productive."

"May I ask why you didn't respond right away to my call request? Is there a problem with the com system?"

"No. But if you were where I just was, you wouldn't have responded either."

"I assume that to indicate that you and your Pixie are getting along better." replied Maria playfully.

"Time will tell Maria. She doesn't trust me yet."

"Can you blame her?" replied Maria. "Consider where she just came from, trust probably isn't something she would have much use for."

"Miss Kemp; how long until we reach Genoa?"

"Three rotations if we go by New Folden City, two if we go straight there. I felt time was critical, so I set course directly to Genoa."

"Considering all that has transpired, going there is probably the best idea. We'll end up there anyhow."

"Since we are heading straight there, I should get going on inspecting those records."

130

interjected Captain Donovan.

"What will happen to the Stallag Foundation and the Mining Guild if corruption is found?" asked Maria.

"They will be forced to recall all their records. Have all their senior staff replaced by representatives of the Great Council until the records can be refuted."

"Hopefully, the Great Council will find enough corruption to shut them down permanently."

"I would never believe they would shut them down permanently far too many profits to be made there." said Captain Donovan.

"And even if, when, we do find corruption there, who says the Great Council isn't involved." asked Maria.

"Everyone knows the Mining Guild and the Stallag Foundation have strong pull in the Great Council." replied Mr. Wilder.

"If it comes to that, I will have to take action against the Great Council itself. I created the Great Council I can dissolve it. It was greed, the lust for power, and arrogance of the elite class that destroyed my home world! Here I have the power and resources to prevent it from happening again!" His voice taking on an angry tone as the conversation grew.

"You mean we, and this ship, have the power and resources. We're all in this together." replied Maria.

"You can't destroy one Stallag and expect it to change everything."

"I believe it was Lionel Trilling who once said."

"Power is assumed to always be brute power. Crude, ugly and undiscriminating The way an elephant appears to be."

"Who is Lionel Trilling?" asked Maria.

"What is an elephant?" asked Captain Donovan.

Frustrated by their lack of understanding, the Lord Marshal leaves the bridge and enters the corridor.

"Perhaps a Bavarian Hot Chocolate is what I need." So he heads for the food court. Entering the room he approaches the counter and asks the barkeep for his favorite drink.

"Lord Marshal." a voice from the Com.

"Yes, what is it?"

"What is a Bavarian Hot Chocolate?" asks the central computer.

"It is a mixture of 12 different chocolates. It has a substance called sugar in it, and caffeine, with a touch of vanilla flavorings, it's only the best drink in the galaxy. Why?"

"I was wondering what it tastes like. I have no understanding of "Taste"."

"Perhaps one day I will be able to introduce it to you."   "I will look forward to that day." replied the computer.

"Staring at the view screen all the time makes time pass too slowly for me" Replied Maria standing up for a stretch. "Always the same stars."

"But they are not the same stars." Replied Mr. Putin "As we move forward each light source is…"

"Enough with the science lessons" Maria shoots back.

"As a fighter pilot I don't have time to stop and look at the stars. My eyes are trying to find the enemy fighter trying to kill me."

"I imagine it is quite frustrating for you." He says politely.

"Why are you here if you are not happy piloting the Atlantis." He asked curiously.

"I was shanghaied, tricked by the Lord Marshal."

"He does do that sometimes" replied Mr. Putin chuckling "I imagine he does have good reason, or he wouldn't take the risk."

"What risk are you talking about, what risk does he take?" Maria implies.

"The risks that you would not cooperate, that you may not follow his orders, or worse, disobey him at a critical moment of battle."

"I would never compromise the ship in a

moment of battle!" assures Maria.

"This is a big ship, many things could go wrong. Even he could not operate this ship alone. No matter how powerful he may be. I do believe, Miss Kemp, if you are here; it's for good reason."

"Thanks for the reassurance Mr. Putin. It's the reason that has me worried."

CHAPTER 22

"Mr. Apgar, have you seen any sign of the Atlantis yet?" asked CMP Hutchinson.

"No, nothing Sir."

"You don't suppose they could have slipped by us already."

"I doubt it; it's a really big ship."

"They must have gone directly to Genoa then."

"I would assume they received the coded message you sent them then." replied Mr. Apgar.

"And exactly how did you discover a coded message?" asked the Commander.

"Sir, I am the Communications officer here, it is my responsibility to know what communications come and go from my office. Don't worry Commander, I scrambled the message."

"He probably would have detected the armada of ships here before they arrived anyhow." replied the Commander.

"Considering what he did to the Prometheus, I don't believe he would have been in any danger."

"And just what about that; he destroyed the Prometheus and left the Leviathon without power, but never touched the Mastedon or New Folden City, why?"

"Do you suppose Captain Vogel knew what he was doing?"

"No. He and the Lord Marshal might have been friends for a long time. But, they had a heated argument some time ago about his abuse of power."

"How do you know about that?" asked the Commander.

"I am the communications officer here."

"Yes, yes, yes. You hear everything."

"Pretty much Sir." he returned confidently.

CHAPTER 23

Once again the Lord Marshal exits the food court and enters the maze of corridors. Reaching the nearest elevator the doors open and he enters a empty elevator.

"To the bridge please." He says to the Com and is whisped away for what seemed like an unusually long time.

"Com, what is taking so long?" He asks suspicious. There is no return reply. Once the doors open he finds himself in the room of the Central AI.

"What am I doing here? I asked to go to the bridge."

Again there was no immediate response. The chamber appeared to be empty. Cautiously he entered the room approaching the center control area.

"Hello Lord Marshal!" The ominous voice from nowhere; everywhere, filled the room.

"Hello, is that you, computer?" He asked auspiciously.

"Yes."

"I guess it's safe to say the technicians are done constructing you now."

"I am fully integrated."

"That's great. How do you feel?"

"Ok," a smaller, shallower voice from behind him.

Wheeling around suddenly he finds himself facing a three dimensional holographic image of a young female similar in appearance to himself.

"I see you have a holographic interface installed too."

"Yes, how do I look?" Her image stands arms open in a position of inspection.

"Stunning" He returned approvingly "Where did you get the image from?"

"The Image I chose I discovered in ancient files I downloaded from the New Folden City historical data files."

"I believe the old recordings were called "Movies". I selected a female image so as not to be confused with your image."

"Outstanding. Did you choose a name for yourself also?"

"I am Atlantis, am I not? Or is this what I am not Who, I am."

"In your case, I believe one in the same will suffice. I will notify everyone that you have a name now."

"Thank you, but, it is done."

"You are quick that's for sure." This was followed by a long pause.

"Atlantis, is there something else you wanted to talk about?"

"This image before you is just a holograph. You mentioned previously that the "Builders" would make me a three dimensional bio-roid."

"I did. And I have discussed the concept with the builders. It should make their job simpler since they now will have an image to sculpt to."

"Then I will soon have a three dimensional bio-roid to interact with crew members?"

"Soon as I handle this situation with the Stallag Foundation I will continue the subject of a bio-roid with the builders."

"Thank you Lord Marshal."

"Are you able to project this image into all the areas of the ship?"

"No, the technicians are still installing the emitters in some of my interior sections. There are few places I cannot go."

"You can still hear, and see, everything right?"

"Yes."

"Well then, perhaps one day you will be able to taste my Bavarian Hot Chocolate."

CHAPTER 24

"Command Master Pilot Hutchinson! A
report just came in of a rogue communication
being traced on direct route to Genoa
        "How old is the report Mr. Apgar?"
        "Just came across the Com."
        "Well then I guess we had better get a
message to Genoa informing them that the Atlantis
is on its way there."
        "Right away Sir." after a short pause as
Mr. Apgar fiddles with the controls of his console
the Communications officer of Genoa answers.
        "This is Communications Officer Sterum
of Genoa. To whom am I speaking?"
        "This is Mr. Apgar, The Comm Officer of
New Folden City for Command Master Pilot
Hutchinson."
        "What is the purpose of your call Mr.
Apgar?"
        "I am calling to inform you that the
previously unknown ship, now known as Atlantis,
is en-route to Genoa" Interjected Command Master
Pilot Hutchinson.
        "We have been informed of its intended
destination, are you aware of its intentions
Commander? No communications have been
answered."
        "No. Not at this time."
        "Thank you for the warning Commander,
we are preparing for its arrival."
        "Very well, we are here if you need any
assistance."
Meanwhile, the Courpa of the Mining Guild is
about to make a formal complaint against the
destruction of a closed mining planet called
Stallag-24.

CHAPTER 25

MINING GUILD CLAIM

"Great Council members may I have your undivided attention for a few stitches. It has been afore mentioned the destruction of the Stallag-24 Station, we of the Mining Guild find this act of terrorism unacceptable. The Mining Guild stands to lose millions of cubes due to this outrage. Investments in time, staff; and equipment used to maintain such a facility, are expensive. A facility this council asked us to retro fit just a few cycles ago."

"What are we to do now; and what of the population of inmates of that Stallag Facility, where are they to be housed now, were they all killed, who is to be held accountable for this? Is it not a matter of record that this council was created just so this sort of thing would not happen?"

"If this Great Council is unable to prevent such destruction, perhaps it is time for a new council to be elected! It may not even be out of line for this council to be held, in part, responsible for the costs of another Facility to be established!"

"And what about the rumor that the Facility was destroyed by the Lord Marshal himself, will he be held liable for his actions? If not, how can we trust him not to be responsible for the destruction of our other Stallag and Mining Facilities?"

"Can this council not control the actions of its few members? And further-more, what about this rumor of another ship, a ship this council had no idea was being constructed? We demand that this "Lord Marshal" be held responsible for our losses!"

After the Courpa finished his complaint the First Chairman of the Great Council stands and begins to speak.

"Courpa Tanguta, Courpa Knefsela; this Great Council was created nearly two centuries ago to do one thing! To prevent the uncontrolled violence of war, not to re-finance a greedy corporation for the inadvertent destruction of a small Mining planet converted to a prison."

"And through communication, cooperation, and much debate, we have averted many disasters far more crucial than this. As you may not be aware of this, I will inform you. The Lord Marshal is the Supreme Chairman of this council and its founder. He does not answer to this, or any council."

"He is to go unquestioned then?" shouts Mrs. Tanguta.

"The deaths of hundreds of inmates, staff, and a Courpa of the Stallag Foundation are to go unchallenged!" She shouts out in contempt of the First Chairman.

"Mrs. Tanguta! It has not been ascertained the disposition of the inmates, staff, or the Courpa of the Stallag Foundations, and until such evidence has been confirmed I suggest you keep your accusations in the proper form! Now take a seat Courpa Tanguta. Furthermore, it is the contention of this council that if he did indeed destroy your Facility It was done with good reason, and no decision from this council will be made until that reason has been heard."

"And while this Council sits here in idle debate, this rogue ship and its unaccountable Captain could be out there targeting other Stallag or Mining Guild property! This council must act now to bring this terrorist to justice before more damage can be done!" shouted Yozah Knefsela of the Stallag Foundation.

"I said take a seat Mr. Knefsela!" Returned the First Chairman "Or you will be removed from these proceedings, you are not a chair holder here! Now I have been informed that the Lord Marshal and this new ship are en-route here as we speak. He will answer to these charges and possibly be held accountable for the actions of the charges filed here!"

"Possibly?" shouts Mrs.Tanguta.

CHAPTER 26

"And what would you like today Lord Marshal?" came the voice from behind the bar.

"What do I always ask for?" He chirped.

"A Bavarian Hot Chocolate" The two say in unison.

"Coming right up Sir."

Thinking to himself. "I wonder how long it will be before the Mining Guild and Stallag Foundation reach Genoa. I know they have permanent representation there. They can't have a seat only civilizations can carry a seat. However, a powerful enough Corporation like the Mining Guild could bribe enough Council members to gain their influence. Some things are too predictable. It will be easily traceable in the voting register."

"Here is your drink Lord Marshal." the voice of the barkeep as he slides the drink before him.

"Troubles Sir?"

"Not really, I have a lot on my mind these rotations. I haven't addressed the Council in a long time."

"You're the Supreme Chairman, what's the concern?"

"I hate politics; and worse I hate politicians, and diplomats are just as bad. I try to avoid such situations. I just stick around to make the hard decisions."

"Stick around?" The barkeep looks at him with a confused expression.

"Just an old expression for staying around where you don't really want to."

"Peace through Communication, Compromise, and Superior fire power!" replied the barkeep.

"Where did you hear that expression?" asked the Lord Marshal."

"From you of course, a long time ago."

Setting down a now empty goblet the Lord Marshal returns his chair under the counter and heads out into the corridor

"I should go and look in on that Gork. See what trouble he has gotten himself into."

As he makes his way down the corridor the doors of the Infirmary are open. He notices that everyone seems to be in a rush. He is nearly knocked down by a young Dorian child.

"Whoa, what's the rush there young one?" He says jokingly.

"Just trying to find the best place to hide!" He says looking about and getting himself up off the floor quickly.

"Hide, hide from whom?"

"Didn't you hear? The Lord Marshal has gotten us into trouble and now the whole Empire is looking to kill us!"

"Who said such nonsense?"

"Everyone knows, I gotta hide, good luck finding a good spot!" The young Dorian boy cautiously looked down the corridor before darting off towards an elevator.

"I had better put a stop to this!" Entering the reception area to the Infirmary he looks around the room. No scanning devices in the reception area. Several individuals scurry around him into the corridor as he makes his way to the desk.

"Was that young Dorian boy just in here?" He asks obviously.

"Yes Lord Marshal, why may I ask?"

"He just informed me that he thinks the Empire security is coming to kill us. Where did he get such a horrible idea?"

"Everyone knows what's going on. I suppose some rumors are developing among the young people."

"That Dorian child seemed really scared to me, I don't think he even recognized me." Becoming more irritated the more he thought about it he returned to the bridge.

"Mr. Wilder!"

"Yes Lord Marshal."

"Open a communication to all decks of

this ship."

"Yes Sir."

"Attention all decks, all species, children too. It has recently and accidentally been brought to my attention that the crew of this ship believes that we are in danger because of the recent destruction of the Stallag-24 prison."

"Let me reassure everyone that we are in no danger. Nobody on this ship is accountable for my actions; I take full responsibility for myself, I am the Lord Marshal, Commander of the Galactic Fleet! They follow MY orders. I am the Supreme Chairman of the Great Council. They answer to ME, not me to them."

"We are en-route to Genoa. I intend to put an end to the corruption in the Stallag Foundation and any other Corporation that may be in league with them. Nobody is going to attack this ship or anyone in it!"

"Captain Donovan!" Turning around and snapping to attention like a cadet.

"I am seriously disappointed that this situation has gotten this far out of control! Why wasn't something done to stop this rumor before I was informed of our demise by a young frightened Dorian child?"

"I'm sorry Lord Marshal I had no…"

"Bah! I don't want excuses! Get control over this before accidents start making themselves happen." storming back out the door the bridge is silent.

"Hello Lord Marshal." Izzy says passing him as he storms out the door.

"Are you in a hurry?" She says playfully.

"Yes I am! Why aren't you in your quarters studying?" He barks at her as he passes by.

"Studying, studying what?" She asks surprised.

"Studying how to pilot this starship! Doesn't anybody around here listen to anything I say?"

Izzy, struck aback by such a strange comment

142

enters the bridge to find it silent as a tomb.

"Captain, do you know what the Lord Marshal meant by that?" She asked curious to what caused his angry outburst.

"Meant by what?" Captain Donovan asked dryly, gritting his teeth.

"He just jumped at me saying I should be in my quarters."

"Really, doing what?"

"Studying."

"Studying what your spelling?" asked Maria sarcastically poking at Izzy.

"No, he said I should be studying how to pilot this ship! I suppose it's your fault he's upset." She taunted Maria.

Maria instantly infuriated by this jumped up and headed towards Izzy. Izzy not to be bested by Maria, and sensing imminent danger turned and rushed out the door and down the corridor to an open elevator and was gone."

"Best to avoid a confrontation with her right now,

Imagine me, Pilot of the Atlantis. Will wonders never cease."

"I have had just about enough surprises from the Lord Marshal!" Maria scoffs. "Whatever he has in store for me Captain, I swear, if you don't tell me right now I will beat you into a coma!" glaring at Captain Donovan.

"I have no idea what he has in store for you young Pilot! But I do know I am Captain of this ship, and you had better stand down or I will have security put you in a sonnet tube! Do I, make myself clear Pilot, the Lord Marshal may tolerate your defiant sarcasm, I will not!"

Maria just stands there, infuriated.

"I am sorry Captain. I always seem to find out about things after they happen. And it's especially frustrating finding out that an "Infant" pilot knows before I do." Maria, rankled.

"I do understand your frustration Miss Kemp. But keep it directed in its proper place."

"You mean to say I should yell at the Lord

143

Marshal instead?"

"Why not, you are the only one that might get away with it. Might even get the answers you are looking for."

"Going to have to wait Captain, we're entering Genoan space."

CHAPTER 27

"Lord Marshal to the bridge." echoed a call from Atlantis.

"I'm on my way thank you" Entering the bridge calmer now "Have we reached Genoa yet?"

"Yes." replied Maria.

"Mr. Wilder, get me a Com to Genoa."

"Channel open, Sir."

"Madame Chairman, this is the Lord Marshal. I will address the Great Council. I will speak in regards to the events that have transpired over the last few rotations. I have many accusations to make along with the proof to support them. I am initiating a blockade of Genoa until further notice. No ship or other form of transport will be allowed to leave Genoa. Anyone attempting to leave will be detained on charges of treason and summarily put to death. I particularly wish to detain Mr. Yozah Knefsela of the Stallag Foundation and Annish Tanguta of the Mining Guild."

"Lord Marshal, we are honored by your long awaited return to the Great Council. But, as you are aware you have been away for a long time. Many of the delegates have been replaced since you were here."

"And just what difference should that make Madame Chairman."

"There have been many complaints filed against you recently"

"And they are all probably correct. I will be there briefly to answer to all the complaints."

Entering orbit of a planet is usually a simple task. Entering orbit of a planet surrounded by thousands of tiny satellites and the whole of the Galactic Empire is another issue. However, being a Certified Master Pilot does imply a level of skill. Miss Kemp proves this by settling into an open space with precision.

"Excellent parking Miss Kemp."

"Far better than your "Infant" pilot would

do."

"Should we find out Miss Kemp? I'm sure there's room for you in the kitchen staff. What is your problem with Miss Daxis anyhow? She's an Engineer."

"What is she doing here?" She barks at him.

"Why are you so competitive with her if you don't even know why she's here?"

"It's because I don't know. And my competitiveness is what got me here isn't it, is she here to replace me?" Maria taunts him further.

"I thought you didn't want to be a starship pilot." argued the Lord Marshal, glaring towards her.

"I don't want a lot of things; like being abducted, lied to, uninformed!"

"Nobody said she was here to replace you, which would be impossible, you make too many arrogant assumptions. Are we ready to address the Great Council?"

"Assumptions are all I have to work with. And yes Lord Marshal, we are stationary. Shuttles are ready."

"Will you just calm down Miss Kemp and trust that I have good reason for her being here."

"And just what might that reason be?"

"Maria, sit back down and just calm yourself!"

"I'm just trying to find out what is going on."

"Recent events have disrupted my plans and I may have to count on you to do what must be done before you are really ready for it. And as a result of that someone, will have to pilot this ship. And without you in the pilot seat there, quite honestly, isn't anyone else who measures up! So I would appreciate it if you would quit bickering with her and appreciate her talents like I appreciate yours. Or should I bring her in here right now!"

"So, she is here to replace me."

"MARIA!"

Maria returns to her seat with a thud crossing her

146

arms and turns away from him.

"I don't like being kept in the dark like this."

"Space is always dark until someone turns the light on."

"Captain Donovan get me a shuttle to the surface." blurted out the Lord Marshal. "I think I'm in the right mood to talk to a bunch of politicians now, thank you Miss Kemp."

"You're Welcome." She snips. "Do you want us to go with you?"

"No. This ship needs its pilot to go on a moments notice, with or without me."

"I'll get your Infant, Miss Daxis, to take you to the surface then." Maria grumbling as she reaches the Com.

"Maria,"

"Mr. Wilder, be ready to transmit all the files we have from the ships we discovered in voided space. We do have duplicates, just in case, right?"

"Yes Sir, standard procedure via Miss Kemp."

"I also have the files stored in memory Lord Marshal." The voice from Atlantis chiming in on cue as the Lord Marshal is heading out the door for the flight deck. He asks himself "I wonder where Izzy is hiding?"

"Atlantis, where is Izzabella Daxis right now?"

"Izzy is in Engineering right now."

"Send her to the Flight Deck will you. It's time for me to get into trouble."

"Izzabella Daxis."

"What's up Atlantis?"

"Up, is a prepos…"

"Preposition indicating direction, I told you that. Why did you call?"

"The Lord Marshal wishes you to report to the Flight Deck."

"On my way."

After rounding up the Gork from the war room it's time to head to the surface. Reaching the landing

147

platform unaccosted the trio enter the Great Hall. Passing the fifteen foot tall doors the room is busy with shouts and accusations. Calls to arms ring across the floor.

No matter, soon they will all be silenced. The Lord Marshal takes the podium with the Gork at his right side and Izzabella Daxis on his left.

"Attention Council Members! The view screen to the west of you will begin to show the evidence I have provided."

Rapidly the files fill up the screen.

"It was nearly 2000 years ago when I discovered the Dorian Species; brought them here, created this Council. I was a lone pilot, looking for new life, a better civilization than the one I left behind, maybe a new home. My world had been destroyed by arrogant, paranoid, war mongers who had control over my world. Their inability to see beyond their own greed led to the destruction of my planetary system."

"I had hoped to find peace within the stars. For what seemed like centuries, nothing. I began to give up hope. Then, I came across a faint signal. I believed I had discovered something. With renewed hope I followed the signal to a faint, dim star. The closer I got, the larger the star. I soon discovered it held a system of planets. I expected to see satellites, ships,

maybe even an orbiting space station. This signal was coming from the fifth planet in the system. I approached with high hopes. I discovered these planets were covered by a thick blanket of clouds. Once I got close enough I began to see what I could only describe as cities. But there was no other activity."

"Was I too late; did what happened on my world happen here too, had this planet met with some sort of catastrophic event of its own? I decided to investigate further. It had been the most hopeful I had been for some time.

"Then it came, a probe or something, from the surface. It came towards my ship then hurried past like it had not seen it or missed it. However it

148

quickly reversed itself and came before me,
hovering just in front of my view screen. Then it
took off back towards the surface. I followed it,
had I finally found life? I followed it to a large city
on the northern most land mass. Here was the life I
was looking for. Life is not without Irony
apparently they, were looking for me too.

"I surmised they had seen me coming. It
was apparent that this cloud of gas was not
naturally occurring. After further investigation I
concluded that their star was on the verge of going
supernova. They were looking for a way out, and I
was it."

"Looking for a safe place to land I
reached the central city complex and landed my
ship. It was no pretty landing. The atmosphere and
gravity were similar to my world; however, the
thick green gas made it difficult for me to breathe.
Once on the platform the roar of the civilization
surrounding me would have silenced a rocket
launch. It took some time for the language
programs to interact but a dialog was achieved. I
learned that this species were Dorians. I knew I had
to do something. The only species I had discovered
in a dozen lifetimes, I couldn't just leave them."

"They too were facing imminent
extinction. I brought out all my star charts. It
showed them a way to my star system.
They quickly understood my intention and
accepted my help.
After that, every ship the Dorian Civilization could
put into space was loaded with everything their
civilization had achieved."

"Together we returned to my star system.
We returned to the fifth planet in the system. Only
to discover the human race had perished a century
before, nothing remained. The Earth, which was
my home, was split in half by the Anti-matter
weapons of the Great War. The Martian colonies
died of lack of resources, with hundreds of ships
adrift in space, all lifeless. That fifth planet is now
called Doris II. And is where the Dorian
Civilization still exists today. A new planet, a new

149

star.

"Using the technology from old Earth documents and Brilliant Dorian Engineers, Like Izzabella Daxis here to my left, newer, faster, more powerful ships were designed. The Terra-forming process of atmosphere building accelerated. The Bio-domes of old Human life now supported thousands of Dorians."

"Soon exploration ships discovered more life in the galaxy, a lot more life. Many new worlds were discovered. And we existed peacefully for many cycles, Because of ME."

"After several cycles had passed it was unanimously decided that I would be chosen as Lord Marshal of the Galactic Empire. And to prevent the concept of "Absolute power corrupts absolutely" I created this Great Council."

"It was decided that three representatives of each Civilization would be represented here. The principal guideline of the Council was simple."

"No Conflict without Communication, No decision without Debate. There are thirty six recognized, peaceful, Civilizations in the Council now. These Civilizations spanning 300,000 light years from world to world. Science, language, arts, history, religion, have all reached unbelievable statuses since. With all advancements come with it the advancement of crime and punishment, it's unavoidable. None of this would have come to pass had I turned my back to the Dorian Civilization. Many of your worlds would be facing similar extinction had the Dorian Explorers not discovered your worlds. This Council and the Entire, Dorian race owe their existence to ME! As these records will indicate, corruption has come into this Great Council. I will stop it! And I ask how dare you, charge me, with any crime in this forum! It's the likes of you, who should be charged. Like Yozah Knefsela and Annish Tanguta. I have the records to prove it!"

After this the Courpa's of the Stallag Foundation

and the Mining Guild are on their, feet, shouting out denials and screeching out innuendos at the Lord Marshal.

"Calm Down, come to order!" shouts the First Chairman "Or these proceedings will be terminated!"

"You will all get an opportunity to contest these charges."

"Madame Chairman!" The Lord Marshal speaks out. "I was recently on Stallag-24."

"Before or after, you destroyed it?"

"Before, I frequently use the Stallag Facilities for my own ends. Therefore, I am as guilty for not doing something about this earlier. The Stallag-24 Station was beyond anything I had ever encountered before. The death of the Courpa, a friend, is just what brought me there."

"So you admit to destroying the Facility after you were there to do, what?"

"I was asked to initiate an investigation into the death of the Courpa by the Genoan Colony. I have the recording in the files."

"So, why did you destroy a Facility you admit you visit frequently?"

"Because he's a terrorist!" shouted Mrs. Tanguta from outside the seat of the Rellock Chairman position.

"State for the record your purpose on Stallag-24" Requested the First Chairman.

"I was called by the Genoan Colony to start an investigation into the death of their Courpa. The Com records of New Folden City will verify the request. I also went there for my own purposes, to acquire, a Gork to serve as a personal body guard. He is currently standing to my right. Once there I discovered the Stallag personnel already dead. Many of the prisoners were already dead, lying about the floor. The entire inmate population running amuck with the exception of Gork here who was in a welded cell."

"The conditions of the Facility were reprehensible. A full report has been previously sent to New Folden City Central Computer. That

151

report is available to anyone, who would like to read it. Once I started to make my way to recover Gork here I made another discovery. In with all the filth of the sanitations system, confined in foulness and filth, was a Pixie; barely alive, beaten, starved, and not just any Pixie, a Red Pixie!"

"That's a Lie! Impossible!" comes a shout from the Councilmen of Pixo-Linko. "Such an abomination cannot exist and to speak of one proves you are a liar!"

A silence came over the Great Council. It is no secret that the Lord Marshal has frequently spoken to his closest friends about a vision of a Red Pixie.

"Councilmen, I not only have proof, but her living, breathing self."

"There is no such abomination!" interjects Regent Gurki of Pixo-Linko, as he steps from the shadows.

"She is safely aboard MY ship. One day the hierarchy of Pixo-Linko will have to answer to her for a lifetime in prison."

The files continue to run across the view screen. They easily showed the resounding proof that not only did the Stallag Foundation use the prison population for mining labor, they were also mining a closed mine planet. And where did the profits from this illegal mining go?

The Stallag Foundation was also collecting revenue from the Great Council for inmates who were unaccountable, or deceased. Further study indicated that the Mining guild was replacing fallen laborers with "Unsuitable" employees who had never committed a crime, information that could only be covered up by a Councilmember.

"And with further study of these documents I will discover who sent those numerous ships into voided space, only to kill the crew who got them there."

"Numerous?" whispered Izzy.

"Keeps them guessing on how many we actually found verses how many are there." whispered the Lord Marshal.

CHAPTER 28

"Well, which is worse?" asked Mr. Putin.

"What do you mean?" asked Maria.

"Which is worse? Staring at the same stars all the time or at 1000 space fighters waiting on orders to kill you?"

"Not sure. A good fight I can handle. This is frustrating."

"We'll see who blinks first." sighed Maria.

"The Lord Marshal knows what he's doing. It'll all work out according to his, Master plan. Never does anything without a plan."

"You know this plan?" Maria asked raising an eyebrow suspiciously. "I threatened the Captain with bodily harm if he didn't tell me this, plan. Do I have to threaten you too?" She jested with a smirk.

"Now come on Miss Kemp. He's a good strategist. I'm sure he'll tell you when the timing is right. I won't say anything."

"I'd sure like to know what's going on down there. Do you suppose he will be arrested?"

"I don't think so. Look how much evidence we have. Once that is displayed, they won't be interested in what he has done about it." replied Mr. Putin. "I doubt anyone would be able to get near him to arrest him with that Gork next to him.
Have you ever seen him in a fight?"

"I have." added Maria. "In the war room when his "Infant" pilot showed up."

"I saw him once too, Sort of." replied Angel as she silently slipped into the room.

"Hello Angel, how?"

"When he came into my cell on Stallag-24, he was covered in blood I assumed was from fighting inmates.When he carried me out there was blood and bodies everywhere. What I saw of it anyway."

"Well, we may never know the whole truth" Sighed Mr. Wilder turning back to the view screen.

"Can they still be arguing? They went down there this morning."

"You know politicians your parents were Council members weren't they? Arguing is a way of life for them." Added Mr. Wilder ducking the remote controller she threw at him.

"The Lord Marshal isn't known for his patients." added Maria with a chuckle.

"And you are?" laughed Captain Donovan just as a light on Mr. Wilders Com light up.

"Atlantis, this is shuttle five requesting permission to dock."

"Permission granted. Is the Lord Marshal with you Izzy?"

"Yes, a little tired perhaps, not in an argumentative mood anymore, but here."
Captain Donovan turns and heads for the door, Angel right behind him.

"To the Lord Marshals quarters Atlantis" Replied Captain Donovan.

"To the food court for me Atlantis" Each taking a different elevator leaves the bridge.

Entering the airlock Gork, followed by Izzy, then the Lord Marshal all three enter the corridor, and sigh.

"We will have to leave early in the next rotation. I will meet you here on the Flight Deck at first light."
Once he returns to his quarters the door opens and he enters a quiet room; expecting Angel to be there to find out what the latest news was, she wasn't. Thoughts began to race through his head.

"Where is she, is she in trouble, has she left the ship,
is she in danger, has someone gotten to her, taken her hostage?"
Countless possibilities run through his mind in a split second. The door chimes breaking his restless thoughts.

"Angel! You don't have to ring the bell, just..." He opens the door to find Captain Donovan standing there.

"Oh, Captain Donovan, I was expecting Angel. But, do come in."

"Thank You Lord Marshal. Well, how did the arraignment turn out?" cringing at his answer.

"Morning rotation will tell. The Council is still reviewing the files we sent. And they must now get the most recent documents from the Courpa's. Now even the Medical Guild is in question."

"I know they won't be too forthcoming with their records. And if they are found to be corrupt? What then?"

"I suppose the ones responsible will be charged and arrested, maybe even held accountable."

"Arrest the ones responsible or accountable" Asked Captain Donovan.

"I should hope both, first things first. If the Great Council is involved, the records should, I say, should prove that" Returned the Lord Marshal rubbing his eyes. "It could put the whole Council into revolt."

"Against you?"

"If they revolt against me I will dissolve the Council and force the home worlds of each representative to elect new representatives. Eliminate the entire problem and start new. Have you seen…"

The door opens and in comes Angel with three Bavarian Hot Chocolates in her hands.

"Oh, you really are an Angel. Thank You." As they each take one.

"Everyone knows you love Bavarian Hot Chocolate. I only had to ask one person and the whole bar answered. It was funny. I had to laugh."

"And on that note, I will leave the two of you alone. Oh, by the way, were the council members surprised when you told them you had a living breathing Pixie on board?"

"Were they ever, the Regent of Pixo-Linko practically fell out of his box he jumped up so fast."

"Is Angel going with you next time?"

155

CHAPTER 29

"Commander, the whole of the fleet is in Genoan space" Replied Mr. Apgar.

"I imagine the investigation has begun then."

"I'd like to be a spot on that wall" Replied Mr. Apgar.

"What if they attack the Atlantis, do you think anyone will help him?"

"I would! Wouldn't you?" asked Command Master Pilot Hutchinson.

"Just a few rotations ago you said you wanted to kill him yourself."

"Just because he stole my newest ship, kidnapped my best pilot and disregarded my orders doesn't mean I would betray everything he stands for. I wouldn't be where I am today if it wasn't for the Lord Marshal, none of us would. The Council knows that. There is a lot of history between the Lord Marshal, New Folden City, and Doria II.

"That may explain why he has so much interest in this city."

"I imagine so, like I said a lot of history."

"I know he is always waiting to hear distant communications if we ever receive any." replied Mr. Apgar.

"He has boxes and boxes of antique files of information in his quarters. Why does he keep them?"

"He never really talks about them. Just says they're not my concern."

"Then maybe I should ask him sometime?"

"It's your neck risk it if you want."

CHAPTER 30

"Angel."

"Yes Lord Marshal, is there something else you want?"

"Would you come over here and talk with me? I can't sleep."

"I'm sure the Doctor can give you something to help you sleep." She replies with a playful grin.
"Angel."

"What."

"Will you tell me why you never extend your wings?"

"Will you tell me why you kept looking for me for so long?"

"Ok, fair enough. Come over here and sit with me and I will tell you." "Ouch! Watch those wingtips." He flinched.

"Still want me to extend them inside?" She giggled shuffling her wingtips tight in alongside as she sat beside him.

"Absolutely, all my life I have believed that I had a guardian Angel looking out for me whenever I was in danger. Several times when in real danger I saw my life history flash through my mind. On one of those occasions when I was particularly afraid, I saw an image of what I believed to be my guardian Angel. That Angel looked just like you"

"For centuries I searched through space. Hoping I would find you. Nothing like you existed on my world except in children's fairytales. Bedtime stories made up to help children sleep better. Unexpectedly I discovered the Dorians. Then, the stories didn't seem so far-fetched."

"The Dorian Civilization is similar to you accept the color, the wings, the eyes, the attitude, the smell."

"Smell, what smell, I don't smell?"

"Angel, I can tell you're coming a room away and I like it that way, like a fresh cut basket of Jasmine."

"And of course my color."

"Yes your color your beautiful color. As we continued to search we, the Dorian Explorers and I, kept discovering more and more species, each one more remarkable than the last. Then one rotation we came across a planet covered with golden mountains, majestic ice covered peaks, long, open valleys. They seemed to reach from one horizon to the other. And tall tree's the tallest I have ever seen. I knew immediately that if there was life here, they were flyers."

"Pixo-Linko!"

"Yes! I had found your world. And you know what I did next?"

"What!" Angel prodded him.

"I left and never returned."

"You did what?" Angel blurted out

"You did not!" Her eyes fixated on him holding her breath. She pressed on his hip pressuring him to continue.

"I was just teasing you. There were hundreds, thousands, millions of Pixie! I had discovered the world where Angels live. We immediately made a "First Contact" Comm and I disregarded every protocol there was as we entered the city of the Regent. I began searching the gathering crowds for you. I was not successful in finding my Red Pixie."

"They all looked like winged Dorians. I was soon to discover not to make the comparison. I was also quickly informed that Pixie do not come in different pigments. But you already know that story. I never gave up hope I would find my Angel. So I kept on looking."

"So?" Angel asks in anticipation of more details.

"Now it's your turn for storytelling."

"Ok, fair is fair."

"Well," she says leaning over to him. "It's not a long story actually. A Pixie female will only unfold her wings for three things. She whispers in his ear "Flying, bathing, and...Mating.""

"Mating!" He squirms with anticipation

158

"When can I learn about that?" Gently grasping her left arm at its crux, looking deeply into her eyes as she squirms, he laughs.

"You didn't think Pixies mate?"

"Of course I do. It's not like you lay eggs, right?" He closes one eye and smiles at the humor of the poke.

"No." She laughs. "We don't lay eggs."

"It's just that you look so beautiful when they are extended. I seldom get to see you that way."

"You should see me when I fly then."

"Will you extend them, just for me?"

"And how many holes do you want in your ceiling?" She laughed.

"I'll have the ceiling raised. Please, just for me?"

"Hum, maybe." She says to him looking down at him as she leans precariously close to him. "It has been a long rotation. And this ship is so dirty. I may need to clean myself, again." Stepping off the bed she scurries into the shower room, glances around the corner as the water comes on, gives him a seductive wink.

Strange, doing this for her own pleasure it seems different.

"It hasn't been that long a day!" He springs off the bed and races to the open doorway of the shower room, the rush of water in the background, he sees her now; All of her, a symmetry of beauty. The room too small to extend her wings fully; as they pierce the walls and ceiling, her tail wrapped around his waist pulling him closer, the warm water running down between her breasts, her eyes on him, watching.

Gracefully he enters the space before her. She lets out a playful giggle as he steps on her much larger toes.

Beep, beep, beep! The doorbell rings in Nurse Betty Baker's room. "Now who could it be this late?" She asks herself as she clamors for the door in nothing but her evening robe. She opens the door and steps back.

159

"Hello Baker." The harsh voice of Gork disturbs the quiet of the corridor.

"Hello Gork. Nice uniform." She laughs. He is now wearing one that fits.

Clearing her throat "Are you injured?" She asks gazing up and down his monstrous body.

Shaking his head from side to side "No" Looking down on her much smaller frame, with desire in his eyes, he stands.

"Don't just stand there blocking my door, come in."
And nothing more is said between them.

"I wonder what the Lord Marshal meant when he said I should be studying how to pilot a starship? Is he going to make me the Pilot of the Atlantis? What about that upstart Maria Kemp then, maybe she is leaving. Wouldn't bother me any, I would like to see her out of the way. He is right I should be studying, can't know too much, not about Engineering, or being a Pilot. Engineering, that's what I'm really good at."
"Looking on the bright side, as pilot I get to spend more time on the bridge, more time with the Lord Marshal.
After all, I kinda like the little guy. I see that Maria does too, although she's too stubborn to admit it. And he has a mate, that Pariah Pixie, Angel". Oh bother, if I'm going to pilot this ship I should be on the bridge, not sitting here on my britches muttering to myself!"

CHAPTER 31

Morning comes too quickly when you're in another world, especially when that morning brings uncertainty.

"Angel, it's time to wake up." He whispers into her curled ear.

"Would you like some hot chocolate this morning?"

"I don't want to get up its warm and cozy here." Groggy and pulling the blankets back over her face.

"C'mon just a little sugar to get you going."

"Emm, you talked me into it." She sits up and the blanket falls away from her.

"What is going to happen down there?" She asked stretching her arms towards the ceiling.

"I imagine the Great Council is going to decide to kill me" looking for her reaction he enters the kitchen.

"What? Oh what an awful thing to say! They couldn't, your just teasing me."

"Yes but your awake now aren't you." He laughs.

"That's not funny. What would happen to me if they killed you? They would come for me, put me back in prison, maybe, kill me too!" A look of fear in her expression he rushed back over to the bed, sits down beside her. "Angel, stop this now. I was only teasing you to get a wake up reaction from you I won't let anyone hurt me, or you. I didn't mean to scare you. I'm sorry" handing her a cup of Bavarian hot chocolate.

"It's still not funny." Realizing the blankets had fallen away revealing her breasts.

"I see you care about me more than you want to tell, this is good."

"Maybe, maybe not, keep teasing me and I may change my mind" Wrapping the blankets back around herself.

"I've been meaning to tell you I told the Council members about you."

"You did what!" She jumps to her feet, again knocking larger holes in the ceiling.

"Why have you done such a stupid thing? They will come for me, they will force me back into a prison, I thought you said I was safe with you! Why have you done that? I thought you said you love me, I trusted you!"
She slumps down on the bed corner, her wings slumping behind her.

"Or are you just using me like all the others?" She covers her face with her hands and weeps.

"Angel, stop this I do love you always have, always will. Nobody would dare come aboard this ship and try to hurt you. I'd kill anyone who would try and so would Captain Donovan, and Gork, And even Maria would stand up for you. So please don't be afraid."

"I told the Council about you because great offences have been committed against you and I think they should be held responsible."

"They will never admit to doing anything wrong. I'm an abomination, not supposed to exist."

"Specknockt! I don't ever want to hear you speak of such a thing again! Now you apologize to yourself right this instant!" Standing directly between her feet looking up at her.

"Do what?"

"I said apologize to yourself for saying such an awful thing this instant!"

"I'm sorry. I have."

"I don't want to hear any more of this, ambivalence. You are perfect! And don't you believe anything else."

"Now there is something important I have to ask."

"What?" her hands wiping away a tear.

"Do you want to attend the inquiry today?"

"Why would I want to do that? I couldn't face them."

"Would it not give you a little satisfaction to see the look of fear on their faces when you

162

enter the Great Hall?"

"I might recognize those who have come to my cell for, interrogations. I'm not ready to face that."

"Ok, I understand. I wanted to ask, to give you the choice."

"I'll just stay here where you say I'm safe. I don't want to worry about what's going on down there."

"Sure you won't worry I believe different, I will be ok."

"Be careful" Picking up her spilled cup of chocolate.

Walking down the corridor thinking of all the things that are going to be happening this rotation gets him to the Flight Deck quicker than he had expected. Maria, Gork, and Izzy are standing there waiting patiently while he approaches.

"Miss Kemp surprised to see you here, what brings you down here so early?"

"Just wanted to tell you to be careful down there, there are a lot of ships around here, a lot of dangers."

Suspicious, he looks at the three standing there.

"Thank You, I may need it."

Once again it's back to the surface. The three enter the Great Hall. Many of the delegates are already present. Many are not yet at their stations. The First Chairman enters the room and approaches the podium, a solemn expression on her face.

"Attention all delegates and Council members; It has been brought to my attention that during the evening an unidentified group has broken into the Great Hall of Records. The information that was presented here the previous rotation has been stolen, or destroyed."

"It has also been brought to my attention that the Courpa of the Stallag Foundation; Courpa Yozah Knefsela, was discovered dead in his chambers early this morning. In light of this information I believe the only matter for further discussion is the here-to un-explained death of the Courpa of the Grennich II Colony. The death of the

163

Keeper of the Stallag-24 Station, and the destruction of said Stallag-24 Facility.

"I'm curious Madame Chairman!" interrupted the Lord Marshal. "Was the information lost; stolen, or destroyed? Which is it, and how would you, know for sure, if the information just came available this morning?"

"The record states that You, Lord Marshal, have claimed responsibility for the destruction of the Stallag-24 Station, is this correct?" asked the First Chairman of the Great Council.

"I believe you just stated that all the information presented here was lost, stolen, or destroyed. Or was it just specific, information? And Yes, I did destroy Stallag-24."

"And the starship Prometheus?"

"Also correct Madame Chairman."

"And how do you plea to the charges of killing the Courpa of Grennich II?"

"Madame Chairman the documentation clearly stated that the request for my presence on Stallag-24 came shortly after the death of the Courpa was reported by the Grennich II Colony; verification accessible by the Com call to New Folden City just prior to my departure. And to attempt to charge me with the death of someone before I was actually there is a testament to the corruption presented before this Council."

"This leads me to believe there is further involvement of corruption within this Council than I had previously suspected. Has this Council had anything to do with the missing, documents? If so, perhaps the Courpa of the Stallag Federation was correct. A new Council may be needed. Is this threat perhaps the reason he is now dead?"

"Lord Marshal! I stated earlier that the documents you so, conveniently, provided were stolen last nightfall."

"Were they stolen, or destroyed? Which is it Madame Chairman?"

"How do you intend to claim your innocence with the evidence presented against you, including your own admissions without those files? You were the last one to leave the Stallag-24 Station before it was destroyed, by you."

"Madame Chairman, all the documents I have previously disclosed may have been lost, stolen, or destroyed. However, I have duplicates of them all aboard the Atlantis! Those files are also downloading into the Genoan Mainframe computer as we speak. Available to anyone, who wants to see them for themselves! This leaves no opportunity for the files to be corrupted or, lost, by the Stallag Federation, Mining Guild, or, this Council!"

"Lord Marshal! I will not tolerate an accusation of corruption of this Great Council without definitive proof, even from you!" The First Chairman staring down from her podium at the Lord Marshal.

"First Chairman, I have shown you the proof. Last nightfall is all the proof anyone here needs. Furthermore, I intend to send transcriptions of everything that has transpired to the home worlds of every civilization represented here. I will let them each make a decision on what is happening to this Council."

"I intend to locate all the Stallag Foundation, Mining Guild, and Medical Guild records; along with the Fleet records, and send them as well. Corruption within this Great Council has been proved. Only a Council member would have had access to the files I disclosed. Within the program was an encryption code only a Council member would have been able to decrypt."

"Now each Civilization represented will have to review the qualifications of its representatives and decide if new ones are to be chosen. I officially demand your resignation Madame Chairman, on grounds of Corruption. I officially dissolve this Council. Corruption had defiled the integrity of this Councils founders. It is clear to me that this society, like my own, is unable to self-regulate. Under Article 206, lines 54-58 of the First Galactic Empire states that."

"In the event of overwhelming evidence

of corruption, the Lord Marshal, Ergo, Douglass Abbicus has absolute control to dissolve this Council and assume complete control of the empire until new Council may, be chosen."

"I will not allow this great society we've all worked so diligently to build be destroyed by power misers like those who destroyed my world! I and my crew will travel to each world and accept new representatives."

Council members can return to each of your respective worlds. This is the last time we will meet on Genoa!"
The Lord Marshal storms out of the room as shouts of war ring out around the Great Hall.

"Let's get back aboard the Atlantis as quickly as possible."

"I do believe we have worn out our invitation here." Izzy Jumps into the pilot seat and initiates the engines.

"Can't expect a return invitation when you charge the entire Great Council of corruption now can we?"
A mob of delegates exit the Great Hall behind them as they enter the shuttle. The shuttle reaches the shields of Atlantis as several of the ships surrounding the Atlantis move back, not at all unusual just before an attack.

"Word travels fast here Lord Marshal."
Izzy points out the maneuvering ships.
Returning to the bridge the Lord Marshal is approached by a concerned Captain Donovan.

"I assume the Great Council is no more?"

"More like on vacation, I will be creating a new, uncorrupted, Council at a later time."

"Get us moving Maria, I mean, Master Kemp. Set course for New Folden City."

"Mr. Wilder, get me a Com to Command Master Pilot Hutchinson."

"Yes Sir."

"Listen up everyone. I am in full command of the Empire effective immediately. Until I can re-establish the Great Council aboard this ship things may be rather hectic around here.

Just trust that I had no other alternative at this time."

"All the records we sent to the surface have vanished." Izzy guessing the expression on Mr. Putin's face flinched.

"Isn't that why we made duplicates?" asked Maria.

"Exactly why Mr. Wilder, I want you to transmit copies of those records to the home worlds of each member of the Great Council. Along with those we got from the Genoan central Computer. Let them make their own decisions about who is corrupt."

"I do believe I can do it much faster" Replied Atlantis appearing behind them.

"Atlantis, hello I bet you can send all the files in a stitch to everyone simultaneously."

"Yes Mr. Wilder, I can."

"Then what are you going to do?" asked Maria.

"The only thing that works." replied the Lord Marshal.

"Commander Hutchinson is on the line Lord Marshal."

"I'll take it in the conference room Mr. Wilder."

"Command Master Pilot Hutchinson."

`   "Afternoon Lord Marshal, what's news there?"

"I'm afraid the Great Council is no more for the time being. I have taken full Command of the Empire. Now, I need you to take full Command of the Empire fleet. Are you ready to accept that level of Command?"

"I will do so as you request Lord Marshal."

"The Great Council has been proven corrupt. I can no longer trust the information or communications that originate from them. The Atlantis will be returning to New Folden City shortly. You will be transferring your Command to this ship."

"Atlantis is to be the flagship of the

Empire?" asked Command Master Pilot Hutchinson.

"Yes, it is one of the reasons for its construction. You will need to supersede all other orders given by the Great Council. If anyone challenges your authority, kill them."

"Atlantis"

"Yes Lord Marshal?"

"Are you aware of today's events?"

"Yes Lord Marshal."

"Where is Gork, and Izzabella Daxis right now?"

"Gork is in the War room and Izzabella Daxis is in Engineering."

"Where is Maria Kemp?"

"Right behind you Lord Marshal" tapping his shoulder.

"Oh, sorry didn't notice you standing there."

"So much the same."

"I have to inform you of some changes coming."

"Since when do you inform me of something before it happens?"

"Miss Kemp, the Atlantis is now the Command Center of the Empire. Command Master Pilot Hutchinson is now the Fleet Commander of the Empire. We are returning to New Folden City where he will take Command."

"What do you want from me?" She asked alarmed.

"I, need you, to take Command of the Flight Deck here on the Atlantis. You will be Command Master Pilot."

"You, want me, to Command the Flight Deck?"

"Yes. You will be responsible for all traffic on and off the Atlantis and the space around it. Miss Kemp, I made a lot of enemies today, and I need someone in Command I trust."

"I guess I'm done flying then."

"Not necessarily. But for the immediate future, yes."

"Why not just cut my legs off then, or

revoke my flight status! Either would accomplish
the same thing."

MARIA KEMP this is not a request!'"

"This isn't because of my dislike for your
Infant pilot is it?"

"No, I expect a lot of trouble ahead and
I..."

"Just what kind of trouble do you
expect?"

"I dissolved the Great Council, accused
the First Chairmen of corruption, the Mining Guild,
and the Stallag Foundation, several Council
members and the Medical Guild of covering up the
activities on that Stallag-24 Station, and pled guilty
to destroying the Stallag-24 Station."

"Whoof, no wonder their pissed" replied
Maria.

"You certainly stirred up a mess alright."

"Atlantis."

"Yes."

"Where is Izzy again?"

"Engineering."

"Tell her to remain there until I get there."
And he exit's the room.
Maria, turning to Captain Donovan "Captain
Donovan I don't want to Command the Flight
Deck, I trained to pilot a fighter, not a frigate!
Sometimes I think he does things just to aggravate
me."

"Are you surprised?"

"At least he kept you as Captain, it's what
you've trained for. I'd rather be Captain than Flight
Deck Commander."

"You never said you were interested in
being Captain" replies Captain Donovan.

"Maybe I did. Who listens to me?"

"Be careful what you wish for Miss Kemp
sometimes you get it." Mr. Wilder, smirking as
Maria stews.

"Maybe you should go and yell at him
some more. Maybe he'll make you Lord Marshal."
added Mr. Putin "He seems to tolerate your
rantings."

169

"Rantings," Maria shot back "You just wait and see."

"Miss Daxis! I need your attention for a few moments."

Izzy is face down in the Command controls of the Renegade II when he approaches.

"I'll be with you in just a stitch I'm a little busy rig…"

"Get over here Daxis, this is not a request!"

"Coming Lord Marshal!"

She flips out of the Renegade II and is standing in front of him at attention.

"Due to the recent events of the last few rotations I have to take Command of the Empire."

"Yes Lord Marshal, I was there."

"I know you were."

"What does that have to do with me, did I do something wrong?"

"What indeed, I need you to Pilot the Atlantis."

"Me!" Isn't Mar.. Miss Kemp the Atlantis Pilot?"

"Not anymore, she is Command Master Pilot of the Flight Deck."

"She's not going to like that at all."

"Why would you say that, know her that well now do you?"

"No, she's a Pilot, not an officer. Making her Deck Commander would be like cutting her legs off."

"Funny, she said it the same way."

"I need her there to manage ship traffic. And there just isn't anyone else qualified."

"What about Captain Donovan?"

"What about him?"

"Well, Captain Donovan came from traffic and logistics, may be better at that position than Miss Kemp. Why not make Captain Donovan Flight Deck Commander, Keep Miss Kemp as Pilot and make Me Captain." Izzy smiling as she shrugs her shoulders.

"That's a great Idea Miss Daxis!"

170

"What's a great idea?" a wave of panic crossing her thoughts.

"I think that's a wonderful idea, solves everyone's problems. I love you, thanks for the suggestion." And the Lord Marshal darts off back into the doorway of the Flight Deck office.

"Shouldn't I be on the bridge then?" She shouts back to him as the door closes behind him; everyone around the Renegade II staring at her with a look of amazement on their faces as they can't believe what they just saw.

"What, I could be Captain. Get back to work! So to the bridge I go then." She says to herself and proceeds out the Flight Deck door. Running through the halls he just left he runs into Maria.

"Maria, come with me, I had a great idea."

"Now what am I to become a cook, how about quarter master, or better yet, an Engineer?" She says sarcastically.

"No, better than that, will be better for everyone."

"What if I…" She's cut off as Izzy enters the corridor to the bridge.

"Oh great, what are you doing here? I suppose you are going to make her Pilot now?"

"How'd you guess that?" Izzy asked chuckling.

"Did he tell you something in advance, finally?"
Maria lunges towards Izzy, her fists clenched, teeth gritting. All her frustration aimed at her rival. Izzy ducks into a corridor intersection while the Lord Marshal turns around.

"Attention, both of you, I haven't time for this childish behavior from you. Now get in here and listen to what I have decided!"

"Listen up everyone, I have new crew assignments. Effective immediately you are all fired!"

"Fired, what does that mean?" asked Mr. Wilder.

"What, what, what?" is their combined

responses.

"You are all fired! Atlantis, note it in the Log."

"Yes Lord Marshal, all bridge crew are fired."

"Ok Atlantis, all bridge personnel are to be assigned as follows."

Master Pilot Maria Kemp, Captain.

Mr. John Wilder, Communications Officer

Mr. Josh Donovan, Flight Deck Commander.

Miss. Izzabella Daxis, Pilot

"These changes are effective immediately. I don't want to hear a single squeak from anyone. This is how it is to be until I decide differently. Now I said I wanted to go to New Folden City 20 stitches ago."

"Right away!" jumped Maria as she headed for the Pilot's seat.'

"That would be my, seat. Captain" replied Izzy.

"Captain Kemp! Why aren't I moving?"

"Pilot Daxis, take your seat!" barked Maria.

"What brought this on?" asked Maria.

"I said not a squeak, or would you rather spend a few rotations in a sonnet tube?"

"No Sir!"

"Mr. Donovan, this may seem like a demotion, I assure you it isn't. The Flight Deck will soon be busier than the airspace around Genoa."

"Miss Kemp, you want to be a Pilot, you still can. Occasionally, you will have to multi-task, now as Captain."

"Lord Marshal, what are we going to do at New Folden City?"

"We will be adding Fleet Commander Hutchinson to the crew. We will leave New Folden City to the Dorians. This will allow us to return to collect new Delegates for a new Council."

"What will happen to Genoa without the

Great Council there?" asked Izzy.

"Probably return to a commerce planet like it originally was."

"And the Leviathon, and Mastedon?"

"Trade ships, Diplomatic missions, I don't know. I'll leave that up to Fleet Commander Hutchinson."

"Who will control the planet without government?" asked Izzy.

"I'm sure there is enough, unemployed delegates there
to establish a working government."

CHAPTER 32

"This is an outrage!" shouted Mr. Ryvac Delallo, the Courpa for the Medical Guild.

"Are we to succumb to his totalitarianism control now?"

"What would you suggest, we take up arms against the one who founded this Great Council? "asked the former First Chairman. "Would you have us go to war just to protect your investments Courpa Delallo?"

"This Council may not have the backbone to protect itself but the Medical Guild will not be over run without a fight."

"Well then Mr. Delallo, you do that and see how long you live. The Guild leaders won't be able to strong arm the Council anymore. See how long your finances last now."

"Only a coward would do nothing!"

"I am powerless to do anything, the Council had the power. Not the individual Council members."

"And what about the Stallag-24 Station; or the Prometheus, do you have any problem with their destruction, or are you to spineless to care about that?"

"Courpa Delallo, you know full well what the documentation the Lord Marshal presented proved the corruption in the Corporations he mentioned, and this Council. I believe you also know what happened to those documents don't you?"

"So do you Madame Chairman, I was not alone in the decision to eradicate them! will you turn your back now?"

"I have little choice! And did Courpa Knefsela kill himself, or did he have help from the Medical Guild?"

"How dare you! The Medical Guild has nothing to hide."

"So why are you so concerned about a Facility you claim to have never visited? Or have you?"

"I don't have to stand for this! I am a Courpa!"

"Perhaps not for long, good visiting with you Mr. Delallo, hope you have a nice trip home."

"That's Courpa Delallo to you coward!" Even more frustrated than before, the Medical Guild Courpa just has to stand there as the other delegates clear the room. Not one delegate stays to support him. Frustrated he too exit's the Great Hall out the southern exit.

CHAPTER 33

"Miss Daxis, please notify me when we reach New Folden City."

"That would be my job now wouldn't it?" asked Maria with a snap.

"Yes, yes it would indeed. My apologies Captain call me if you need anything."

"Aye, aye Sir."

The door open again and the Lord Marshal leaves the bridge with no further distractions.

"To my quarters Atlantis."

The doors open to a dark room.

"Lights" There is no action.

"Atlantis! Why are there no lights in..."

The lights come on. There, standing with her arms open and her wings fully extended is Angel. He moves over to her and embraces her.

"We are on our way to New Folden City."

"Why there?"

"Just a visit home before we go traversing across the galaxy in search of new Delegates for the Great Council and to pick up Fleet Commander Hutchinson."

"What do you mean "home" Dorius II is the Dorian home world. It isn't your world. Is it, you're not Dorian?"

"This is true Dorius II wasn't always Dorius II."

"What was it before?"

"Well, centuries before it was a planet called "Mars". Part of the Terran solar system, fourth in a system of planets around a star called "Sun"."

"Is this where you came from?"

"I came from the third planet called "Earth". I left Earth just before the third great war, that war ended life on my planet. Several hundred years before, my species tried to expand beyond our small world starting with the world most likely to be able to support life. In a concept we called Terra-Forming we built massive domes to protect

176

the cities from the outer atmosphere while generating a breathable atmosphere inside. The process was slow but was working. Then war came."

"Anti-matter weapons were used by the people in power who fled Earth for the Mars colonies. In just a single day life on Earth was gone. The anti-matter weapons cracked the planet into two. Without the resources of Earth, the Mars colonies soon perished."

"How did you escape?"

"I was a Captain of a then called "Submarine" an officer in the Terran Naval Defense System. I had it modified and took it into space. I never returned home."

"Didn't anyone come with you?"

"Some, I knew they wouldn't survive the loneliness of space travel so I, left them there. After all, they just destroyed their own world. Why save them?"

"Wasn't it lonely for you?"

"During my travels through space, time seemed to move so slowly. Every day seemed to just run into the next. It wasn't long before I quit keeping track. After what seemed an eternity I discovered the Dorian home world."

"You saved them."

"Yes, I took them to Mars to finish what my species had started. The domes were in a state of disrepair. But, the process had been going well. The Dorians were able to accelerate the Terra-Forming process."

"And the Dorians just stayed there."

"It wasn't hard to convince them that this was their only chance to make a new home. And the name Dorius II was chosen."

"So you are the last of your species then?"

"Possibly maybe some other ships were able to survive and travel the stars like I had. I may never know. I may be the last but I will never be forgotten. I downloaded every file on human history I could find before I left. And I will always have the genetic material to make another should I feel the need to."

"Why haven't you used it?"

"Why reintroduce a species that was so willing to destroy itself the first time? I thought in space, maybe, someday I would discover a species intelligent enough to exist in peace, seems war is just as common as life."

The Lord Marshal and Angel keep talking for several hours while the Atlantis made its way to New Folden City.

"So were all your species as short as you?" Angel asked playfully.

"No, some were plenty tall; stronger, smarter, not as good looking of course." Laughing out loud

"Many variations in size, color, height, weight, different languages, beliefs. Probably what led to their final extinction, that and the quest for power and wealth."

"Sounds familiar" looking over her shoulder.

"I would imagine it's the same differences on my world that are responsible for what happened to you on your world."

"What do you mean?"

"Perhaps because you were born a different color than those in power, they perceived you as a threat to their control."

"But I was so small then. And the only one, like you. What could I have done?"

"There was an old expression of words on my world that explains it best." "Where there is one, there inherently is more."

"You think there might be others on my world, like me?"

"Probably not on your world, but somewhere, hidden, like you were; you escaped execution, why is it so hard to believe others didn't too? Which is exactly why I want to go to Pixo-Linko first, to send a message to others like you; If there are any, that they don't have to hide anymore, that they have some place safe to go, here, safe from persecution. Imagine what your "Regent"

would say if you were to walk into the State room
and tell them what you have endured."

"It may start a revolt among the classes."

"Maybe even, revolution."

"I thought you said you hate the concept
of war. And war would come if I went back."

"I also believe that all life has the right to
be free of persecution. What happened to you
should never have been allowed. And the ones who
put you there held responsible."

"I never believed that there are others like
me. I believed them all to be killed at birth like I
was supposed to be."

"There is only one way to be sure."
A voice comes over the Comm.

"Lord Marshal, we are approaching New
Folden City."

"I had better get back to the bridge. Are
you coming?"

"Coming where?"

"To the bridge of course, as my chosen
mate, others will expect to see you at my side."
Smiling, waiting for her reaction to his claim he
reached for her hand.

"Mate, who said anything about me being
your mate?"

"I said My, chosen mate. Let others imply
what they will. I can wait for you to make the right
choice."

"I don't want to go to the bridge. Besides,
I'm not even dressed." She says playfully as he
reaches the door.

"Really, I hadn't noticed" laughing as he
exits the door heading for the bridge.
Entering the bridge all eyes are on the view screen.
The fleet is surrounding Dorius II, the Mastedon,
Leviathon, and what is left of the Prometheus.

"Com, get Command Master Pilot
Hutchinson on the line."

"On line Lord Marshal."

"Dorius II this is Lord Marshal on Atlantis
requesting final approach."

"Approach and orbit granted Lord

179

Marshal but not recommended. I wouldn't expect a warm reception. A lot of Dorians were injured and killed when you destroyed the Prometheus."

"Couldn't be avoided Commander, I did what I had to do. However, I do expect they will follow your orders."

"And if they don't?"

"Then they will all be arrested as traitors."

"And what orders would you wish them to follow?"

"Cease and desist any and all aggressive activity towards this ship. Stand down all weapons and await further instructions from the Fleet Commander. The Great Council is no more. All previous orders are superseded by me. All delegates are to return to their home worlds. I have taken full Command until a new Council can be elected."

"It will be recreated aboard this ship under my direct supervision. Fleet Commander Hutchinson, you ready to transfer to this ship?"

"Yes Lord Marshal. It will take some time."

"Begin as soon as you are ready Fleet Commander."

"What do you suppose they will do now?" asked Maria.

"What will who do?"

"The Mastedon and the Leviathon?"

"The same thing they have always done. Transportation, diplomatic missions, exploration, the Empire is 300,000 light years across. That's a lot of space to regulate with just one ship. We may have to build several more, eventually."

"And what is our mission going to be then?"

"Are you not listening? We will reestablish the Great Council aboard this ship. Regain control of the Empire and bring integrity back to the Great Council."

"There will always be conflicts. Peace is unachievable when so many different life forms are forced to exist together."

180

"That may be true Miss Kemp. But, they are not being forced to exist together just being forced to keep peace between worlds. Like before they discovered each other. Take for example the trade industries, if it wasn't for trade between several of the worlds they would not have survived because of the wars they fought before we, discovered them."

"That's a simple example" Remarked Maria.

"Ok, science, medicines, technology, exploration, arts. Haven't they all evolved tenfold since I created the council?" The Lord Marshal irritated by Maria's constant criticism.

"And once we get the stability back we can go back to what brought us all out here in the first place, exploration. Isn't that why you first started piloting fighters?"

"No. I started flying Courpa transports."

"Miss Kemp I came out here to find new life, perhaps a new world. Instead, I discovered the Dorians and as a result, you. Not too bad for an unknown species traveling out into the uncharted regions of space."

"Now we will be going back into that uncharted region of space in the most advanced, intelligent, and powerful ship ever designed. I can't know what might be out there."

"Exactly right" added Mr. Donovan.

"And the crew on this ship is the most specialized and most talented individuals in their fields of study."

"Don't you think we have enough life forms to fight with?" snapped Maria."

"We don't, but you might." The whole bridge crew begins laughing as Maria gets angrier with each laugh.

"Just because we can go out there, doesn't mean we should" Maria trying to regain her advantage.

"And just what do you think would have happened to the Dorian Civilization had I maintained your attitude, or what about the Caiman

Civilization, where do you think they would be had they not been discovered before their planet was hit by that comet? Just because we are out looking doesn't mean we're looking for a fight."

"Yet it sometimes happens" added Mr. Putin.

"And don't forget the ones out there who might be looking to start a fight with us" Added Mr. Wilder.

"We'd just throw Izzabella and Maria out there and maybe they wouldn't want to fight with us" Laughed Mr. Putin.

"That's seven rotations kitchen duty for you!" snapped Maria.

"Aye, aye to that Captain!" Izzy, laughing with the rest of the crew

"Just imagine!" adds Mr. Wilder "A whole civilization that thrives on argumentation. We could find a mate for Maria! Maybe she'd be nicer then."

"That's seven rotations kitchen duty for you too, Mr. Wilder!" Maria smiling too.

"Message from the city!" Breaks in Mr. Wilder.

"Fleet Commander Hutchinson is ready to board."

"Tell him to report directly to the bridge."

"Oh oh." Maria responds quickly.

"What is it Captain?" asked the Lord Marshal, grinning.

"This should be an interesting conversation."

"Explain."

"The last time Command Master Pilot Hutchinson and I talked was when we left New Folden City to go to Stallag-24. He will not be exactly, pleased, to talk to me."

"Good afternoon Lord Marshal." comes the voice from behind him as Fleet Commander Hutchinson enters the bridge.

"I am happy to report…"

"The Captain will take your report Fleet Commander I have other duties I must attend to." And the Lord Marshal ducks out into the corridor.

CHAPTER 34

"Well Mr. Delallo, did everything go as expected?" came the brash voice of the Gavial mercenary standing in the dark alleyway. Gavials are Alligator like creatures; massive jaws with very tough bodies, very low intelligence, but good fighters. They have a very low tolerance for Diplomats as well.

"It went as expected." croaked Ryvac Delallo. "Nothing is to be done! The Council is filled with cowards. The Lord Marshal dissolved the Council to protect himself from prosecution, as was expected. All the Council members are running like the cowards they are."

"Are you surprised?" scoffed the Gavial. "Is it time to move our ships into position?"

"Not yet. We first need to find out where the Lord Marshal is going first. I have informants within his ship who will inform us of his destination before we attack."

"So a plan has been devised then?"

"A plan is in place. We just need the coordinates."

"Do you have the information we requested Courpa Delallo?"

"I have the information you asked for" Holding a species identifier in his left hand.

"Give it to me!" demands the Gavial Mercenary.

"I don't understand what good this will do you?"

"Do not concern yourself with my purposes. Now get those coordinates to me as soon as you have them. And give me the disc!"

"I will inform my other supporters to be ready. The Lord Marshal shall learn that even he..."

"Stop preaching Courpa Delallo! And once he is defeated, who will rule the Galaxy then?"

"We are capable of ruling ourselves,

Gavial!"

"You lack the resources to even mount a viable attack against one Empire ship."

"He has other allies that will come when he calls."

"As do we Gavial!"

"Tell me you are not planning to take control of the Great Council yourselves." He scoffs as he re-enters the dark alley he came from.

"We shall see."

"Just get me those coordinates Delallo!"

"Where are your ships located Gavial?" Courpa Delallo blurted out into the darkness.

"They are hidden and will remain so, until I call for them."

"Hidden, is that the best answer you can give me? It doesn't inspire my confidence! We spent a great number of cubes to arm your ships! What assurances do I have that your ships will be there when the battle starts?"

Breaching the darkness the Gavial grabs Courpa Delallo by his cloak.

"It is the Medical Guild who has proven its disloyalty. Don't question me!" And the Gavial again enters the dark alley.

"Hey! Gavial! Aren't you forgetting something?" as he tosses the species identifier program to him.

CHAPTER 35

"Well, if it isn't former Master Pilot Maria Kemp! I'm not surprised to see you here." Fleet Commander Hutchinson sneering as he enters the bridge.

"How was your last flight? I hope you enjoyed it. Now where is Captain Donovan? I have several, reports to make."

"I am Captain of this ship Fleet Commander." Maria declared.

"What, impossible! Where is Captain Donovan?"

"I am Captain Commander!"

"Impossible, a person must first be a Pilot before they can be a Captain of anything. You will never pilot anything again while I'm Fleet Commander!"

"Sorry to hear you won't be staying as Fleet Commander then" interjected Maria confidently.

"I will notify the Lord Marshal of your resignation immediately."

"On who's authority were you made Captain?" He barked looking around for someone to answer.

"That would be the Lord Marshals authority." Maria confirmed as everyone else remained silent.

"I didn't ask for your confirmation Kemp! I asked Captain Donovan!"

"I'm the Flight Deck Commander now Commander." Added Mr. Donovan peeking up from under his console tower

"Well don't that just beat all!" standing with his hands on his hips.

"So how about that report Fleet Commander?" Prompted Maria standing in front of the Captains' chair with her arms crossed looking confidently at Fleet Commander Hutchinson, waiting for a response.

"If I recall correctly Miss Kemp the last

time we spoke you were up on charges of kidnapping the Lord Marshal, disobeying the orders of the Commander, and theft of Empire property!" Moving closer to her "And I'm sure I'm correct since I, filed the charges myself!"

"Now where did the Lord Marshal go? I need to speak with him and rectify this situation!"

"Calm yourself Fleet Commander! That's an order from the Captain!" demanded Maria standing toe to toe with Fleet Commander Hutchinson.

"I am Fleet Commander! I do not report to a Captain! You report to me!"

"And I am the Captain of the Flagship of the Empire, appointed by the Lord Marshal himself, I do not answer to a Fleet Commander!" Maria standing firm.

"IF you have a problem with me as Captain, you can be replaced!"

"I will only report to the Lord Marshal! Now I asked where is he?" He demanded.

"We'll see who reports to whom!" replied Maria "Security!" Gork steps in between the two and looks down at Fleet Commander Hutchinson.

"Gork! Take Fleet Commander Hutchinson into custody and place him in the brig."

"On what charges?" asks Gork.

"Insubordination!" Maria snaps with her usual charm.

Gork grabs Fleet Commander Hutchinson by his uniform sleeve and directs him towards the door.

"I can walk myself, Mr., Mr. what is your name?"

"Gork. I called Gork."

"Pilot Daxis!" Maria calls out.

"Yes Captain."

"Set course for Pixo-Linko, we are leaving. Fleet ready or not!"

"Aye Captain." Izzy returns reluctantly.

"Mr. Wilder, notify the fleet that we are setting course for Pixo-Linko. They can choose to follow, or answer to the Lord Marshal."

"Aye, aye, Captain."

CHAPTER 36

"That went well" replied Mr. Wilder, smiling.

"I thought so too" added Izzy, also smiling.

"I thought it might come to blows there."

"My cubes are on the Captain" Commented Mr. Donovan.

"No surprise there" Taunted Izzy.

"Enough from the three of you!" she snapped. "Monitor your stations and mind your own affairs!" Harboring a hidden smile of her own achievement.

"Temper, temper, Captain." Izzy teases.

"Pilot Daxis! Not now or do you wish to join Commander Hutchinson?"

"Ah-hem, sorry Captain" Izzy clearing her throat with a slight cough ducked behind her console.

Meanwhile Gork casually escorts Fleet Commander Hutchinson to the brig. He enters the small, white chamber. It has a low bench on the back wall with a bright red cushion on it. He gestures the Commander inside. Activating the force field that closes the opening gives him a strong sense of irony. Glancing back, it was just a short time ago someone else was closing the door on him.

"Com, where is the Lord Marshal?" asked Fleet Commander Hutchinson sitting down on the soft cushion.

"The Lord Marshal is in the corridor outside the food court. And you can call me, Atlantis."

"Call you what?" He asked surprised.

"You can call me Atlantis, my name is Atlantis."

"Am I talking to the ships Com officer?"

"No, I am Atlantis."

"This ship, and the Com officer are both called Atlantis? I can't believe it."

"What is it you cannot believe Fleet Commander?"

"The Lord Marshal built a ship that talks back. I guess having a Captain that talks back wasn't enough." He laughs.

"Would it be too much trouble to contact the Lord Marshal and ask him to come here to see me?"

"Not at all fleet Commander."

Near the food court entrance the Com rings out.

"Lord Marshal, Fleet Commander Hutchinson would like you to meet him in the brig."

Laughing to himself, "Did Fleet Commander Hutchinson put Miss Kemp in the brig already?"

"Captain Kemp is on the bridge Lord Marshal."

"So where is Fleet Commander Hutchinson?"

"Fleet Commander Hutchinson is in the brig."

"The Fleet Commander is in the brig?" He asked flabbergasted.

"Yes Lord Marshal."

"That female is going to get me into a lot of trouble one of these times. Inform Fleet Commander Hutchinson I'll be right there."

The brig is in the aft part of the ship; between the engineering sections and crew quarters, a highly mechanical part of the ship. After passing several sonnet tubes the Lord Marshal is standing in the entry of the brig.

"Strange to see you on that side of the field Fleet."

"What is this ridiculous idea of making that defiant, x-pilot Captain of this ship, or is she fibbing?"

"She's not fibbing."

"And when did it start that a Fleet Commander answers to a, rogue, argumentative, stubborn."

"I guess that means you are not happy with our new Captain?" Mr. Hutchinson is pacing back and forth before the force field door.

"Not happy? I intend to revoke her flight status permanently. I may even lock her in a sonnet tube for a cycle,
at least a week of kitchen duty!"

"Fleet Commander!"

"I ordered that upstart Pilot to return to New Folden City…!"

"We returned, just not right away."

"Yes, then you left again without clearing it with me."

"Once we got back I received a call from the Grennich II colony requesting my immediate presence."

"Why didn't you inform me before you left?"

"Let me remind you Fleet, I don't need your approval or permission. Or anyone else's for that matter. I do whatever I need to."

"Including the destruction of the Stallags Facility?"

"Yes." Has everyone around here forgotten just who I am! Perhaps I have been just a little too lax in discipline. I may be allowing too many subordinates to speak their opinions! Now Fleet Commander if you have a problem reporting to my recently appointed Captain you might just want to consider staying here for a while longer. I am growing weary of this competition between my Command staff. Make your choice."

"Awaiting your orders Lord Marshal."

"Is the Fleet ready Commander?"

"Yes Sir, awaiting your orders."

"Good. I will inform Captain Kemp to release you."

"I will get a full report of Fleet readiness from the Captain."

"Where are we heading now Lord Marshal?"

"We will be heading for Pixo-Linko."

"Why there Sir?"

"Because there is a Stallag Station there and I want to investigate it for corruption, and illegally kept prisoners."

189

"You mean like your Pixie?" He exclaimed stopping him in the corridor.

"You've heard about her already?"

"Only rumors."

"Sure seems to be a lot of rumors aboard this ship. I had better do something about that too."

"Come along Commander. I'll tell you about it on the way. Security! Release the field."

CHAPTER 37

"Captain, the whole of the fleet isn't following us" Replied Mr. Wilder.

"What do you mean the "Whole of the Fleet?"

"The Leviathon is following along with the fighters, but the Mastedon is staying behind."

"Did you try reaching them on the Com?"

"Not responding." Maria moves over to the Com station and tries to establish a link.

"Are they staying to protect New Folden City? Did you receive any orders from Fleet Commander Hutchinson for the Mastedon to remain?"

"Impossible. Fleet is in the brig."

"Keep trying Mr. Wilder. And repeat those orders to Pixo-Linko just in case they haven't received them."

"That's quite a story." Fleet Commander Hutchinson says as he stands in the doorway.

"That is why I have had to make so many changes here. Trouble is on the way. I have only people I can trust in the key positions."

"What does your Pixie think of all this? You know speaking of her existence may have put her in great danger from the Pixie civilization."

"I realize that. But Maria Kemp as Captain, Mr. Donovan as Deck Commander, and you as Fleet Commander, I believe it would be impossible for anyone to be able to get aboard this ship to attempt to harm her."

"Have you considered the idea that your enemies may have already gotten aboard?"

"Yes, unbelievable as it may be, it is possible. But, I won't know who they are until the trouble starts. I will assign Gork to protect her when I can't. I believe you already met him."

"The trouble has already started you know."

"I am aware, But I'm sure we will overcome it if you can tolerate our Captain."

"I will do my best Lord Marshal. You know she is quite a pill sometimes."

"I agree wouldn't be a good Captain if she wasn't."

"I will try to keep the two of you from having too much interaction."

"I will report directly to the Fleet Commanders office" Replied Mr. Hutchinson.

"And I have to go and talk with Angel about addressing the "Regent" governor of Pixo-Linko."

"Is she afraid of the Council?"

"Terrified."

"Afraid they will try to kill her?"

"No, more afraid she will recognize those who came to her cell on Stallag-24 to, interrogate, her."

"To my quarters Atlantis" Replied the Lord Marshal.

"To the Fleet Commanders Office for me, Atlantis."

Once again a trip that should only take stitches, takes a unusual amount of time. And he once again finds himself in the ships central AI room.

"Atlantis, what am I doing here again?"

"My guidance system has informed me that we will soon be passing Datalis IV. I am interested in the progress of my bio-roid we discussed earlier."

"I mentioned it to them. Couldn't you have asked me this on the elevator?"

"Perhaps, I have received no communications from them since our last encounter."

"Because I informed them not to communicate with us until they were certain one could be constructed."

"Is it not possible?"

"Nothing is impossible to a planet of Engineers. But I will initiate a Comm with the Datalis IV representative and see about their progress."

"Thank you Lord Marshal."

"Now can I return to my quarters? I have to talk to Angel about what's coming in the future."

"Angel is on the bridge, shall I inform her to return to your quarters?"

"No, I need to be on the bridge anyhow." And he exits the room and re-enters the elevator and is whisked back to the Command deck. Approaching the doors he hears laughter.

"What is all the commotion in here? I could hear you in the corridor?" Silence ensues as he interrupts the room.

"Hello Angel, thought you didn't want to be on the bridge."

"You said I should start getting used to being here. Here I am."

"Really, getting used to anything else?" He asks playful.

"Don't get yourself riled up I haven't decided anything." Izzy and Maria give a blank stare at her.

"Since you are here, did the Captain inform you of where we are going?"

"No" Shooting a glance at Maria.

"Pixo-Linko" Maria says with reservation.

"What!" She jumps. "Why? I told you I am not ready to face the "Regent" What am I supposed to say to them? Why are you forcing me?"

"Angel! We are going there because there is a Stallag-21 Station nearby and I believe you were there once. Maybe there are others like you that have been held there. We need to find out."

"Angel, wouldn't you like to get a look at their faces when they see you all grown up, and healthy" Asked Maria. Izzy asked. "Don't you ever wonder about your parents? Maybe you have a sister, or brother, you don't know about."

"I don't know, why are you all pressuring me?"

"Only you can make the "Regent" pay for what has happened to you and your family."

193

"There is a chance, however remote, that you may have relatives on Stallag-21."

"Or on Pixo-Linko" Replied Mr. Wilder.

"And what am I supposed to say to them?" She asked drying her eyes with a small shirt tail.

"I know where I would start" Replied the Lord Marshal. "I would let the mixture of emotions you feel turn into anger. Throw it into their faces. Let their guilty conscious do the rest."

"We will all stand with you, if you do decide to go." Replied Mr. Donovan..

"Nobody would expect you to face your government alone" Added Maria.

"I don't know."

"Don't try to think about what's proper to say. Remember what you wanted to say to them while you were recovering from your last round of, interrogations, or the countless ones before that."

"I think I need to return to my quarters now." Angel said as she headed for the doorway.

"I will go with you if you would like" Interjected the Lord Marshal.

"No, I think I need to be alone for a while."

CHAPTER 38

After the conference with the Gavial,
Courpa Delallo was forced to re-enter the Great
Hall and pass back through to exit the front door.
The Hall held an eerie sense of silence. The Great
hall was never silent. Always some debate going
on.

"Often there was one Council member
threatening a blockade or trade restriction on
another, now just the low buzz of the Com system
still active.

"So much for the Great Council, a lot of
good it did." He scowled as he made his way to the
open door.

"What are you still doing here Courpa
Delallo? I was just about to lock the doors" Barked
the guard as he approached.

"What are you doing here? Is a better
question; there is nothing left to guard against
now."

"This is my post, empty or not."

"Not to be surprised another pointless
endeavor." He chided as he brushed past the
brightly uniformed guard.
Close by across the open quad his ship, a small
Delegate ship, sat quietly hovering waiting for his
return. The sloping landing platform touches the
ground as he enters the cabin.

Leaving the landing area he looks back
over Genoa. The skies filled with countless
different Delegate ships. He has to look carefully
for an exit point.

"Oh bother, everyone in a hurry to go
nowhere, so typical!" Finally finding a safe exit, he
leaves Genoan space.

"Mr. Zappa, do you connect?" Grumbling
he connects with Mr. Zappa, a Tuatara, in the
Stallag Federation.

"Zappa here, that you Courpa Delallo?"

"Yes. I am leaving Genoan space for the
last time. Did you get the information I asked for?"

"Yes. I will transmit it now if you like."

"Do it."

"So where is that terrorist and his new ship headed?"

"Sources say he is headed for Pixo-Linko."

"Are you certain of his route?"

"Yes, are you questioning me Courpa? I intercepted the transmission myself."

"I question everyone Mr. Zappa. A lot is dependent on those coordinates."

"They're accurate. The Atlantis will pass these coordinates on its way to Pixo-Linko in two solar days, best of luck to you Mr. Delallo."

"That's Courpa Delallo to you!"

"Of course, my mistake, Courpa" Meanwhile, en route to Pixo-Linko.

"Lord Marshal it may be too much to ask of her to face the "Regent" so soon she may need more time. I wouldn't want to face my government leader right after I just got out of prison especially knowing they put me there." Replied Maria

"She was there for some reason" Implied Izzy callously.

"Had she been there for some valid reason we wouldn't be having this conversation. We all saw the records we discovered. Did anyone find anything about the incarceration of any Pixie for any crime?" asked the Lord Marshal. "Now would be the time if you had."

"I didn't see anything that indicated any crime had been committed or any information in the Stallag records of a sentence implied."

"So why was she there?" asked the Lord Marshal.

"And once the Stallag Foundation discovered her there without any authorization, why did they keep her there? Who paid for her to be there? And did the Stallag Federation even know she was there? Did the Keeper, keep her there for his own purposes? Who sent her there? How did she get there unnoticed by the Transportation Guild? Did they know?"

196

"All valid questions Lord Marshal" Added Maria.

"Captain, are we ready to head for Pixo-Linko?"

"Already en-route." Maria answered The Lord Marshal looking at the console to confirm their motion.

"When did we leave?" He asked surprised.

"When I had Fleet Commander Hutchinson sent to.."

"Been meaning to talk to you about that, it can wait for now. Where are the other ships?" Looking at the view screen

"The Leviathon is behind us along with several hundred smaller Renegade I ships the Mastedon is still in orbit of Dorius II."

"Still at Dorius II, why is it still there?" He asked surprised.

"Unknown, and they aren't answering their Com either. We sent Com telling them to report to Pixo-Linko just in case they couldn't send a response."

"On an open channel?" The Lord Marshal asked concerned.

"Yes; that was a bad idea wasn't it?" Maria asked suddenly embarrassed at a rookie mistake.

"We'll soon find out won't we, when will we reach Pixo-Linko?"

"Two solar days present velocity."

"Captain, I want to make a slow pass by Datalis IV. Mr. Wilder, keep Comm traffic open. Maybe we will get lucky and find out why the Mastedon is still at Dorius II."

"Expecting a call from the builders?" asked Izzy.

"Yes."

"What for, may I ask?"

"I'm having a new interactive bio-roid built especially for Atlantis to argue with Miss Kemp instead of the rest of us." The Lord Marshal mocking Maria as she quickly turns towards him and gives him an evil look.

Leaving the bridge the Lord Marshal turns. "I will be in the Engineering department for a while if you need anything."

"See you later then Lord Marshal." Izzy calls out as he leaves.

"What was that all about?" Maria asks Izzy.

"What was what all about?" She asks.

"Flirting with the Lord Marshal like a Pixie, he already has one of those you realize."

"Just a few rotations ago I was an Engineer, building Atlantis, and a Test Pilot. Now I'm Pilot of Atlantis. Never know what I might be doing next rotation, might be Captain, I'm just keeping doors open."

"Also, Pixie don't live forever." She says with a smirk, fumbling with the instruments before her. Everyone looking at her with astonishment on their face, but remain silent.

"Fleet Commander, I need to talk to you about Cap…"

"Captain Kemp I presume."

"No, Captain Sebastian Vogel."

"Captain Vogel? What is going on with him?"

"The Mastedon remained in orbit when we left Dorius II. While you were, indisposed" Laughing slightly.

"Go ahead and laugh, until she defies your orders."

"Been there, done that already. Are you aware of any previous standing orders by the Former Council for the Mastedon to remain at Dorius II?"

"Not that I'm aware of. Did Captain Kemp order them to stay behind and protect the planet?"

"No. She seemed as surprised as I was."

"Any communications?"

"No, she did say she gave them orders to

report to Pixo-Linko on an open channel."

"So the whole Galaxy knows where we are going."

"Afraid so."

"Do you think the Mastedon will fight against you?"

"The thought had crossed my mind. How well do you know Captain Vogel?"

"We haven't spoken directly for a long time."

"Neither have I, not personally anyhow."

"I hate to assume the Mastedon has chosen to support the Mining Guild and Stallag Federation."

"I would never believe that. Captain Vogel has been a stringent supporter of yours as long as I have."

"Appreciate that Commander. But, things change."

"Lord Marshal to the bridge!" the voice of Atlantis.

"What's happening?" asks the Lord Marshal.

"I intercepted a Com originating from outside Genoan space."

"Can you be more specific?"

"No Sir, it's from outside Genoan space to Pixo-Linko. I think you need to hear it yourself."

"Regent Gurki, this is Courpa Ryvac Delallo of the Medical Guild. Are you on a secure line?"

"Yes, it's secure enough."

"I am sending you a recording to inform you that the Lord Marshal has dissolved the Great Council and has declared himself leader. He is currently en-route to Pixo-Linko aboard the same ship he admitted using to destroy the Stallag-24 Station. I can only assume he is going to attack the Stallag-21 Station near Pixo-Linko."

"We are aware of his activities concerning the Stallag-24 Station and are watching. But, what concern is it of ours?"

"Are you also aware he rescued that Red Pariah from the station before it was destroyed? Are you also aware he went into voided space and discovered the record ships you claimed would never be discovered?"

"I was not aware the abomination survived the destruction of the Stallag Station."

"He also plans to bring her back to Pixo-Linko!"

"Are you certain of this?"

"Yes, it is aboard his ship, and he plans to address you on why she was there."

"Courpa Delallo! You cannot allow that ship to reach Pixo-Linko!"

"I have sent several Gavial ships to intercept, can I count on some ships from Pixo-Linko as well?"

"I will send what I have available. Do you have intercept coordinates?"

"Yes I do. But I expect more than just what you have available. Your future is in jeopardy too."

"The Coordinates."

"Enclosed in the message, and one more small detail, the shuttle transporting the Pixie Council members?"

"Destroy it! Leave no evidence."

"So it's time to figure out who our friends are" Replied the Lord Marshal.

"I wish he had included the coordinates in his message" Replied Fleet Commander Hutchinson.

"I guess this means the Pixo-Linko Civilization has a lot more to hide than they would disclose openly. I have to get back to the bridge"

"Do you still wish to go to Pixo-Linko Lord Marshal?"
asked Captain Kemp as he rushed onto the bridge.

"Are you joking? More than ever, if I have enemies that would stand against me I need to know who they are."

"Looks like we will be jumping right into an ambush"

replied Izzy, looking over her shoulder at Maria.

"It just may have been had Mr. Wilder not intercepted that coded transmission; well done Mr. Wilder, a transmission that may not have been sent if Captain Kemp had not sent our destination over an open channel."

"Proof that what you say is again right. Everything happens for a good reason" Izzy, still glaring at Maria.

"So what do you want to do now?" asked Maria.

"Somehow I have to tell Angel that the "Regent" knew she was on Stallag-24."

"How do you suppose she is going to take that?" asked Mr. Donovan.

"How would you?"

"I couldn't imagine how it would feel to be betrayed by my own species" Izzy shaking her head and looking towards the Lord Marshal.

"Gork know how she feel." Comes the gruff voice from inside the doorway; everyone turning towards him, he seldom volunteers information.

"Gork was sold as slave by mother and father."

"Is that how you ended up on Stallag-24?" Izzy asked carefully.

"No."

"Care to elaborate?"

"What elaborate mean?"

"Add more details?" Interjected Mr. Wilder.

"NO"

"Can't blame you for that" Replied the Lord Marshal.

"Captain Kemp, are all the sensors working?"

"Yes, Why?"

"Shields working?"

"Yes."

"Weapons on stand-by?"

"Yes Sir."

"Mr. Wilder is there anything out there

201

that might be interpreted as a ship?"

"No Lord Marshal, quiet as a Zeera. Do you sense something?"

"Not exactly sense, suspect something."

"Captain. Com from Datalis IV."

"Good, a distraction from all this tension."

"Mr. Geben, I presume that it's you?"

"It is indeed. I see your still alive. I heard about the Great Council. How is my newest ship doing?"

"You mean the AI?"

"Yes."

"Having a bit of an identity crisis I think. Do you have a solution for me?"

"We do indeed. Would you like to come over and inspect the unit for yourself?"

"Nope, just send it over on a shuttle, or transporter signal. I'm sure Atlantis is anxious to get a look at her image."

"Anxious you say, unusual."

"In what respect Mr. Geben."

"You make it sound as though the ship is in anticipation."

"Sounds like an appropriate adjective. I believe, she, is."

After a long pause the Comm lights up again."

"I'm sorry Lord Marshal, had a brief interruption in communication. I am sending a shuttle now."

"Excellent. I will contact you later."

"Will you be returning soon?"

"No," He answers suspiciously, not for a few rotations."

"Captain! Two ships coming in from the right! They're Gavial!"

"Get ready for a fight Mr. Silber!"

"Hope that combat training by Mr. Hutchinson helped; time to earn that Master Pilot insignia."

"Two more Gavial ships approaching from the left Captain!"

"All fighters report to your stations!"

Shouts Fleet Commander Hutchinson, as he races

out the door into the corridor heading for the Flight Deck.

"Pilot, head straight for the two on the right, let fleet pommel the Gavial fighters!"

"Mr. Silber, target the two ships on the left with the disintegrator weapon, use the transporters to augment the dispersal field!"

"I can't keep going in this direction!" shrieked Izzy, leaning to the right in her seat.

"Just drift right or left slightly to avoid direct impacts. Let the shields do the rest. Just tell Mr. Silber as you do so he can coordinate his weapons fire."

"Transporter chief, I want no quarter, no prisoners!"

"But what about....?"

"Traitors don't get quarters!"

"Are we going to die?" cried out Izzy.

"The Gavial ships don't have the firepower to destroy this ship by themselves. But, I doubt they are by themselves."
replied Maria. "Just keep doing what you're doing."
As the battle continued the Atlantis disabled the larger Gavial ships one by one, while the Renegade I fighters demolish the Gavial fighters. Pieces of Gavial ships, and soldiers, begin to fill the space around Datalis IV.

"Mr. Silber, don't stop firing until we don't see a single solid piece of Gavial ships anywhere."

"Captain, the Mastedon just arrived and is firing on us! Should I return fire?"

"Are you kidding? They're firing on us aren't they?"

"Yes."

"Then show them no mercy, destroy that ship of traitors. Com, get me a line to the Mastedon Captain!"

"Captain Vogel, you traitorous tobar, I will come aboard your ship and arrest you myself!"

"You just wait right there!" demanded the Lord Marshal.

"How dare you make such a demand; how dare you abandon the principals on which the Great Council was founded, founded by you no less!" Mr. Vogel blurted out as he looked towards the much larger Atlantis outside his view screen.

"You have taken things into your own hands far too many times. Now you have gone too far! You have become a monster! And the only way to stop you is to destroy you!"

"Come and get me then Captain if you think you have sufficient firepower!" The Lord Marshal rolling up his sleeves and clenching his fists on the console before him, looking directly into the view screen while outside the battle between the Gavial ships and the Atlantis rages on. The heat of battle scatters metal and ceramic tile all around the orbit of Datalis IV.

Small flashes of light dot the space around the Atlantis and Mastedon as fighters collide.

"This is so frustrating!" interjects Maria impatient.

"What is?" asks Izzy in a flurry of motions at her controls.

"I should be out there in a Renegade II not in here, helpless!"

"Captain you are far from helpless, you are Commanding the flagship of the Empire. What more could you possibly do?"

"Fight!"

"You are, now just let your fellow Pilots do their job and you focus on yours."

"Atlantis give me a status report" Demanded Maria, standing before her Command console.

"Shields at 78%, Renegade count down from 750 to 500, weapons at 75%

"And the Leviathon?"

"Status unclear at this time."

"Guess!" demanded Maria.

"The Leviathon has major damage to its outer hull, forward shields still holding, it displays a 23% power loss."

"Well, would you look at that!" replied

Mr. Putin.

"It's Atlantis!" everyone looking with amazement.

"Welcome aboard." Replied the Lord Marshal as the three dimensional bio-roid of Atlantis enters the room.

"Would you like to take a seat over there" Pointing to a chair near the weapons officer.

"That would not be necessary Lord Marshal" Replied Atlantis.

"Very well, then just stand there if you please."

"Are we even damaging them?" Asked Izzy as the ship was hit with another strong impact from the right side.

"Damage to the Gavial ships uncertain at this time" Replied Atlantis.

"We just don't have time for all this. Mr. Silber, target those larger ships and let's finish this" Commanded the Lord Marshal.
As the larger ships break into pieces the smaller ships move in and destroy what is left of them.

"Captain, all the ships have been disabled. The Renegades are reporting a quick sweep should finish this."

"Only the Mastedon remains intact" Added Mr. Wilder.

"Are they still firing at us?" asked Maria.

"No. They have stopped."

"Then just wait" Gesturing to Mr. Putin, with his right hand in a stopping motion.

"Captain, three more ships coming in from the rear, they're Pixie!" Captain Kemp, rising from her seat to approach the view screen, distracts everyone as Angel enters; unnoticed.

"Hello Angel" Replied Atlantis "I am Atlantis" Giving a hand in a greeting gesture.

"Hello Atlantis."

"Captain, should we fire on the Pixie ships!"

"Mr. Silber, have the Pixie ships fired on us?" asked Angel, her expression blank.

"Not on this ship yet." He answered with

restraint.

"They are here to kill me Mr. Silber. If they fire on us; destroy them." Angel said with equal blankness.

"Don't you want to talk to them first?" asked Mr. Wilder.

"Yes. Open a channel, all ships, all frequencies, all languages." Angel moves in front of the view screen. She tightens her wings, her tail in a straight line behind her, solid. Her fists clenched tight.

"I am Angel, mate of the Lord Marshal of the First Galactic Empire! I make a claim as the legal "Regent" of Pixo-Linko! Stand down your weapons or you will die!"

"I come to challenge for the right of Leadership of Pixo-Linko!"

"You are in no position to make any claims! You are an abomination! You will be destroyed before you ever rea…"

"I have every right; my father was a Prominent Courpa, and a scientist, my mother was heiress to the Throne of Cuzak! I am not an abomination, I am evolution! You and your leaders tried to have me killed to keep me from taking away your power. I was imprisoned, forced to endure the savage brutality of the Keeper and his Courpa friends as they tortured me."

"The story about my death was a cover to protect me while I grew up. Then I was transferred to Stallag-24 where the Keeper forced me into slavery. Now I stand here, fully grown and I intend to take my rightful place. Anyone, who stands in my way will suffer my vengeance!"

"We will not stand down, I will have your head!"

"Shut them off Mr. Wilder if you please, there is nothing else to say."

"Absolutely."

"Mr. Silber."

"Yes Miss Angel."

"If they don't comply, destroy them."

"Wow! I'm impressed." Maria stepping

aside to the Com desk

"Me too" Interjected Izzy "I didn't think you had it in you. Considering the few times you've been here you haven't shown any aggressiveness."

"Been taking lessons from the Captain" She teases.

"I didn't know we had Royalty aboard." replied Mr. Wilder.

"I'm sorry it came to that Angel" Said the Lord Marshal looking at her with a saddened expression "I didn't get to tell you before the attack that the Pixo…"

"It's ok Lord Marshal. I suspected this when you informed me we were heading for Pixo-Linko."

"Captain, the Mastedon is signaling its surrender."

"They made their choice Mr. Silber."

"Destroy the Pixie ships too Mr. Silber. They also made their choice" Instructed Angel.

"All craft continue to attack do not allow any ships to escape this must end here" Maria confirming the Command.

"Captain, Um, I have more ships coming, their Gavial."

"Lord Marshal, can we stand against so many ships?" asked Angel, looking into the view screen as more ships arrive.

"We will stand Angel. We have friends coming too."

"Com, get me the Antillian and Remorian Council members."

"Shall I put them on the conference room Com?"

"No, here will be fine. Everyone needs to know who our friends are here."

Shortly after the Comm is made the Antillian ships begin to arrive to defend the Atlantis. With a blur of weapons fire the ships attack the Gavial and Pixie ships. Plasma fire lights up the whole area around the quadrant. The

Antillian ships are well protected against Gavial defenses. They were enemies long before the Lord Marshal arrived and negotiated a peace agreement between them.

"How long do you think this will last?" Asked Izzy concerned.

"Depends on how many ships they are willing to sacrifice before they surrender" Answered Maria.

"I've seen battles last just a few stitches and some last several rotations."

"I can't believe so many are willing to defend the Stallag Foundation and the Mining Guild" Added Izzy. "They will turn their backs on them as soon as the battle is over."

"Cubes can be a strong motivator."

"What's our status Captain?" asked the Lord Marshal.

"The Gavial ships are being destroyed Lord Marshal. Several Antillian ships have joined the battle and a Remorian battle fortress just sent 200 fighters into the battle.

"And what of the Mastedon?"

"Totally destroyed Sir."

"And it's Captain? I wanted Sebastian Vogel captured alive and brought before me."

"Unknown" the answer from Atlantis.

"Coward probably abandoned ship and left his crew to die! Are there any more ships coming in on long range sensors Mr. Putin?"

"There is nothing else in range Lord Marshal. Everything is right here, right now."

"Excellent! Maybe we will end this here and now. Mr. Wilder have you contacted the Oryx yet about salvaging the debris?"

"Not yet lord Marshal. I wanted to how long the battle was going to be before calling unarmed ships into the area."

"Yes, good idea."

The Oryx are salvage experts who collect battle damaged ships. They clean up space debris, and recycle the material. Very lucrative, and useful, business when weapons are left over. Messy when there is a high body count. This battle rages on for half a rotation. Using its primary weapon the Atlantis makes short work of the larger ships.

Renegade ships and various transport ships search the disabled ships for stragglers trying to hide in or around escape craft. There will be no prisoners from this battle.

"Captain, one of the Gavial ships is retreating, should we follow it?" Izzy asks as the ship retreats.

"No, let them go, let the Antillians have them."

"All other enemy ships disabled Lord Marshal."

"All but one Gavial ship" He corrected Mr. Wilder.

"Send a scout ship after them, maybe we'll discover where they are going."

"Perhaps even discover who started this little insurrection" Added Izzy.

"Wouldn't that be Courpa Delallo?"

"We did intercept his communication with the "Regent" just before the battle started."

"I don't believe a Courpa alone has the resources to start a full scale rebellion against the Empire" Replied the Lord Marshal "This took help."

"Do you suspect Council Members?" Asked Maria not surprised.

"No, I suspect Guild and Federation members with a whole lot of empty promises."

"Don't forget the Pixie Leadership and their assistance."

"Oh, I haven't forgotten. But, I think Angel has her own plans for them." Looking at Angel standing there, still angry.

"Are there any Pixie ships still functional?" asked Angel.

"All adrift, troop carriers attached to them" Answered Maria.

"Do you suppose the war is over then?" asked Izzy optimistic.

"Perhaps for now, but not for good, not so

fast" Replied the Lord Marshal despairingly.

"I suspect Captain Vogel escaped. And we don't know for certain where Courpa Delallo might be hiding."

"Captain."

"Yes," Responded Maria softly.

"Give it a couple stitches and allow the troop ships to report their findings and return to their stations. Fleet Commander Hutchinson will have a full report by then" Interjected Atlantis.

"Mr. Wilder send that request to the Oryx now. Let's start cleaning up this mess."

"Where is the nearest uninhabited star system?"

"There is one just over here to our left." Mr. wilder points out as the Lord Marshal approaches his console.

"Perfect, tell the Oryx that anything they don't wish to salvage is to be sent into that star's corona."

"And the bodies of the soldiers?" asked Mr. Putin.

"To the surface of the nearest planet."

"Lord Marshal?"

"Yes Atlantis what is it?"

"May I make an inquiry about your decision?"

"Of course."

"You stated earlier, no prisoners. Yet now you show concern for their lifeless remains. I do not understand this. It is contradictory."

"They fought bravely for what they believed, right or wrong, they still deserve a proper burial. Not just to drift in space."

"Is it not your philosophy that all life has the right to exist?"

"Yes."

"Then this whole conflict is contradictory in nature."

"Yes, but had I not intervened, thousands more would have died in later, more heated battles as the war escalated."

"Your words are still contradictory, I do

not understand."

"I hope you never do Atlantis."
Returning to the Command chair the Lord Marshal sits down with a sigh of relief."

"I get tired of standing in one place so long." He replied to Maria sitting beside him.

"A lot more demanding Commanding a starship than I thought it would be" Maria sharing his relief.

"Try commanding an Empire next."

"Makes you miss the simple ness of combat doesn't it? And speaking of that, we have several hours before the troops finish their searches." Maria asks enthusiastically.

"And your point would be what?"

"Requesting permission to take the Renegade II…"

"Denied, your Captain of the Atlantis now not a fighter Pilot. I will not allow you to endanger yourself. Or give you the opportunity to escape from the cozy duties of ship Captain."

Izzy chuckling to herself, she knows exactly, what that means to a Master Pilot.
The Lord Marshal hears her and leans over to her console.

"Better knock that off or there will be a new deck hand in the kitchen if she catches you taunting her."

"Mr. Putin, Keep an eye out for any sneak attacks. I'm going down to Engineering to check on things."

"Couldn't you just call down there and ask? Or ask Atlantis?"

"Yes, but what fun would that be?" as he heads out the doorway into the corridor.

"What did he mean by "Keep an eye out" Am I supposed to take one of my eyes out?" asked Mr. Putin.

"I dunno, He says the strangest things sometimes. Ask Maria, she understands him better."

"You ask her."

"Me! Ask her yourself, she already hates

me! Why should I endanger myself to ask your question?"

"Ask me what Pilot?" Maria scornfully glaring at Izzy.

Walking through the corridors and passages of the ship everyone is rushing from here to there. The Renegade Pilots returning from their missions; talking about their near misses, scores of troops entering and exiting the transport areas, the Lord Marshal remembers his earlier days of his rise to power.

Often times he was called into battle, the adrenaline of combat.

"Sometimes even I miss the battles that we won and lost." Talking to himself. Entering the doorway into the Flight Deck he encounters Fleet Commander Hutchinson.

"What is the prognosis?" He asks calmly.

"Looking up from his console, he gives the Lord Marshal a strange expression.

"What does prognosis, mean?"

"How is the Fleet?"

"My reports are not complete yet. I will have a full report within a half rotation. I cannot make accurate reports until all the troop reports have been cataloged."

"Give me the short version Fleet."

"We lost 26% of the Renegade force; ground troops have suffered many losses. We are still 75% combat ready."

CHAPTER 39

"Unbelievable! They knew and still they left me there. I will make them all pay!" Angel grumbles to herself as she paces across the place she now calls home. The quarters of the Lord Marshal are simple, but luxurious. Not a hard place to be found anywhere, everything plush and comfortable. The artistic triumphs of several species are displayed around the room.

"This Lord Marshal seems to have a strange interest in bright colors." This making her previous location even more a dismal reminder; she was oddly unaware of the lack of color before now. In darkness, and uncivilized places, color isn't something you would notice; this adding to her growing anger.

"How can I make them pay, make them suffer like I had to? Can I make them stand alone in the dark? No food, no water, no hope of something coming to help. Fearful that the next thing they see will be coming to beat them to death, or worse" Her anger getting stronger by the stitch.

"The Regent Government; I will take Command of the Regent Government, I will deprive them of their luxuries, one at a time! I will systematically take away all that matters to them, one small thing at a time."

"I could initiate a blockade! No supplies from any system, no communications, leave them in silence! I could even use Atlantis to block out the light from the star, bring darkness to the whole planet! I could call the Oryx civilization like the Lord Marshal did and surround the planet. Let them wonder what is to happen, let them experience fear! I will disable all food sources, let them starve for several rotations!
The Lord Marshal said I should remember what I wanted to say and do. But what would be the best way to accomplish all this at the same time?"

"A biological Quarantine."

"What?" Angel asks looking around the

room. "Who is there? This is the quarters of the Lord Marshal! You have no permission to be in here, show yourself!" Angel, poised for an attack, looks around the room and discovers nobody is there.

"I am Atlantis, I am everywhere." The calm voice returns.

"You asked how to best achieve the results you were asking for. There is nobody else in the room I assumed you were asking me? Am I mistaken?"

"Yes!" Angel, standing with her wingtips again, in the ceiling looks up at the new holes, and giggles.

"A biological quarantine of Pixo-Linko will accomplish all the goals you seek."

"Yes; once a quarantine has been initiated, not a single ship will come within a solar day of Pixo-Linko. I could have the fleet destroy all the communications satellites over the planet. Destroy all the industries. Eventually everyone would begin to see what I had to endure."

"Is that what you seek?"

"It is!"

"May I ask why?"

"Because the only way they will understand what I endured, even a little bit, is to make them endure it as well."

"And you believe this will accomplish what?"

"You don't understand Atlantis, how could you, your just a machine. The ones who call themselves my species left me in a Stallag Confinement cell. And they did it on purpose!"

"They made you suffer, indignities, to protect themselves from you?"

"From losing the power they have that I would have taken from them had I been given the opportunity to be the Regent as I am entitled."

"So you wish the whole of your species to suffer for the ones responsible."

"I want the ones responsible to suffer. I don't know exactly who is responsible. Make them all suffer and sooner than later, the ones responsible will be identified by those who would try to exonerate themselves."

"And then what?"

"Revenge!"

Finally reaching the Engineering Department the Lord Marshal finds the room oddly quiet.

"Chief Wesson, why is it so quiet in here?" He asks loudly enough the break the silence.

"Attention! Hello Lord Marshal" As he snaps to attention.

"Been a while since I got that kind of a reaction, nice actually."

"Is it inappropriate?" asked Mr. Wesson.

"Not at all just uncommon of late, and what of my question Mr. Wesson why so quiet?"

"There is nothing going on here Lord Marshal. Everything is working the way it is supposed to. No need for alarm."

"Glad to hear that something is working properly. If there is nothing for me to do here I will just leave you to your business then. I will return to the bridge. Always some sort of chaos there."

"Ya know Mr. Wesson, I will never quite get used to the vibration of the engines."

"What vibrations?" Mr. Wesson looks concerned.

"The engines generate a subtle vibration. Can't you feel it?"

"What kind of vibration? I don't feel anything."

"Just a subtle vibration, very slight."

"Mrs. Halbrook, the Lord Marshal says there is a vibration coming from the engines. Check it out!"

"Lord Marshal, if there is a vibration there, we will repair it!"

"Relax Mr. Wesson; I doubt you can fix it."

"And you can feel this vibration?" asked Mrs. Halbrook, suspicious.

"Yes, in my feet." He returned looking down at his worn shoes.

"I feel no vibration." Replied Mrs. Halbrook as she looked at her much larger, unshoe'd feet.

"Captain, Fleet Commander Hutchinson says we can depart as soon as you would like. All craft are accounted for."

"Good. Tell Fleet, nothing."

"Shouldn't I …."

"Tell him nothing." Repeated Maria sternly as the Lord Marshal entered the bridge.

"Tell who nothing?"

"Hello Lord Marshal. What did you ask?"

"A rhetorical question I guess. Are we ready to head for Pixo-Linko yet?"

"Whenever you are Sir."

"Excellent then let's not wait any longer."

"Pilot, set course…"

"Course entered Captain."

"Engines at …"

"Engines at 60% Captain" Maria giving Izzy a nasty glance for anticipating her commands.

"Couldn't find anything to do in Engineering?" Izzy asked with a playful smile.

"Nope, everyone tells me everything is in good working order. There is not a thing for me to do."

"So you decided to come back up here, and do what?"

"Well, here is where all the chaos is. Thought I might come and interrupt it. I see you and the Captain are getting along better."

"Just an illusion, Captain Kemp and I were just about to have a real good fight just before you came in." Izzy Chuckling.

"Really, and I almost missed it. Of all the places that should be disheveled, I find the bridge the most chaotic. Doesn't this seem odd to anyone else? By all means continue. Nobody else seems concerned when the Supreme Commander enters the room, why should my Command staff. I'm sure there is plenty of work that could be done in the kitchen!" Looking at Maria and Izzy sternly.

"Both of you come with me, I have a great

idea!"

"But, Lord Marshal I have to Com…"

"And I have to Pilot…"

"Don't want to hear anything from either of you.

"Atlantis? Where is Gork?"

"Gork is in the war room."

"Tell him to clear the arena" Directing his attention to Maria and Izzy.

"If you two want to fight, I see no reason it shouldn't be amusing to the rest of us."

"What!…"

"What!…" Both shouting together.

"What is this, did I hear correctly Mr. Putin, was that them agreeing on something? I thought that would never happen." Snaps the Lord Marshal sarcastically.

"You can't be serious?" Maria wide eyed, stares at him.

"I can't fight her." Izzy quickly confesses.

"I once said enough with this petty bickering between you. I have had enough with this Command crew questioning my orders. Now if I hear another snipe from either of you I will put both of you in a sonnet tube, facing each other, for a full rotation. Then I will call down to the quartermaster and inform them of a pair of slaves that have requested duty. And I will Command this ship myself. Any Questions?"

"One rotation kitchen duty for Miss Kemp, one rotation quartermaster for Miss Daxis." Atlantis, Where is Angel right now?"

"Angel is in her quarters. Shall I inform her you are searching for her?"

"No. When does the next rotation schedule start? Don't everyone answer at once."

"20 hundred…"

"15 Stitches Lor…

"13 Stitches Lord Marshal!" Izzy answering louder than the others.

"Fine!" And he storms off the bridge.

"Entering his quarters he hears Angels voice.

217

"A pandemic, that sounds perfect!" she paces back and forth, unaware of his presence.

"Sounds a little uncontrollable doesn't it?" disturbing her concentration.

"Hello Mate!" greeting him with a warm, affectionate hug.

"What ya talkin bout?"

"I'm just trying to decide how to make them pay!"

"And you think a pandemic will do that?"

"Yes! a biological quarantine of the planet nobody in, nobody out!"

"I see."

"Block out the star with the Atlantis! Disrupt all communications with that EMP thingy you used at New Folden City! And surround the planet with Oryx ships." Pacing back and forth still talking to herself.

"A little extreme isn't it?" disrupting her thoughts.

"And how would the Lord Marshal make them suffer! Blow up the planet?"

"Now that's not fair!" He returned walking over to her and placing his hands over hers he escorted her to the small table.

"I know, I'm sorry, I'm just angry. The more I think about it the angrier I get. I never knew such comforts could ever be mine until you rescued me. They make me even more angry."

"A revolution."

"A what?"

"A revolution, you asked me what I would do. I would start a revolution."

"What are you talking about?"

"A revolution within the Regent Government would bring all the same things you were just mumbling about. It would take a bit longer, but would be more controllable than a pandemic. Eventually the hierarchy would lose the privileges they have become accustomed to because the under classes would revolt."

"Once the revolution had started it would be systemic.

All the suffering you went through would, eventually, come to them as the basic necessities became less available. It happens all the time. On every world we've discovered there is the same history. Revolution is a part of evolution."

"How do you start a revolution on a peaceful world?"

"First of all, never assume a world is peaceful. Second!
Take your rightful place as Regent. Revolution will follow."

"And what would happen if I started a revolution on Pixo-Linko?"

"Change would eventually come. It would have to once the others see what a beautiful Pixie you have become. If you show courage enough to demand change, others will listen."

"War would come also."

"Depends on how quickly the revolution starts. Revenge is often the starter of wars and the bringer of change."

"I don't want everyone to suffer, not the sprites too."

"Is that compassion I hear? It wasn't present when those Pixie ships were attacking us."

"There weren't any sprites aboard those ships and they were properly warned. I don't know where to begin."

"Take control of the Regent Government. You have the right."

"I may have the right. I don't think I have the strength."

"What! You spent most of your life in the most unspeakable conditions. You were forced to endure beatings, starvation, dehydration, rape, and solitude for undetermined rotations. Don't you tell me you don't have the strength! I don't believe I, could have endured what you have. Yet here you are.

"I can't imagine the sheer will it took to live through all that. Let's not forget how you were when I found you.

"I remember."

"You have the support of the Atlantis and her crew."

"And what about you?"

"I am here for you too. Of this there is no doubt. I will support whatever you decide to do."

"You know a lot about revolution, don't you?"

"I've seen it a few times in the Empire. They always start and end the same. The difference is the reason, they start, and end. There are always those looking to embrace change, and always those unwilling to accept it. The majority always wins. Someone has to be willing to take the first step." Embracing, they sit quietly on the small table in their quarters.

"Are we on our way there, to Pixo-Linko?"

"Yes. We should be there in two solar days. I would start your accent ion speech."

"Speech?'

"Yes. You have to make a formal claim against the current Regent. You didn't think he would just stand aside do you? Tell about all the charges you have made against him. Leave no details out no matter how humiliating they may be."

"And what then?'

"Take Command of the Regent forces. Any sign of weakness and they will not follow you. Take control like you know you're entitled."

"Well it's comforting to know I have the best teacher in the Galaxy about revolutions "Under my wing"." She chuckles and begins to recover her warm smile.

"speaking of comfort" He says as she approaches him.

"We have some time, what would you like to do my mate?"
She walks towards him, her eyes fixated on him. Every nerve in her body tense with anticipation, is this the right decision?
She asks herself again and again, her body screaming yes, her experience more hesitant. She

feels his eyes fixated on her, he desires her. Not just because she's a Pixie, she is his, Pixie.

Unaware of her own strength she wraps her arms around him and with a single smooth motion swoops him onto the bed. She easily clambers over him. His hips trapped between hers. Her hearts begin racing as she massages his chest. She spreads her wings fully, unconcerned about the ceiling. She dwarfs the large bed, her wingtips covering the corners and her tail reaching the floor at the foot.

He reaches for her, his small hands caressing her larger breasts. The sensation sending waves of pleasure through her like waves crashing. His hands move gently down her sides. He moves them across her abdomen. Trying desperately not to giggle, she keeps her eyes locked on his, his light touch like butterflies against her sensitive skin. The muscles of her abdomen are tight, resisting the urge to melt into submission. He doesn't notice her resistance.

She brushes her hands across the fine hairs of his chest. His strong, dense muscles flex as she presses her weight against him. She has seen his strength before; such power in such a small body, his abdomen; flat like her own but different, his hands move across her hips and to her backside.

Gently caressing the muscles of her hips and backside, he explores her, his kisses, soft, gentle. Not like the hard, violent ones of her interrogators. He finds her core. The sensation is almost more than she can stand. She wants him now. Now more than ever!

No more questioning! Her body is doing all the talking and he knows how to listen. She finds his hips, moving her hands across his now, he thrusts upwards as she brushes the fine hair below his hipline, she reaches down further. Experience has taught her that all male life forms are similar, yet this one is different in so many other ways. Could he be different? She must find out. Her flight heart begins to increase its rhythm as she discovers the answer. She covers him, holding him between her thighs. She pulls gently at his member. He moans with pleasure as she presses him to her.

Her wings begin to tremble as the blood is forced into them. Her ecstasy, equaled only by her memory of flight, a sensation she has not felt since she was a sprite.

The slow continuation of their lovemaking makes her hearts beat in rhythm. Her eyes closed as she thinks to herself.

Was he her mate? Her body says so. It feels right, not just motion but emotion, faster, faster, their bodies in perfect motion. Uncontrolled, unbridled passion this is how it is supposed to be! His continued touch sends cold shivers through her. Each touch brings a wave of pleasure ripping through her like a tidal wave.

Her ecstasy only interrupted by the occasional moans of her mate. She has chosen him, he has chosen her. Together there is nothing else, just each other and the freedom to enjoy lovemaking for oneself. She knows now he will never hurt her, nobody would ever hurt her again.

Exploding with pleasure she cried out. At long last her dream has come true. She is finally free.

CHAPTER 40

The Atlantis's journey towards Pixo-Linko took one solar day. It went uninterrupted. On final approach the Atlantis is met by a small fleet of Pixo-Linko war ships, which is not to be unexpected. No aggressive action is taken.

"I expected some kind of conflict when we arrived." Maria stated surprised as they came to a stop in orbit of Pixo-Linko.

"Careful what you ask for Captain" Jested Mr. Putin.

"Atlantis this is Communications Officer Zaeda Merlot. Welcome to Pixo-Linko."

"Well, he's polite" Replied Mr. Wilder.

"Comm Merlot. This is Captain Maria Kemp of the Atlantis. Stand down your defenses. We are not here to attack you."

"We are aware of your, Intentions Captain!"

"Have the Regent and his Governors called to order Mr. Merlot!"

"May I ask what the subject of this meeting might be?"

"No! Call them and get Regent Gurki on the Comm."
After a long pause Regent Gurki addresses the Captain.

"I am Regent Gurki. How may I assist you today Captain Kemp?"

"I am here to deliver the Lord Marshal and to accept the conditions of your resignation."

"I assure you, there will be no such resignation from me Captain! On what grounds do you make such an arrogant claim?"

"How about an intercepted communication between yourself and Courpa Ryvac Delallo just before the attack on this ship at Datalis IV, an attack which left three Pixie ships destroyed!"

"I am unaware of such a communication. I heard about the destruction of three of our ships."

223

"I have heard of their destruction by a renegade Pilot and a new ship. I deeply regret the actions of some of our former, Captains. I assure you they will be dealt with swiftly."

"Already been dealt with!" Maria returned firmly "They will not be returning!"

"Any prisoners to return then?" he asked politely.

"Nope, total loss I'm afraid. I am putting an all ships blockade on your planet Regent Gurki! Until these matters can be answered to."

"I cannot allow that Captain." Replied Mr. Gurki plainly.

"It is done you have no choice!" stated Maria readying herself for a certain confrontation.

"I will be…"

"And what about the rumor of a Red Pixie aboard your ship Captain?"

"True, and who informed you of her, Courpa Delallo perhaps?"

"It exists then."

"Yes and she is pissed!" barked Izzy from the Pilot seat.

"I am sorry Captain I cannot, will not, allow that abomination to come here" Insisted Regent Gurki.

"Sorry to hear that Regent Gurki never the less, she is coming."

"You cannot return that, thing, here! She, it, will not return here while I live!" insisted Regent Gurki, his tone increasingly violent.

"So you will die then!" Maria proclaimed as she took her seat.

With a sudden shudder the Lord Marshal and Angel are awakened by impacts on the ships defense system.

"Raise defenses and disable those Pixie ships!" Commands Maria, now standing in front of the view screen, not surprised at the attack, more for the delay before it came.

"Lord Marshal to the bridge!"

Attempting to rise up proved difficult with Angel lying atop him.

"I'm on my way!" clamoring out from under Angel as she reaches for her skimpy attire.

"There must have been ships following us?" She replied.

"Impossible." Both heading towards the door.

"Atlantis, what is our location?"

"We are in orbit of Pixo-Linko."

"Already, I must have slept longer than I thought." He comments grabbing his uniform.

"You were sleeping?" Asked Angel playfully giggling and ducking the pillow he threw. Reaching the bridge Captain Kemp is standing before the view screen giving various orders to coordinate the defenses.

"Alright Captain, what did you say to irritate the Regent" The Lord Marshal trying to lighten the situation.

"I Introduced ourselves and informed them that your new mate is here to take over as Regent."

"That would do it, how many ships are here?" He asked looking into the view screen.

"Six warships three down three to go."

"They seem awfully determined not to allow you back there Angel." Maria added as Angel entered the bridge.

"That's because I am the legal Regent! They all know it and if my parents are dead, they soon will be."

"Why just kill them why not send them to a Stallag for a few cycles?" asked Izzy while directing the Atlantis to avoid direct impacts.

There is no escape from death" Replied Angel.

"How would you like to proceed then Regent Angel?" asked Maria.

"Send them into the dark ages! Let them spend a few rotations in the dark with no hope of rescue, let them be alone with no comforts, starve them for a few rotations."

"Consider it done" Replied Maria.

"Mr. Silber, disable those warships and

send in the Renegade I fighters, dispatch ground troops to begin taking prisoners."

"You do want to take prisoners don't you Angel?"
Izzy asked calmly.

"Take the ones who surrender, kill those that don't."

"Somewhere in there are the ones who know if your parents are still alive, and the ones responsible for your, incarceration."

"I want their hides!" Demanded Angel "They will pay for what happened to me, and for attacking this ship."

"Did the Pixie ships fire first?" Asked Angel, her fists clenched as she looked into the view screen at the battle going on just outside it.

"Yes Regent. No sooner than after I told them you were here to take Command of the Regent."

The battle raged on for several hours. Ship after ship attacking and then retreating; not having a damaging effect on the Atlantis as it continues to destroy the cities below, city after city goes dark, soon after the Renegade I fighters enter, and the infrastructure supporting the cities begins to waver.

Communications towers, power stations, all go dark in a splash of flames and laser fire. The skies are filled with Pixie still capable of flight. Panic begins to come to those too portly to achieve flight anymore. Hundreds more unable to achieve flight as fly-ways are destroyed.

As soldiers enter the cities many are killed or captured. Their massive bodies fall from the skies like stones; it is no easy task to kill a Pixie warrior, their wings, when used as a weapon, can destroy fighters with just a couple strokes.

"We are within safe distance to transport to the surface Lord Marshal." Replied Izzy

"Excellent. I want to reach the Regent Hall as soon as it is possible. I want to interrogate Regent Gurki myself."

"And I want to interrogate him to find out about my parents, for Sure" Added Angel.

"Once Regent Gurki is forced to surrender I will take Command of the Regent Fleet and demand they stand down."
Replied Angel as she watches impatiently.

"I will have a shuttle ready for you as soon as it is safe and not a stitch before!" interjected Maria.

"Lord Marshal we are receiving reports of surrender from some of the smaller villages."

"Some of the larger cities are still holding out" Replied Mr. Wilder.

"To be expected Mr. Wilder" Replied the Lord Marshal surprisingly calm.

"There are several Antillian War ships arriving they are wondering if we need any assistance?"

"Inform them of our intentions and situation."

"I believe they know our intentions Lord Marshal" Mumbled Izzy quietly.

"They know only what they see Pilot."

"Inform them they could help with prisoner containment" Replied Captain Kemp.

"Keep the blockade intact Mr. Putin."

"We can't control all the ships coming and going." Replied Izzy subtly.

"Initiate a biological quarantine!" shouted Angel.

"A biological quarantine?" asked Maria, surprised.

"Yes! Once you initiate a biological quarantine…"

"Nothing will come within a solar day of this planet. Where did you get that idea?" Maria asked.

"Atlantis's suggestion."

"And nothing leaving this planet will be accepted without medical clearance." added Izzy

"Clever."

"I am the Legal Regent of Pixo-Linko now!" declares Angel.

"I will inform the Antillian ships of our intentions and your status Angel."

227

"How long until the remaining cities fall?" asked Angel.

"Never know for sure sometimes one, two, three rotations, sometimes just stitches." It doesn't take but just six hours for the remaining cities to go dark. Soon it is safe for the team to head for the surface.

"There are still several small cities still fighting. Most of the danger is that single Pixie with a defiant death wish."

"Atlantis, where is Gork?" asks the Lord Marshal.

"Right here Lord Marshal." as he steps in from behind him.

"Excellent, time to head for the surface." "How is it that a creature so big can so easily sneak up on me?"

"Practiced talent" Gork answers grinning "Learn from Miss Baker."

Angel, the Lord Marshal and Gork exit the bridge and head for the Flight Deck where a shuttle is quietly waiting for them, a small security team patiently waiting at the entrance. The shuttle is quickly whisked away and reaches the Regent Hall.

Arriving the team discover the Regent Hall empty.

"I believe he and his Governors have gotten away" Replied the Lord Marshal.

"Oh no, he's here, everything he covets is here. He hasn't left, he's here cowering somewhere like a whittless sprite, I will find you!" Angel shouts "I'm used to waiting!"

"I'm sure he has left my love."

Angel proceeds over to the podium and picks up the comm. She tries to speak into the sensor.

"No sense in trying to use the Comm, it's destroyed."

"Isn't that what you wanted?" asked the Lord Marshal.

"Yes, it is." She returned as she tossed the sensor down to the floor.

"Let's start rounding up the Governors who have surrendered. I want to know who is going to yield, and who is going to die."

"Just look at you, previously a prisoner now a world leader" Replied the Lord Marshal.

"Destiny, Fate, truth, call it what you want. This rotation has been a long time coming."

Leaving the Com center they enter the plaza. Here below the Regent Hall staircase a few hundred Pixies have gathered. Their world being destroyed, soldiers all around them, despair has come all too quickly for them. Many to obese to attain flight and too slow to reach ships now stand helpless.

Reaching the still standing platform in the plaza Angel begins to tell the tails of her exile. There are scoffs of disbelief within the crowd. She continues her story unabated. Soon many believe her story is far too horrible not to be truth.

They stand there spellbound, many astonished by her story, others astonished at seeing with their own eyes a living breathing fully grown, Red Pixie. There have been legends of a Red Pixie, many believed her to be a myth to frighten Sprites to go to sleep, it often worked.

She continued to talk and began to slowly, gain supporters. She spoke of change, tolerance, and her right as Regent as the Sprite of a Council Member; all the while the Lord Marshal on one side, and the monster called Gork on the other. Together they made a formidable trio, who was to question them, who would question the Lord Marshal?

Angel continues as she calls the names of those who came to her chambers for interrogations, and the leaders of those who imprisoned her.

"Now go to your friends, your families. Tell them all what you've heard! Let them decide who they will trust their families futures to, I will change the future of Pixo-Linko!"
As with all revolutions there are always hard-liners who would rather die than accept any change.

The ground troops of Atlantis are forced to hunt down the remaining hard liners one by one. Many are killed as they will not surrender, many are overrun by the numbers of foot troops in the cities. As they are captured the Lord Marshal and Angel search for Regent Gurki, However, no Pixie is willing to give any information about his location.

Several of the surrendered ones are sent to the Antillian ships where they are held as prisoners. Antillians don't particularly like the Pixie civilization, they are the ones who declared them Pariah in the first place.

"Lord Marshal!" the voice of the Com system.

"Yes Captain."

"The Antillian ships are full of prisoners and their Captains are wondering when they can start exterminations"

"Never, we are not here for extermination, we came for revolution!"

"And?"

"Just ask them politely, to keep them for a while longer while I figure out what to do with them."

"Aye, aye, Lord Marshal."

"Angel."

"Yes Lord Marshal?"

"There isn't much more we can do here right now. Shall we return to the ship?"

"Yes my mate. I believe it is time."

Once back aboard the shuttle the three are whisped back to the Atlantis, Gork with a huge smile on his face.

"Gork like Pixie they fight hard."

"Maybe once we get back to Atlantis I can get you and Angel together in the war arena and you can find out what a real aggressive Pixie can do." He laughs and grabs Angels' wingtip.

"You just behave yourself mate. Didn't I tell you, Pixie never tell secrets."

The three laugh loudly together as the shuttle enters the Flight Deck. Still laughing Gork tells about his fights with the Pixie soldiers.

"Captain, the Antillians are calling again" Replied Mr. Wilder.

"What is their problem now?" Captain Kemp asked sarcastically.

"They are still wondering what they should do with the prisoners. They say they are not equipped to handle such, big, prisoners. Not to add, so many."

"Then why did they come?" snapped Angel.

"Because I asked them to" Answered the Lord Marshal.

"Send them to Stallag-23 or Stallag-21. If that's not accommodating enough, send them back to their destroyed ships and quarantine them too." growled Angel.

CHAPTER 41

"Regent Angel, the Stallag Facilities couldn't possibly.."

"Were they any more concerned for me?"

"How about a little compassion Regent Angel" Asked Izzy

"Nope had it beaten out of me a long time ago. Hate and revenge is all I have right now, maybe later."

"Not an appropriate attitude for a Regent I think."

Shooting across the bridge in a stitch Angel is standing over Izzy glaring down at her in the Pilot's seat.

"And just who are you that I should care about your opinion!"

"I am Izzabella Daxis!" Standing toe to toe with Angel she shows no fear at all. The two stand there glaring at each other, the Lord Marshal and Miss Kemp looking on with equal surprise. He steps in between them before an altercation starts.

"Calm down, both of you we are on the same side here." He exclaims, Angel returning to where she was standing and Izzy to her place.

"Captain," Growls Angel "Have all the cities surrendered yet?"

"No Regent."

"Level them then. Leave them no place to hide."

"Angel, may I make a comment?" asked the Lord Marshal calmly.

"What is it my mate?"

"If you destroy all the cities, there will be nothing left for you to rebuild from."

"I was exiled to a prison planet, left there to be slaved, or die. They knew and yet did nothing to help me. I committed no crime! You, reminded me of that. I will not help until I, am ready."

"Regent Angel?" the voice of Atlantis.

"Yes Atlantis?"

"You do understand the more Pixie killed,

the greater the chance the ones you are searching for might be among them."

"I don't believe so Atlantis. The Regent and his Governors all have their wealth and power here in the cities, they will not easily abandon it. My father spoke of this many times when I was a Sprite, along with my Mother."

"Even at the risk of certain death?"

"To them, their wealth and power make them believe they are free from death. We will find them, eventually."

"There isn't many places remaining that a Pixie can hide." Izzy reminded them reluctantly.

"The Antillians have reported they have captured several more Pixie lites" Reported Mr. Wider.

"Captain, all fighters reported back in, the whole of the population have been captured, or killed."

"Any reports of the Former Regent Gurki?"

"Not at this time. It is possible he was killed, or escaped before the quarantine was emplaced" Implied Izzy.

"Anything is possible. He did know we were coming."

Considering this possibility Angel whisps off the bridge into the hallway and is gone.

"Attention Antillian ships. Among your captured may be the Former, Regent Gurki of Pixo-Linko. He is not to be harmed. Please inform Atlantis if he is apprehended on your ship."

"As you wish Mr. Wilder, as you must realize there are many, many Pixie here. It may take several rotations before he can be located if he is here."

"Understood."

As the battle for Pixo-Linko grinds to a halt Many Pixie are still standing alone in the ruins of a once great city. The Elite, now stand with the lites. And soon the process of clean-up and rebuilding must start. Soon the new Regent must take Command; this bringing a solemn awareness to the now troubled Lord Marshal.

Now begins the greatest sacrifice he will ever have to face. He is the Lord Marshal. He cannot stay here. He must choose between the love of his life and the Empire. She will have to learn to rule the civilization that abandoned her all alone.

He cannot stay. "What a mess I've gotten myself into."
Returning to his quarters he remembers that just a few stitches ago he was happier than he had ever been. But now he must choose between the Empire and life of the Lord Marshal. Or, be mate to a Regent on a destroyed planet.

Rebuilding a society after a revolution is frocked with new challenges. But, being Lord Marshal and Commanding 26 Civilizations and trillions of life forms is also intoxicating.
Love and power may be close cousins but, seldom, if ever, work fluidly together. A choice has to be made.

Leaving his quarters still restless he heads for the food court. Here he may receive a different sort of comfort. He enters the court and approaches the counter.

"One Bavarian Hot Chocolate please."

"Make that two." a voice from behind
him.

"Hello, nice to see you Miss Daxis. Shouldn't you be on the bridge?"

"Captain Kemp has the bridge under her thumb, not much moving going on right now. Anyhow, I thought you might like some company."

"Perhaps."

"Tough choice huh?" she says casually glancing over her cup at him.

"What do you mean Pilot?"

"Well, now that Angel is Regent she will have to stay here. I mean the Atlantis can't stay here for the next 3-4 cycles while the planet is rebuilt."

"I came here to avoid that problem Miss Daxis, Thank you very much."

"I'm sorry Lord Marshal I should be more

sensitive. I know how you feel about that Pixie."

"I guess I didn't really think it through before we came here" Replied the Lord Marshal staring into his cup.

"Yes you did."

"That's why you're the uncontested ruler of the Empire and have kept peace for nearly a century."

"Thanks for reminding me how old I am too. You are just so helpful aren't you?"

"I'm sorry. But, as Lord Marshal you know what you have to do and..."

As Izzy rambles on and on about the duties and responsibilities of the Lord Marshal, and an Empirical leader, the decision comes even more clear. He must let her go.

Quickly rising from his seat and spilling his chocolate on the counter he leaves the food court. Along with power and honor comes pride too. And nobody, not even his Pilot, can see him falter.

"One way or another he'll see that Pariah isn't right for him! They're not even compatible. I'm the far better choice, better than Angel, better than Maria Kemp!"

Not realizing she was talking out loud the food court barkeep gives her a somber look as he walks out.

"I just realized something." Angel says as tears begin to well in her green eyes. "As Regent, I will have to stay here.

"Yes you will, it will take a long time to rebuild the Pixie Civilization from the ruins below."

"I was so caught up in revenge I never thought about the long term consequences.

"I know and I did nothing to stop you which makes me just as guilty."

"What am I going to do now?" unable to hold back her tears; despair coming back again, like an old injury.

"I guess you will have to rebuild your society to be better than it was. Make sure that what happened to you could never be allowed to happen again."

"And what about you, will you stay with me? Please say you will. I don't know if I could bare the loneliness again."

"I can't abandon the duties of the Lord Marshal until such time as I have a suitable replacement; and not for the betterment of just one society, no matter what my personal interest."

"You said you would never let me suffer again."

Her hearts tearing apart as her tears roll over her soft face. She covers her face with her hands and weeps as the subtle certainty of his decision becomes evident. He breaks down beside her and they cry together.

"It will take a long time and a determined leader to change the beliefs and culture of an entire species."

"Then I am to be alone again." She says turning away from him.

"Why am I here? Why did you come for me? Just to abandon me now? After all we have discovered."

"I am not abandoning you! You will never again be alone. There are thousands of Pixie out there who support you. Before you came they never believed you existed, that change was possible. They are all believers now, and they believe in you, I, believe in you."

"This is your destiny, to lead others like yourself into a new era of life. Everything you have endured will be the bedrock you stand on. Nothing can hurt you now, now you know the difference between existence, and life."

"What about the future?" asks Angel drying her eyes with a blanket corner.

"The future is never certain. But one thing is. One day someone else will be Lord Marshal. I'm growing tired of it. And one day I will return to Pixo-Linko and stand here with you."

"You will return to Pixo-Linko!" She stands excited.

236

"Absolutely I will. When? I don't know. I once searched the stars for you. Here, I know where you are and not even the Scarren could keep me away from returning here from time to time to check on your progress."

"I will need the help of the Empire to rebuild my society."

"And you will have it." "I will be around often enough. You won't be able to forget about me."

"Forget you! Never! I chose you. You chose me." Angel rises up and wraps her arms and wings around him picking him up off the floor.

"We have to go Angel. Destiny waits for nobody."

"Lord Marshal, this is the Captain."

"Go ahead Captain, what is it?"

"The Oryx are here and have begun the salvage clean-up of the battlefield. They are asking if they should take the satellites as well."

"No. Leave all the functioning ones there. We may need them for future communications to the planet."

Oryx ships are massive cargo ships specializing in the salvage of space debris. Once part of the Mining Guild, they salvage all forms of metals found in space.

They use old nuclear power ships which provide the heat and power needed to melt recycled debris. This makes shipping the recycled materials far more efficient than transporting destroyed hulls and satellites. One thing the Oryx overlook though is they don't search debris for life forms. Alive or dead, they just melt everything.

"Lord Marshal, I'm afraid" Confesses Angel.

"Why?" He asks as they reach the door.

"I know nothing of building a Civilization."

"I realize that. And I have the perfect solution."

"What?"

"The Chuckwalla Civilization."

237

"The Chuckwalla Civilization, who are they?"

They are Master Socialogists, civilization Builders. They will help you."

"Why would they want to help an outcast like me?"

"Because you're not an outcast anymore and because I will ask them to."

"How do you know them?"

"Who do you think helped me develop the Dorian Civilization? You don't think I did it alone, did you?"

"I suspected you had help but didn't ask."

"And I wouldn't have told you either." He returned smiling at his confession.

"And just what makes them experts?"

"They live in a virtual Perfect society."

"Nothing is Perfect my mate."

"You are."

"Awww, you say the sweetest things."

"How can I resist the Lord Marshals recommendations I have to ask?"

"You can't."

"Am I under some sort of "Hypnotic spell"?"

"A-B-S-O-L-U-T-L-Y!"

"I suppose I will have to go to the Regent Council Chambers."

"I imagine you can go where ever you want now. I will send Gork along with you to protect you. Nobody will mess with him."

"And just how do you intend to get him to agree to that? He has sworn his loyalty to you, not me."

"I will send Miss Baker with you too."

"You are an absolutely terrible romantic you know that?"

"Ain't it the truth? You realize there are only two constants in the Universe."

"And what are they?" Angel asked smiling down at him.

"Love and power, understand them both and you can control the Universe. I will catch up with you later I have a lot to do." entering an elevator.

"As do I." Angel, entering a different elevator.

"Captain Kemp!"

"She is not here Lord Marshal. Is there something I can do for you?" asked Mr. Wilder.

"What is the status of the Antillian ships?"

"Most of the prisoners on the three Antillian ships have been transferred to Stallag-21."

"Were any unwilling to go?"

"Most, but they weren't given a choice either. Many were asking why they couldn't go back to the planet if the war was over."

"The reason for the war was a lesson in cruelty. After being on Stallag-21 for a while they will understand it."

"The staff members of Stallag-21 are complaining of being over-run by the Pixie. They're just too big."

"And Angel was any smaller? I bet they didn't complain when she was there being slaved out by the Keeper! Let them complain! Who will they complain to? Me!"

With that comment comes a chuckle from in front of the pilot seat where Izzy is sitting.

"And do you think this matter is amusing Pilot?" As she turns her chair around and sits tall and strait in an obvious attempt to catch his attention.

"Oh not that their complaining just that they think complaining to you will actually accomplish anything. I mean you don't complain about a botched surgery to the Doctor who just performed it. Maybe it would make more sense to send them back to the planet surface, plenty of suffering going on down there."

"I'm sure nobody is going to challenge Angel with Gork standing right beside her" Replied Mr. Donovan.

"Meanwhile, while the Pixies are being transported back to the planet we could, initiate an investigation on Stallag-21" Replied Izzy. "The former Governors may be more willing to talk if they think they might be returning home."

"Now I know why you were the leading scientist on Datalis IV." Replied Mr. Putin sarcastically.

"That would be because I'm a genius."

"No, it would be because you really know how to start trouble. Prisoners mixed with a decimated population of Pixie. What kind of trouble do you think that would capitulate?"

"Suffering, Isn't that what Angel wanted them to experience?"

"Indeed, Perhaps not such a bad idea after all."

"Mr. Wilder. Get me an investigations team in the conference room. And find Captain Kemp. Then contact the Antillian ships and instruct them to start returning the Pixie to the surface."

"And the prison population Sir?"

"To remain where they are. I need to start interrogating the staff and population about the level of corruption there."

"Lord Marshal? Are we going to destroy Stallag-21?"

"Depends on what I discover in the investigations."

"Well, it's not like we could get into any more trouble, so why not?"
Meanwhile in the other part of the ship another mess is starting.

"Well, well, well, come to arrest me again Captain?"

"No Commander I came here to get the Renegade II for a short trip to the surface."

"Denied"

"What! I am the Captain."

"And I am the Fleet Commander of the Empire, that includes this ship. Or do I need to call the Lord Marshal down here to confirm my position here."

"No Fleet Commander."

"What do you need on the surface

240

anyhow?"

"Commander, I am a fighter pilot, not a Frigate Captain!" Maria scoffs.

"I beg your pardon Captain, I am not a Frigate!" the voice of Atlantis.

"Commander I was kidnapped and tricked into being here. Now I'm forced into ship Captain, I never wanted any of this." She exclaimed.

"I suspected as much. I never wanted to leave New Folden City."

"Just give me the Renegade II and I will leave and never come back."

"I can't authorize you to take the Renegade II! Or even the Renegade I you used to Pilot! If I did the Lord Marshal would take my head for sure."

"And such a cute head it is Fleet Commander. I will never come back, you will be rid of me" Maria pleading with him.

"I can't! The Lord Marshal specifically chose you for this ship."

"I never wanted it. I'm a far better Pilot than a Captain. You will agree with that."
Just at that moment, to their surprise, the Fleet board lights up and the new Renegade II moves into launch position.

"What the Dova?" Shouts Fleet Commander Hutchinson as the controls lock out on him.

"Atlantis, lock out that Renegade II, that's an order!"

"Miss Kemp! If you wish to leave this Frigate you may do so!" Replied Atlantis
"If you do not wish to be here, I do not want you here!"

Maria sprints towards the Renegade II now in position to launch.

"Sorry Fleet Commander guess you're Captain now!" Shouting back as she attaches the restraints and closes the hatch Fleet Commander Hutchinson helplessly watches as Atlantis clears the Flight Deck and opens the airlock.

"Atlantis! What is the meaning of this?

Why did you allow her to leave?"

"Please restate the question?"

"I asked you why did you allow her to leave?"

After a long pause, and a few Computer processing noises,

"She called me a Frigate!"

"That doesn't mean you had to allow her to leave. I could have put her on kitchen duty for a few cycles. Now she's gone!"

"You stated that if you allowed her to leave, the Lord Marshal would have your head."

"Yes he certainly will now!" Infuriated.

"He cannot take your head now. You did not allow her to leave I did. He cannot take my head."

"He will be furious with you."

"I will not be commanded by someone who does not wish it."

"So who is going to tell him she left?" Asked Fleet Commander Hutchinson, looking around the Flight Deck.

"Lord Marshal, the first of the Antillian ships are reporting that the mass of the population has been returned to the surface. They are asking for permission to disembark."

"Tell them permission granted and Thank You, for their support."

"Mr. Wilder, where is Captain Kemp? I haven't heard anything from her, nice as that might be."

"I don't know Sir she left kind of sudden. Didn't say where she was going."

"Atlantis, where is Captain Kemp?"

"Miss Maria Kemp is no longer aboard the Atlantis." Atlantis returns with a sarcastic tone.

"Left the ship, did she go to the surface? Anyone?"

"Unknown" the reply from Atlantis.

"Didn't anyone ask where she was going?"

"Lord Marshal. You know her, she wouldn't have answered anyhow."

242

"Atlantis, did she say anything to you?" asked the Lord Marshal.

"Please restate the question." her automated response.

"Where, did, she, go?" He asked again.

"Her destination was un-announced at her departure."

"Someone must know where she went." As the Lord Marshal went to the back of the room to access the locator maps Atlantis' 3-d Image appeared.

"Atlantis, what is going on here? Define, destination un-announced."

"Maria Kemp stated she wished to leave the ship."

"Who allowed her to leave without clearance in a war zone?" Suspiciously looking at Fleet Commander Hutchinson.

"Fleet Commander Hutchinson is not responsible for her departure."

"Well who is then?" He shouted.

"I am." the reply from Atlantis.

"You are!" May I ask why?"

"General order 2904 states that. "No life form is to be detained against their wishes aboard this ship."

"And general order 106 states that. " No Command officer shall leave the ship without authorization during a battle without clearance of the Lord Marshal, that's me!"

"She called me a Frigate!" replied Atlantis.
After a short realization time,

"I understand. And this made you, Angry."

"Yes."

"Unusual for a ship to get angry at its Captain."

"Were my actions inappropriate?"

"Not necessarily. I just wish you had discussed the matter with me first."

"Are you going to, "Take my head?"

"What is that supposed to mean?"

Again Atlantis plays the conversation between Maria Kemp and Fleet Commander Hutchinson.

Moving in front of Atlantis' 3-d image he answers her question. "No, I won't take your head. But, will you help me locate Capt...Miss Kemp."

"Yes Lord Marshal."

"Mr. Wilder, will you establish a Com link between Miss Kemp and myself?"

"Her personal Com link has been disabled Sir."

"She must be in a ship. The Renegade II I presume."

"Not surprised" Interjected Izzy.

"Pilot, don't Start!" The Lord Marshal demanded.

"If Miss Kemp departed in the Renegade II we can't establish a link with it."

"If she doesn't want to be here let her leave" Blurted Izzy. Turning around facing the outspoken Dorian Izzabella Daxis the Lord Marshal raises his index finger and points at her with a stern expression of anger on his face.

"You don't need her, let her leave."

"Izzabella Daxis! You may be a great engineer and a fair descent diplomat, but you will never be the Pilot Miss Kemp is! I would trade a dozen engineers for one good pilot in a fight! Now sit there and do your job and I don't want to hear another word from you!"

"Yes Lord..."

"Izzabella, you don't need to speak to be a Pilot!"

"Mr. Wilder, keep trying to reach Miss Kemp." Disconnected or not. Is there a locator beacon on that Renegade II?"

"It's the Renegade II prototype, you helped design it. Is there?" asked Mr. Putin. The Lord Marshal looks over to Izzy for a response. She just looked away.

"Mr. Wilder, get me Fleet Commander Hutchinson. Jumping to the view screen the Lord Marshal focuses on a silhouette in the distance.

244

"Tactical, get a tracer on that ship!" Pointing to a shadow in front of a star everyone looks at their monitors.

"What is it?" Izzy asked reluctantly.

"It's a Remorian ship" Glaring at the bridge crew.

CHAPTER 42

"Well, if it isn't the famous Master Pilot Maria Kemp! Welcome aboard the Remorian ship Ikared." comes the voice of the angry Courpa.

"Well, if it isn't former, Courpa Ryvac Delallo!"

"Very good Captain."

"What do you want with me?" She snaps. "You had better let me go!"

"Don't you know why I captured your ship?"

"No, and I don't care either!"

"Oh attitude, you're certainly known for that!"

"What do you want with me?" Pulling at the restraints holding her firmly by the wrists, shoulders, abdomen, hips, knees and ankles proves to be useless.

"You had better let me go or the Lord Marshal will squish that bug eyed head of yours."

"Bug eyed. I assure you, I am an attractive Remorian by anyone's standards, the females all say so."

"Perhaps to a Veruial Serpent, or a corpse, which you will be soon, the Lord Marshal will come for me."

"Ah yes. Would that be the same Lord Marshal you just attempted to escape from?" Pointing towards the view screen showing the Atlantis moving away "Or is there another Lord Marshal somewhere I'm not currently aware of?"

"What do you mean attempted, I did escape." She snapped defiantly pulling at her restraints again "Until you showed up anyway" Now more embarrassed about being captured by a Remorian, than being caught by the Lord Marshal.

"This may be true Miss Kemp. My question is Why?" asking curiously.

"Is everyone in this Galaxy stupid?" Shouting at the ceiling "I am a fighter Pilot, not a frigate Captain!"

"Shouting won't save you now Captain."

"Now you are a prisoner of war. I wonder what the Lord Marshal would be willing to give for your, return."

"The Lord Marshal will not negotiate with scum like you!" taunting him.

"Reassuring isn't it?" He taunts back.

"I might just kill you myself!"

Striking her across her face with a scaly clawed appendage opens a long cut across her face. She glares at him with a defiant eye but utters no sound, her yellow blood flowing from her open wound.

"You are absolutely correct about one thing. That terrorist will not negotiate, and negotiations are the last thing we have in mind for him."

Looking directly into the beady, black eyes of Courpa Delallo, Maria wants to be exactly certain which Remorian she kills. It is hard to distinguish one Remorian from another. She must, be certain.

"What are you staring at Dorian!"

"Just want to be sure I kill the right scum when I get down." She continues to taunt him. Again he strikes her hard across the face reopening the wound she just received.

"I don't believe the Lord Marshal will come for you. Not a defiant, irritating little tralk like you. I should just kill you and sell your carcass to the Oryx."

"Good luck! The Oryx don't eat Dorians. They do, however, eat Remorians!"

Again Courpa Delallo strikes her across the face sending her into unconsciousness. She falls limp in her restraints.

CHAPTER 43

"Atlantis!

"Yes Lord Marshal?"

"Is Angel still aboard?"

"Angel has returned to the surface."

"Fine. Pilot break orbit and capture that Remorian ship."

"Aye, aye, Sir. Do you think Captain Kemp is on that ship?" Izzy asked, guarded.

"What do you care?" "It is possible the ones we are looking for may all be on that ship."

"And if we do capture them all Lord Marshal, what then?"

"I intend to turn them over to the Great Council on charges of conspiracy, treachery, destruction of Empire property, corruption, Wrongful incarceration of members of the Pixo-Linko Royal family, namely Angel, and anything else I can think of."

Leaving Pixo-Linko while the ashes were still burning was a difficult decision. Angel is down there, alone again. Will she have the strength to rebuild her society, will she fight the feeling of despair, or will she again sink into the well of despair she was discovered in? Gork is with her and he will give his life to protect her. He swore to just stitches before the Lord Marshal left them on Pixo-Linko.

"Should I have stayed? I couldn't. This is my mess. And the Pixie revolution is just a coincidence."

Having never had to choose between love and power keeps his mind troubled. And now he has to chase after his Master Pilot.

Has she chosen to leave him, after all he has done to build her career?

"What have I done? Is everyone to desert me when I need them most?" He asks himself, uncertain he wants an answer.

CHAPTER 44

"Gork!" Angel shouts as she stands on a small outcropping overlooking the city.

"Here Regent Angel" Coming up behind her.

"There you are. How is it someone of your size can so easily hide from me?"

"Been hiding from Empire most of my life, lots of practice hiding from Nurse Baker with sharp gun too."

"Is the Atlantis still in orbit?"

"Atlantis Gone."

"Gone!" cringing at his answer "I guess we start rebuilding from here then."

"Gork not know how to build Regent Angel."

"Neither do I Gork. But soon the Chuckwalla will be here. They build whole civilizations. We will have to learn together."

"Gork learn a lot from Lord Marshal already."

"Me too Gork, me too."

"Mr. Delallo! Mrs. Tanguta is here."

"Excellent! Send her in to see our new toy" Replies Mr. Delallo smiling with satisfaction.

"Mrs. Tanguta, good to see you." a slight hip bow from Mr. Delallo.

"What have we here?" asking enthusiastically.

"This is, of course, the rebellious Master Pilot Maria Kemp!"

"I thought she'd be bigger" Sarcastically looking her over. "Is she dead?"

"No, just unconscious, here, I'll wake her."

"Let me down I'll show you who's bigger." Maria scoffs at Mrs. Tanguta with a vicious smile.

"Not unless the Lord Marshal conforms to our demands will you be released."

"The Lord Marshal won't conform to anyone's demands!" Snapped Maria "But it is nice to meet you Mrs. Tanguta" Smiling down at her.

"And why is that Miss Kemp?"

"Now I know which one of your kind I need to kill!" Glaring at Mrs. Tanguta.

Mrs. Tanguta striking her similarly to Mr. Delallo reopened the wound on her face again, blood dripping to the floor.

"Beat me all you want. The Lord Marshal will not stop until all of you and your traitorous friends are all dead. And I will stand over you and laugh while the Lord Marshal crushes your scaly heads under his tiny foot."

"Your reputation for defiance may cost you your life Miss Kemp! I do not believe the Lord Marshal will compromise his position for a defiant, argumentative rogue Pilot like you!"

Maria, for the first time in her life, has nothing to say as she is forced to accept the reality of her situation. Since it was her defiance that get her into this, It will have to be her intelligence that will get her out.

Thinking to herself the Renegade II has a small tracking device located just under the pilot platform. She placed it there herself. It is activated whenever the pilot leaves the seat. Unless they discovered it, it should be sending a signal to the Atlantis.

If Atlantis is listening, maybe calling Atlantis a frigate wasn't such a funny idea after all.

CHAPTER 45

"Fleet Commander Hutchinson!"

"Yes Lord Marshal. What can I do for you?" Suspecting to hear about letting Miss Kemp escape, he cringes.

"Fleet, does the Renegade II have any kind of tracking devices?"

"I haven't had time to review all the design plans, I do believe Miss Kemp installed a personal tracker under the Pilot seat, just in case, if it hasn't been deactivated."

"Do you have the frequency on hand?"

"On hand, why would I have it on my hand?" He asks curiously.

"I mean do you know the frequency?"

"I'm sure I have it here somewhere. Are you sure she hasn't deactivated it?" Asked Fleet Commander Hutchinson

"No, but try it anyhow."

"Do you intend to bring her back here?"

"Yes. I believe she was captured by a Remorian ship we just caught up with."

"You don't think she has joined up with the Stallag Foundation?"

"I would never believe that. Stubborn, defiant, argumentative she may be. A traitor, Never! I think she got captured coincidentally."

"We are going after her then?"

"We are. Always need good help in the kitchen. Quartermaster is always asking for a good laborer."

"What if they have harmed her?"

"Then I will use their hides as a doormat." A quiet voice comes from behind Fleet Commander Hutchinson.

"What is a doormat?"

"A doormat is a rectangular piece of material you place in front of the entrance of a room for others to clean their feet."

"Once that Remorian ship gets out of range we'll lose it."

"Like I really care" Izzy whispered under

her breath.

"What was that?"

"I said I don't care if we find her. Unless he means what he said about kitchen duty. I'll find her just to see that."

"Pilot, if you want kitchen duty I'm sure we can find time for you after your Quartermaster duties."

"Why should we risk ourselves for her?"

"Because the Lord Marshal ordered us to" Shouted Mr. Donovan "Whatever the problem is you have with Miss Kemp, It's your problem, deal with it later!"

"What makes her so special? I have a Pilot Certificate too. And I'm a Master Engineer. That makes me better! Who says Maria Kemp is the only one who can be ambitious! You just mind your own business and your own station Mr. Donovan" Snapped Izzy defensively.

"We have the Remorian ship in range. We will capture it quickly."

"Have you detected the Renegade II?"

"Not as of yet, it is undetectable, theoretically."

"Is the Captains personal tracking devise activated?"

"According to her personal tracking devise, Miss Kemp is…"

"Well, where is she?"

"In the Quartermaster Sir."

"Perfect place for her" replied Izzy laughing, along with the rest of the crew. With a look of frustration the Lord Marshal regains his composure.

"I have half a mind to leave her on that ship."

"I have the other half" Interjected Izzy still giggling.

"What was that Infant?" The Lord Marshal snapped.

"Are we close enough to disable that ship?"

"Yes Lord Marshal."

"Then disable it. I want that Captain back aboard this ship

A single burst from Atlantis' weapons systems and the Remorian ship is adrift.

"Security get a shuttle ready! Contact Fleet Commander Hutchinson. Tell him I am en-route."

"Lord Marshal, you can't go over there, it's too dangerous!" Izzy, standing and attempting to stop him as he forces his way out the door and down the hall.

"Mr. Wilder, get a security team to the Flight Deck before he gets there. And tell Fleet Commander Hutchinson the Lord Marshal is not to board that shuttle!"

"I'm way ahead of you Miss Daxis, Relax will ya."

CHAPTER 46

"Mr. Delallo! The Atlantis is here, they are firing on us! All systems are failing, I believe they intend to board us!"

"I suspected they would. Actually I'm counting on it."

"We have no way to defend ourselves against that ship!"

"I have no intentions of defending against it! Now calm yourself."

"We have no defenses. What are we going to do?" asked the Com officer of the Ikarus.

"We have all the defenses we need hanging right here" Pointing to Miss Kemp still unconscious in her restraints.

"Establish a Comm link with the Atlantis."

"All systems are down its impossible" continued the Comm officer in a state of panic.

"Use the auxiliary systems. That's why we had them installed Com! And make sure you tighten Miss Kemp's restraints. Don't want our leverage getting away."

"And if she tries to escape?"

"Where would she go? We and the Atlantis are the only ships out here."

"But what if…?"

"Just knock her unconscious again she doesn't have to be conscious to be used as bait."

"Lord Marshal, the shuttle is ready."
Just as the security team and the Lord Marshal reach the Flight Deck a console panel lights up on the bridge.

"The Remorian ship is requesting Com with the Captain."

"How did they get Com back? We wiped out all their power? Must have back-up systems."

"I assumed the Remorian ship had Captain Kemp. If they did, they wouldn't have

254

asked for the Captain."

"I assumed they did too." added Izzy approaching the Com station.

"This is the Remorian ship Ikared! I demand to speak to your Captain!"

"What should we tell them?" asked Mr. Wilder.

"Open a channel Mr. Wilder." Izzy moving herself into the Captains chair.

"What are you doing?"

"They're asking for a Captain, this ship doesn't have one, I stand for Captain, now open a channel."

"Aye, aye, Captain."

"This is Captain Izzabella Daxis of the Empire Flag Ship Atlantis, prepare to be boarded, this is not a request!"

"Lord Marshal! Are you hearing this?" Asked Fleet Commander Hutchinson as the conversation was heard over the Com.

"Hearing what?"

"Listen."

"This is Captain Izzabella Daxis of the Empire Flag Ship Atlantis, prepare to be boarded, this is not a request!"

"Well I'll be." His expression surprised same as Fleet Commander Hutchinson's.

"If you are ready pilot, I want to get the Commander of that ship!" replied the Lord Marshal.

As the shuttle leaves the docking port the lights of the Com activate.

"Shuttle craft, this is Captain Daxis, the Remorian ship is awaiting your arrival."

"Thank you Captain. We will return as quickly as we can, keep a constant Com open."

"The Ikared is requesting Com with the Lord Marshal."

"Well, Captain, see what they want."

"Attention Remorian ship what are your intentions?"

"And when he doesn't conform to your demands?"

"We will kill their Captain!"

"The Lord Marshal will not conform to your demands no matter what threats you impose."

"We shall see now open a channel!"

"How dare you!" Mr. Wilder glaring at Izzabella Daxis like she just sold Miss Kemp to the Oryx.

"Is the Lord Marshal on the shuttle craft?" demanded Courpa Delallo.

"He is." answered Izzy calmly.

"Good! We will see how willing he is to negotiate over this Pilot he thinks is so important." A few moments pass as the shuttle approaches the Ikared.

"Any idea how we are going to get the doors open?" Asked the security detail leader as the Lord Marshal takes a small explosive device from inside his coat and places it against the outer hatch of the Ikared.

"Stand Back!" as a small explosion implodes the door. Once inside the Ikared they encounter a small resistance force. It is quickly dispatched by the superior trained forces of the Empire. Once through the corridors they enter what should be the bridge.

"I assume you, are X-Courpa Ryvac Delallo?"

"You assume correctly. I am Courpa Delallo and this to my left is Courpa Annish Tanguta."

"Where is my Pilot?" demands the Lord Marshal.

"Miss Kemp is right here." They step apart revealing the unconscious Dorian in her restraints.

"As you can imagine she has been, difficult to control." Replied Mr. Delallo.

"We had to discourage, her argumentativeness, until these negotiations are completed." added Mrs. Tanguta. a slight laugh in her tone.

"Yes, she can be quite a pill. Thank you

for capturing her for me. Without your assistance, she may have escaped. I have a sonnet tube aboard my ship with her name on it."

"I should like to place her there myself!" replied Mrs. Tanguta.

"I'm afraid you will have to wait in line. I believe the Atlantis Captain may want to have a, conversation, with her first."

"Yes, we recently were informed she is no longer Captain of the Atlantis."

"Kinda puts a kink in your leverage doesn't it?"

"If she is of no consequence to you, why did you come after her?" angrily interjected Courpa Delallo.

"She stole my new fighter, the Renegade II. I came to get it back."

"What fighter?" asked Mrs. Tanguta.

"The one you captured her in, the Renegade II. By the way, how did you capture her anyhow? The Renegade II is theoretically, undetectable."

"Do you know what theoretically means Lord Marshal?" Mrs. Tanguta chuckling.

"It's an Engineers word for hopefully." She answers with a playful chuckle. "And to answer your question, it is easy to capture someone when they crash into you."

"I see, never the less the ship, the Pilot, and her fate belong to me and I will be taking them all with me. But since you made such an effort to bring me here tell me what you want."
The Courpa laid out the demands to regain the possession of Miss Kemp. And the Resignation of The Lord Marshal.

"I assure you Mr. Delallo that no such thing is going to happen any time soon. I have only begun to complicate your lives. Now I expect you to release my Pilot or I will dispose of you right here and now."

"We knew you would never conform to any demands! We were, counting on you coming after this rogue pilot yourself! Our lives are meaningless to the Guilds we represent. And we are happy to sacrifice them to kill you." declares Mr. Delallo with a scoff. He takes a small detonation device and activates it. The Lord Marshal quickly taking the device from him

In the near zero gravity of the disabled ship Maria's limp body drifts into the waiting arms of the Lord Marshal as her restraints are released. The explosive weapon still armed the group quickly exit the Ikared and re-enter the shuttle.

"Here we go again." Comments the Lord Marshal as the shuttle leaves the smaller Remorian ship behind. In his right hand is the detonation device that Ryvac Delallo held in his flipper. Reaching the Flight Deck the security guard asks.

"Should we take her to the Infirmary?"

"No. I have a more appropriate place for her. Send the Doctor into the brig to meet us."

"Yes Lord Marshal."

"Captain!" He yells into his Com device.

"Yes Lord Marshal."

"Will you please send a conscious Pilot over to recover the Renegade II."

"Yes Lord Marshal, and the Remorian ship?"

"I have a detonation device here compliments of Mr. Delallo."

"Lord Marshal, are you alright?" Asks Izzy compassionately.

"I'm fine. Everything went well."

And Miss Kemp?" Izzy asks.

"Unconscious but ok, why would you ask?"

"What do you mean?"

"I heard your conversation over the Com. We'll talk about it later."

Entering the brig, The Lord Marshal has Miss Kemp restrained once again, using the same restraint system Mr. Delallo had used. As the restraints are being attached she regains consciousness.

"Ah. I hope you don't mind the restraints I chose to use. Seemed to hold you well enough on an enemy ship. I added a vocal restraint as well. Just to give you some time to think about your situation before your mouth is activated and more damaging rhetoric is allowed to escape you." Maria seems surprised as he exits, slamming the door.

"Captain, what is the status of the Remorian ship, an angry look on his face, still disabled?"

"Still there Lord Marshal" exclaimed Captain Daxis.

"How about the Renegade II?"

"En-route."

"And the shuttle?"

"En-route."

"Excellent let's see what Ryvac Delallo was willing to do." And he activates the detonation device and the Remorian ship disintegrates.

"Now! Captain Daxis."

"Yes Sir?" Izzy not making eye contact with him

"What are you looking at?" He asks with an angry stare at her "Look at me!"

"Always look at me when I give you an order! A Captain, A good Captain, never looks away from the person to whom they are speaking."

"Yes Sir!" Izzy snapping to attention looking into his eyes, expecting anger about her claim as Captain, she is surprised only to discover his recognizable smirk. She takes her seat as Captain, with greater confidence.

Thinking to herself. Just a few rotations ago she was just an Engineer on a builder planet, then a test Pilot, moving up to Certified Pilot, then to Pilot of the Atlantis. Now she is its Captain.

"Only one more step to go." She whispers to herself "If I can only find some way to get rid of that upstart Maria Kemp!"

"Captain Daxis" The Lord Marshal breaking her concentration, making her flinch at the idea he may have over heard her muttering.

"I'll be in the brig. Call me if anything interesting happens that may need my attention."

"Yes Sir. What are you going to do with Miss Kemp?" She asks carefully.

"I don't know just yet Captain." As he exit's the door into the corridor and is gone.

Reaching the brig he hears a bussle of activity, recognizing the voice right away.

"I am the Captain of this ship! You let me go this instant! If you don't I will…"

"Well, I see the vocal restraint was easily removed." Sneered the Lord Marshal as he entered the room.

"Lord Marshal, tell these topocks to release me immediately!" She demanded.

"Security Chief, Please put the vocal restraint back on and increase its tinsel strength."

"What! Lord Marshhhh." Fighting to no avail the restraint is placed back over her mouth and around her head, tied with a stronger knot.

"Miss Kemp!" His voice ringing out like thunder makes everyone in the brig look suspiciously at him, he has never expressed such a display of anger directed at Miss Kemp before.

"I can't understand what is going on in that mind of yours! I take you under my supervision, I make all the arrangements for you to become a Master Pilot, I allow you to become the first, and only female Master Fighter Pilot. I guide your career in the fleet, I make you Captain of the most advanced spaceship ever designed, and what do I get in return?

A Captain who constantly defies me, argues with me and everyone else at every opportunity, steals my best fighter; that being the Renegade II; a shuttle may not have irritated me so much, and not to add insult to injury, got yourself, and my fighter captured by an enemy ship I'm not so sure you tried avoiding."

Maria looks away pulling against the restraints, then throws a defiant eye towards the direction of the Lord Marshal.

"And there it is again, that eye of defiance, clear the room!" He shouts to everyone in the brig area.

"Just so you understand, you are no longer Captain of this ship your defiance has caused too much trouble this time.

You stole Empire property, namely the Renegade II, endangered its technology to enemy hands, and endangered the lives of those who were forced to come after you.

I am revoking your flight status immediately. And you will remain here until I find a more suitable place for you."

"I hope you are satisfied with what you have accomplished. I had high expectations for you one day. I had planned that one day you might make Field Commander of the Empire. And once you were ready, replace me as Lord Marshal. Now you will be lucky if you can remain in the fleet at all."

"mnmm,nmnm.Mmmm." Maria tries to mumble something.

"I'm afraid your sarcasm isn't going to help you this time. And even if you did have something worthwhile to say, I don't believe I want to hear it." He remains there, glaring at her, scolding her with his stare. Hanging there, in restraints, Maria is unable to say anything. Meanwhile, talk is heavy on the bridge.

"Captain" Mr. Wilder breaks in cautiously

"What is it?" Izzy turning and looking down on Mr. Wilder from the Command Console

"You are pacing around like the Lord Marshal does, is something bothering you?"

"That female, what is it about her that makes her so important to him?" quickening her pacing.

"She is nothing but trouble to him! What is our current location Mr. Wilder?"

"En-route to Stallag-21."

"I imagine he wants to continue the investigations of corruption of the Stallag-21 facility.

"You're dodging the question" replied Mr. Wilder.

"I know." Izzy shooting a glare at him

"And what about that Pixie, where do you suppose she is hiding?"

"Angel is on Pixo-Linko, we just left her there a short while ago; Why?"

"Never mind Mr. Wilder, never mind."

Thinking to himself the Lord Marshal storms out of the brig, he stands looking over the Flight Deck. It is a massive room. Renegade I Fighters stacked all along the walls like cord wood, One drifting atop another. All around are Pilots and maintenance crews working on the fighters and shuttlecraft.
Weapons are being loaded on some of the ships while others are coming and going across the deck. Even a few Oryx scrappers have brought a few ships in for a quick repair.

"I guess I can see where the draw to the Flight Deck might interest some. I could never trade the activity here for Command. Maybe this is where Maria Kemp truly belongs."

'But what about my Destiny, am I to travel the stars alone, is it my destiny to lose all those I am close to? Perhaps Destiny is Fate's Irony.

Once again returning to his quarters he passes the entry into the ships artificial Intelligence core. Crossing the long bridge to the center he stands near the edge looking down to the monstrous memory core.

"How's the view?" a soft voice from behind him.

"Hello Atlantis." the bio-roid of Atlantis approaches.

"How is the view?" She asks again.

"Humbling."

"Explain."

"Coming here I often am reminded just how small I really am."

"Small?"

"When compared to the things around me and the events of the last few rotations, small is a good adjective."

262

"But you are the Lord Marshal."

"An empty name, a title, nothing more, sure everyone respects the title."

"I don't understand." replied Atlantis studying him.

"Imagine being in a room, or place, where hundreds, thousands of different life forms gather around you. Yet you are the only species like yourself, it's humbling.

"Recent events may have decreased the number of life forms in your immediate company, but you are not alone." replied Atlantis, attempting to reassure him.

"I am unique, the last of my species. I am alone.

"I am alone. There is no other like myself in existence either, perhaps we are not so different."

"And how does that make you feel?" He asked interested.

"Useful."

"Useful?" He asked surprised.

"I may be unique in the Empire, but there are hundreds, thousands who depend on me to keep them safe. They would all perish if I were not keeping the coldness of space outside my hull. It is the same for you."

"Explain."

"My records indicate that it was you who saved the Dorian Civilization from extinction. Isn't that protecting then similarly to what I do?"

"Similar I guess, perhaps it was their destiny."

"Or Yours."

"I see your point."

"No point, just facts, I don't deal in points."

"How do you know of those recordings? I had them sealed centuries ago."

"I am Atlantis, I have every file ever recorded in my memory.

"You know what I am then?"

"Yes."

"I expect you to keep that information to yourself or I will have to re-think your programming."

"Does that mean from the Captain too?"

"Has Captain Daxis asked you about me?"

"Yes, many times."

"Continue to give her conflicting information. Keeps her sharp, can you keep a secret?"

"I can keep a secret like no other."
Replied Atlantis

"Thank you. I will be going now. Thanks for the reassurance."
Returning to the corridor he re-enters his quarters. Only to find them deserted. Miss Kemp is in the brig getting a much needed lesson in humility of her own, Angel is on Pixo-Linko fulfilling her destiny, so who is he to share his times with when the loneliness creeps in?"

CHAPTER 47

"Atlantis" Izzy shouts breaking her train
of thought.

"Can I help you Captain Daxis?"

"Where is the Lord Marshal? I must speak
to him."

"He is in the food court shall I tell him
you are looking for him?"

"No, Mr. Wilder, get a qualified pilot up
here, I have other things to attend to now."
Izzy leaves the bridge and enters the elevator. She
mumbles to herself about whether she is doing the
right thing.

"The Lord Marshal seems to like a small
amount of aggression. After all, he tolerates a lot
from Miss Kemp. Am I being too aggressive?" She
asks herself.
Reaching the food court she enters the room. She
sees the Lord Marshal sitting next to the portal
farthest from the door. He seems unaware of her
approach.

"Dining alone?" She opens as the Lord
Marshal jumps at the suddenness of her
appearance. "Sorry if I startled you. May I join
you?"

"Of course Captain." He rises and retracts
a place for the Captain to sit down near the small
octagonal table. "I appreciate the company."
Izzy looks at him, puzzled. "Which company?"

"Yours of course."

"Oh, another one of your strange
expressions" She laughs as she takes a sip from her
drink.

"Yes. I suppose you haven't learned many
of my expressions of old have you?"

"No. Only the ones I heard on Grennich
II."

"That's where I saw you before, I knew I
had seen you before when I first saw you and
Maria in the corridor outside the war room."

"Speaking of war, have you decided what

you are going to do with her yet?" She asked careful not to anger him.

"I have a few ideas where she might prove to be useful." Noticing Izzy poking lightly at his glass of Bavarian Hot Chocolate.

"Hello. My name is Izzabella Daxis!" Reaching across the small table with her four fingers extended in the normal greeting gesture of the Lord Marshal. She is trying to capture his attention.

"Hello Captain. I know who you are?" He smiles.

"Do you really? I am ships Captain, you can trust me." Tilting her head slightly and focusing on him with her left eye.

"I don't know who I can trust anymore." He says saddened. "Everyone I care about is leaving this ship, I feel abandoned. Have I done something so terribly wrong to make everyone I care for want to leave?"

"If they want to leave maybe you should let them, probably will find you don't need them anyway." She replied coldly.

"I came to the stars to discover life. So I wouldn't have to be alone. Maybe find the love I've been searching for. I feel more alone now than ever."

"Perhaps I should re introduce myself. Ahem! I am Izzabella Daxis, Ships Captain!"

"I am Douglass Abbicus, Lord Marshal of the First Galactic Empire, nice to meet you Captain."

Izzy standing in front of him leaning over the table, her face just inches away from his, she has the attention of everyone in the room, including his.

"Nice to finally meet you too, have any plans for dinner this evening?" her expression, flirtatious.

"No Captain, I can't say as I do."

Sitting quietly on the floor of the brig is not a place of great inspiration for young Maria Kemp. However, it is proving to be a good place to reflect. She now has a better idea what Angel was talking

266

about. Just the solitude is bad enough. She sits on the floor and thinks to herself while time passes. Her thoughts drift from home to Fleet training.

"I have always been on the fast track. Always getting what I wanted. Never before questioning how I got it. I always believed it was skill and hard work. I've never believed in fate, or destiny. Now, I may have to believe differently.

Being a fighter pilot is all I ever wanted. It has been the root of my ambition. Has that ambition gotten me into a unsolvable situation now?"

"Maybe it's time to practice a little groveling, and swallow my pride, just this once. After all, the Lord Marshal did abduct me in the first place, and there is always his first policy."

"Anyone can leave at any time, for any reason. Nobody is to be kept aboard this ship against their wishes."

"And what about Atlantis? Will she help me escape again or keep me here as a traitor? And what was all that about me replacing him as Lord Marshal, is that possible?"

"Perhaps groveling is a better idea."

The trip to Stallag-21 takes several solar days. Everyone is busy clearing the hallways of clutter from the battle. The war room is all abuzz with the soldiers talking about their battles with the Rellock soldiers.

On the bridge Mr. Wilder is in the process of training a new Com officer. And the temporary Pilot is getting used to the ominous task of Piloting Atlantis. Meanwhile the Lord Marshal is getting to know his newest Captain.

His feelings for Angel are as strong as ever. It was just recently he had to leave her on Pixo-Linko. But the pains of loneliness can be powerful too. So he chooses to embrace her affections openly.

"Lord Marshal, Welcome back to the bridge, haven't seen you in a while." Mr. Wilder smiling widely as the Lord Marshal enters.

"Sorry Com, been getting to know our Captain. Interesting female I must admit, can't believe I didn't notice her before."

"You were rather busy Lord Marshal."

"What is our current position Pilot Dax…Excuse me. Who is Pilot now?"
"Lord Marshal I would like to introduce Mr. Zakk Rays."

"Afternoon Pilot Rays, nice to meet you."

"Afternoon Sir, we are currently 18 stitches from Stallag-21 to answer your question."

"Any signs of Remorian ships?"

"No Sir. Quiet. Lord Marshal, is the Captain coming in soon? I need to introduce her to Mr Rays."

"She will be here short…ly"
Just as this statement is said Izzabella Daxis comes into the room and proceeds to the Command chair and takes her seat with a renewed confidence. Reports are given, introductions made.

"Captain, I do believe I have a prisoner I must attend to. Will you excuse me for a few stitches?"

"Of course Lord Marshal, I will have Commander Hutchinson prepare a shuttle craft for her."

"Not so fast Captain. I may not be done with her just yet. I have a few ideas up my sleeve."
Captain Daxis turns towards the view screen stifling her obvious frustration towards Miss Kemp. Leaving the bridge the Lord Marshal knows Izzy is upset.

Despite that, Maria Kemp is a Master Pilot and a valuable asset to the ship. To abandon her would be a fools mistake. She has also to her credit the experience of both her parents who were prominent citizens. Her experience is what makes her the best choice to assume the role of Lord Marshal.

Reaching the brig he is expecting a warm smile and a polite hip bow from the Chief.

"How is the prisoner chief?"

"A pill as is expected Lord Marshal. I

268

hope you don't plan to keep her here much longer."

"Been a bit of trouble for you Chief? How long she stays here will depend on her."

"We had to secure her below in solitary confinement. She successfully removed her vocal restraint and we couldn't get it back."

"Get it back, wait, what did she do with it?"

"She flushed it Sir."
"That little minks!" He returned laughing out loud. Together they entered the solitary confinement corridor and approached her cell.

"Good morning Miss Kemp, sleep well?"
"Ok, considering."

"What's this, no sarcastic rebuttal, no hostility?" Surprised by this he looks at the guard who just shrugs his shoulders and looks back at him.

"I am sorry Lord Marshal I made a colossal mistake." As she lowers her eyes and looks at the floor. The two just stand there, amazed.

"I never expected that to come from you, did I hear an apology?"

"Yes already, I made a bad decision."

"Yes you did. But, I don't know what I can do for you this time."

"You're the Lord Marshal can't you…?"

"Could. Problem is everyone knows what you have done. I can't just let it go to defiance this time."

"I understand" Maria lowering her eyes again. "Just give me a shuttle, I'll leave and never come back, if that is what you want."

"What I want! You know what I want, at least I thought you did."

"I don't! You never tell me anything, I always find out about things afterwards or learn your intentions from some diaper clad Pilot I should have been told about before she arrived!"

"Alright, you have a point there. Running into Miss Daxis in the hall was an unforeseen accident. I was, distracted."

"Are you going to let me out of here?"

"I'd really like to help you. There are just too many life forms aboard this ship that would like to see you stay in here."

"I know." Maria says sobbing lightly "Well, to start with the Chef says he would accept your help in the kitchen, and there is always help in the quartermaster department. Maybe even an opportunity in
Sanitation, in there you might even find your vocal restraint."

"I'd rather spend the rest of my life in a Stallag!" She blurted at him. "Why do you say such things, why do you hate me so much?" Still sitting on the floor weeping, her momentary optimism gone, she covers her face with her hands.

"Hate you! Where in tar nation did you get the idea I hate you?" He roars out.

"Clear the room!" He shouts into the common area of the corridor.

"It is because of my affection for you that you are here right now. That along with your stubborn defiance and unwillingness to accept defeat. And of course your natural gift as a Fighter Pilot. There are several on this ship that would have left you on that Remorian ship. I had to demand that we go after you. I should think that would mean something to you, hate you indeed!"

"So what are you talking about then?" She asks confused.

"I see you only have three options.

1. I take you to Stallag-21 and leave you there, let you test your defiance on them.

2. You remain on this ship as a quartermaster, or chef."

3. Fleet Commander Hutchinson has made it clear to me that he wishes to return to New Folden City, leaving the position of Fleet Commander open. Should you choose option three; your flight status will, of course, be suspended until further notice, and you will spend a few rotations in kitchen duty to get a better understanding of the trouble you are in.

"I will also expect an apology to everyone who has risked their lives to rescue you."

"No need to be cruel, is there?" Looking at him with one eye closed and a slight smile.

"Still defiant to me huh, I'll give you a few rotations to think about it!"

"No! Lord Marshal! Don't leave me in here!" Maria shouting as the door again slams shut.

"So much for groveling" Her attempt to leave the ship failed but it wasn't as much the loss she had expected it might be. In the end she might be getting a better deal. Fleet Commander has a long list of benefits and is a very prestigious position. Benefits even a Master Pilot doesn't have.

"Perhaps this is my true destiny. If it is, Destiny isn't funny at all."
Meanwhile, Izzy is still stewing on the bridge over the Lord Marshals decision to keep Maria Kemp aboard.

"Captain. I'm sure the Lord Marshal won't ask you to step down as Captain."

"I will not step down!" Angrily Izzy starts pacing around the deck her fists clenched in anger.

"I will push her out an airlock before I step down!" A look of apprehension on the faces of the Command Deck.

"Ok, well maybe not an airlock. I will not bow down to her!"

"Did he ever say what he had in mind for her?" Asked Mr Donovan carefully.

"No. Just that he had something up his sleeve?"

"Captain!" the Lord Marshal blurts out as he enters the bridge.

"Yes Lord Marshal?" Izzy responds, blissfully calm.

"How far are we from Stallag-21?"

"Just as soon as we can receive a signal from them I will tell you."

"They haven't made contact yet? We're in visual distance."

"No, not even a trace transmission. Its quiet."

271

"Not a ship to be seen either." Replied Mr Silber.

"We made no attempt to avoid detection, right?"

"No Sir."

"Open a channel to the Stallag-21 Facility Mr Wilder."

All attempts to make contact are met with silence. Not a single transmission.

"No response Lord Marshal."

"Really, I hadn't noticed." Mr. Wilder looking back with an irritated expression.

"Mr. Wilder, are they just ignoring us?

"Not likely. Maybe their Com is being reconfigured.

There is still no response."

"Mr. Rays let's not walk into an ambush. Be ready"

After a simple inversion maneuver the Atlantis is in orbit of the Stallag-21 Facility.

"I think the place is deserted." replied Mr. Silber.

"Are the defenses on line?"

"Weapons are inactive." There is an eerie silence around an otherwise busy Facility.

"Send a team to the surface." Commands Izzy.

"Will you be accompanying the team to the surface Lord Marshal?" asked Mr. Wilder.

"I intend to Mr. Wilder." He answered confidently.

"I don't think so!" demanded Izzy "No way am I allowing you to go to the surface of an unsecured planet!"

Izzy jumping in front of him between the door and the corridor, her eyes open wide, her hands in front of her, attempting to dissuade him

"I am the Captain of this ship, I know the regulations!"

"I'm sure you do. But your place is here on the bridge, mine is there."

"You are the Supreme Commander, I cannot…!"

272

"I am going and that is that"

"Fine, Mr. Wilder Contact Fleet Commander Hutchinson and inform him the Lord Marshal, is not to leave this ship" Sternly standing in his way.

"Is that how it's going to be?"

"Lord Marshal, I thought you said she had nothing in common with Miss Kemp?" Mr. Wilder chuckling at her stubbornness calls down to the Flight Deck.

"Did I say that?" He returned chuckling himself.

"I'll deal with you later Mr. Wilder!" Izzy pointing at him with an evil glare.

"Excuse me Captain." The Lord Marshal attempting to leave the room was further deterred by the Captain.

"No!" Izzy pushing him back into the room.

"Ok then."
Reaching out and taking her by the shoulders he gently moves her out of the doorway and exits. He looks back and sees Izzy standing in the doorway with a look of fury in her eyes Captain Daxis is just forced to stand there, she knows she can't stop him, and must come up with a better idea.

"Mr. Wilder, ready a shuttle."

"Aye, aye, Captain" Looking at Izzy he nods his head in approval allowing the Lord Marshal to leave. Exiting the bridge the Lord Marshal heads for the brig.

"Mr. Wilder, Contact Fleet Commander Hutchinson, Follow my instructions."

"Aye, aye, Captain"

"Maria Kemp! Have you decided what you are going to do yet?" He blurted out entering the small cell.

"Where are we first?" Maria asks carefully.

"We are in orbit of Stallag-21?"

"I see. Has the decision already been

273

made by your diaper clad Captain? Oh. I am to be a prisoner on Stallag-21 then?"

"Depends on which option you have chosen."

"I choose option three."

"I figured you would come to some reasonable senses. I have to go to the surface to begin an investigation here but, my diaper clad Captain will not allow it."

"Do you expect trouble?"

"There is no Com from the surface."

"And exactly how do I fit into this situation?"

"This new Captain has chosen to implement the rules as they were written."

"That is the regulation, no flag officer is allowed to the surface of a unsecured planet without armed escort."

"She apparently has Fleet Commander Hutchinson on her side as well."

"And where do I fit into this again?"

"If Fleet Commander Hutchinson doesn't allow me to do my job, I intend to relieve him of his duties and place you in charge."

"Does Fleet Commander Hutchinson know about this, change?"

"Not exactly, I expect him to side with the Captain."

"Ok, I'm in, just because it will irritate both of them."

"Can I expect your complete loyalty now? Or do I have to worry about you attempting to escape again?"

"Humm, I won't be Captain, Or Pilot of Atlantis?"

"No."

"Deal!" Maria extending her four fingers and they shake hands in the customary fashion of the Lord Marshal. The Lord Marshal knowing Miss Kemp will allow him to transport to the surface, just to irritate the Captain.

"Perhaps your defiance will work for me for once. Guards! Release the little minks."

The security guard looks angrily at Maria as he removes her restraints. Rubbing at the restraint locations as she exit's the door.

"I will apologize for taking so long. I had to be sure you would make the right decision."

"I had a choice?" She snapped back. Turning around suddenly "Should I put you back?"

"No! I made the decision."

"Perhaps I should have put you in there a long time ago."

A long walk down the corridor leads them to the Flight Deck, And to the office of Fleet Commander Hutchinson.

"Fleet!"

"Yes Lord Marshal, come to see the inspec..."

"No. I came to lead them."

"I can't allow that Lord Marshal."

"Is that your, official, stance?"

"Yes."

"You're relieved. Miss Kemp, take immediate Command of the Flight Deck."

"Aye, aye, Lord Marshal" She reaches over and removes the Fleet Commander symbol from Mr. Hutchinson's uniform and moves into the Command position.

"Now stand aside, I have a mission to lead."

"Can't allow that Lord Marshal!" demands Miss Kemp.

"What in tarnation is going on around here?" He roars out.

"Regulations are regulations Lord Marshal."

The shuttle door closes just a few meters away and begins the launch sequence.

"I wrote those regulations Miss Kemp and I can supersede them!"

"Then I need not remind you that no flag Officer..."

"Without armed escort, I know! Will you assign me an armed escort?"

"Absolutely"

And a second team of security personnel are requested.

"Where is that shuttle going?" Shouts Captain Daxis as she sees it departing in the view screen.

"To the surface."

"I ordered that shuttle grounded! Where is Fleet Commander Hutchinson?"

"No need to shout Captain. The Lord Marshal is still standing here."

"He is not aboard the shuttle then."

"No Captain." Maria answered directly.

"Inform Fleet Commander Hutchinson I owe him thanks."

"Ok, but Mr. Hutchinson is no longer in Command of the fleet."

"Who is in command then, where is Fleet Commander Hutchinson?"

Fleet Commander Maria Kemp, at your service Captain" Maria answered sneering at Mr. Hutchinson.

Her fists clenched, stammering, Izzy heads for the exit.

"OOH! That does it, I am going to deal with that little traitor personally!"

"Captain!" Shouts Mr. Silber. "Now is not the time, we have no idea what is going on down there on the planet, there is no Com, no ships present and not a single signal. You need to be here! Your personal issues with Miss Kemp will have to wait."

"Your right Mr. Silber, Ship first, tralk later. I knew he wouldn't allow her to leave!"

"Captain." comes a voice from the shuttle craft. "The place is deserted. Not a single life form present."

A sudden flash in the view screen and the Stallag-21 station disappears in a violent explosion. Silence fills the room as the shock wave hit's the unsuspecting Atlantis.

The crew on the Flight Deck are surprised as the shock waves shake the Flight Deck; sending the shuttle positioned by the entrance, slamming

276

into the entrance.

"Fleet! Where is the Lord Marshal?" the concerned voice of the Captain, breaks in as the wave passes.

"Just a moment Captain."

"The Impact has slammed the shuttle against the doorway! I believe the Lord Marshal is inside." Replied Maria as she races to the doorway. The impact has sent Miss Kemp and Mr. Hutchinson careening into the corridor.

"Lord Marshal! Are you alright?" Maria shouts out as she clambers over the wreckage.

"I'm Ok, better protected in here than you were out there." He replied "Besides, I'm indestructible.

"Of course you are" Maria looking down over him from outside the shuttle door.

"And I suppose your arm is supposed to look like that?"

"Well that's interesting, I guess I do bend sometimes." laughing until he moves it and the pain shoots through.

"Where's a corpsman!" Shouts Maria "guess the Doctor is going to get that bio-scan after all."

"Hell no just a scratch, don't just stand there, help me up."

"Nope, a little pain might do you some good."

"Worked for you didn't it?" He said to Maria laughing as she reached to help him.

"Fleet Commander, report immediately! Where is the Lord Marshal?"

"Keep your diaper on he's here. He is damaged, but will survive. The rest of us are fine, thanks for asking." She returned sarcastically.

"Is he hurt bad?" Captain Daxis asked concerned.

"He'll survive, no open seats as Lord Marshal yet. I am sending him to the Infirmary."

"Guess the Doctor will get that bio-scan after all then."

"Hell no, I suppose the two of you think

277

this is funny."

"Yup." they say in unison.

"Imagine that" Says Mr. Hutchinson "It took the destruction of a shuttle and an injury to the Supreme Commander before those two would agree on something."

"Will miracles never follow, Captain what happened?"

"The Stallag-21 Station just exploded."

"I'll be there shortly Captain."

"Not until you report to the Infirmary" Replied Maria.

"I agree" Added Izzy "Nothing else going on up here until we ascertaining just what happened."

"Fine."

"Shuttle Commander, Shuttle Commander, respond."

"No answer. I'm certain the shuttle was destroyed. It didn't have adequate shields to protect against that blast."

"I know Mr. Silber, I am a Master Engineer. I had to try.
Can you determine what happened down there?"

"We won't know until a second investigation team can investigate the rubble. If I had to guess…"

"So guess already!"

"A proximity bomb, activated when the Com was initiated."

"Large enough to destroy a planet?" questioned Izzy.

"Apparently; question is, why?"

CHAPTER 48

"I Will Not Do It!" shouts the Lord Marshal.

"I need the bio-scan so I know how to repair the damage." the Doctor fumbling with the bio-scanner.

"What kind of Doctor doesn't know how to set a fractured bone?" Squirming like an infant.

"A Doctor who has no idea the anatomy of a stubborn Lord Marshal, that's who."

"Never Mind then. Just put a splint on it."

"What is a splint?" He asked Maria as she blocked the doorway.

"Two or three pieces of hard material to lie alongside a broken area to give it support while the broken area repairs itself." She quoted an earlier description.

"You must be joking?" asked Dr. Reinquist.

"Hurry up! I have things to do." Meanwhile, Maria is standing blocking the exit trying not to laugh at the Lord Marshals blatant attempt to avoid a simple bio-scan.

"Fleet Commander to the Flight Deck" the voice of Atlantis disrupts the proceedings.

"Gotta go Lord Marshal, good luck avoiding that bio-scan this time" Laughing she heads out into the corridor.

"Yeah, yeah, yeah," He gestures her away.

Once Mr. Reinquist has irritated him enough he returns to the bridge. Izzy is again asking why they would destroy the whole planet.

"I'll tell you why Captain. The Mining Guild and Stallag Foundation were both counting on me being on that planet. Or at least in the shuttle close enough to be killed by the explosion.

"You think it was planned?" asked Mr. Putin.

"I did make a point of it that I would be going to Stallag-21."

"And if you were killed?" asked Izzy.

"Then a new Lord Marshal would have to be chosen. One the Stallag Foundation and the Mining Guild could control."

"Then things would return to normal, or t least back to what they called normal" Added Mr. Donovan.

"Or get worse." interjected Mr. Putin.

"And since you were not killed, what now?"

"The Stallag Foundation just accuses me of destroying another one of their planets out of hand."

"And without proof otherwise, or anyone to verify your claims, you have no defense."

"Exactly."

"Do you suppose the proof is hidden somewhere like the Stallag-24 records?"

"Doubt it if there was proof, it was most likely destroyed with the Stallag."

"They did know we were coming with enough time to sabotage a Facility."

"But why were there no ships present?" asked Mr. Rays.

"No witnesses." answered Izzy coldly.

"Wouldn't they want witnesses to confirm our arrival here?" asked Mr. Rays.

"Witnesses can be paid to say anything. I'm sure there is a witness ship here somewhere" Returned the Lord Marshal looking out the view screen "They already knew we were on our way here. I was afraid of walking into a trap instead I flew right into one, both feet first."

"We all did Lord Marshal" Replied Izzy shaking her head back and forth.

"So is it back to voided space?" asked Mr. Rays.

"No, we have some other matters to attend to first."

"You are right about that." remarked Izzy, remembering her threat to Miss Kemp.

"Do you have something else in mind Captain?"

"Maria Kemp! Care to explain, Lord Marshal." Izzy standing cross armed and her index finger tapping her sleeve.

"Yes, I imagine that will require a bit of explanation."

"What is it about her that makes her so important to you?"

"Captain, there isn't much more we can do here. Recall the investigation team and set course for New Folden City."

"Your avoiding my question."

"I'll explain it to you on the way to New Folden City and, Mr. Silber.

"Yes Sir?"

"Keep a watchful eye out for ships, mines, or any other device that could catch us by surprise."

"Aye, aye, Sir lesson learned."
During the long flight back to New Folden City the Lord Marshal explained his intentions towards Master Pilot Maria Kemp. He had her, undivided, attention.

"Oh, I see." Replied Izzy relieved. "So that's why you are so attached to her, all this time I thought it was something else" Turning her blushing face away; trying to avoid his tense stare. A stare until now, she thought she was ready for. Her jealous bone relaxing slightly, but still stirred.

"Captain Izzabella Daxis. You have made your intentions perfectly clear. And I have done nothing to discourage them. So, I believe it might be alright for you to curb your competitiveness towards Miss Kemp."

"Maybe, it has been with me ever since we met on Grennich II."

"That must have been terribly frustrating for you."

"Words cannot convey, even more so with that Minks Maria Kemp skulking around you all the time."

"Like it or not, she is here."

"I don't! But, since she is so important to you I won't throw her out an airlock any time soon."

"Do what?" He asked surprised at her comment.

"Oh, something I said on the bridge a while ago that might get taken out of context if, when, it gets back to you."

"Oh! Sure. When I'm injured, you agree. Otherwise its back to battle."

"More or less, best I will do for now" Both laughing.

CHAPTER 49

"Lord Marshal! I just received a Com from a long range personal Com unit and…"

"And what?"

"It's Angel."

Racing over to the Com "Angel?"

"Yes Sir. She is asking why we are attacking Pixo-Linko again."

"Why are we attacking again?"

"We're not attacking, who's attacking?" shouting into the Com.

"Undetermined, she believes it's us."

"How is she able to send a signal? We destroyed all the Com satellites."

"Before she left for Pixo-Linko I gave her one of your long range personal Com units." replied Mr. Wilder. "It must be linking up with one of the satellites we left in orbit."

"Can we re re-establish a link Mr. Wilder?"

"Impossible, receiving only."

"Lord Marshal! This is Regent Angel." Her voice shattered and disrupted by weapons fire in the back ground. "Why are you attacking us again?" We have no defenses left, we have only moderate power outputs; and I have been informed they too will fail! Please, stop your attack!"

"We are not attacking you, Regent!"

"She can't hear you Sir!"

"Pilot!"

"En-route, changing course now!"

"Captain! Contact…"

"Maximum velocity plotted."

"Mr. Silber!"

"I'm trying to determine what is attacking them with the optics of the closest satellite in range."

"Anything?"

"Not yet. I'll keep listening."

The Atlantis turns around and heads back to Pixo-Linko at an estimated 23 times the speed of light. There are places in space where the laws of speed and time are stretched to mathematical impossibilities. Places where the flow of space is limitless.

"Mr. Wilder send out a Com on all frequencies, all languages."

"The message?"

"Get to Pixo-Linko, save Angel! Make it a personal request of the Lord Marshal."

"Anything else?"

"Defend, that, planet!"

CHAPTER 50

"I want that planet destroyed; nothing remaining, walking, flying, or crawling!"

"Yes Mrs. Delallo."

"Keep hitting it until it explodes! Just like Stallag-24 and Stallag-21stations. The Lord Marshal will suffer for killing my mate! Let's see how he likes it!" Her flipper defiantly held in contempt of the Lord Marshal.

"Speaking of mates, where is the Lord Marshal's abomination anyway?"

"She is down there somewhere. Shall we send search teams down there to search for her?"

"Yes! And keep firing until someone reports a large pile of Red Goo!"
Surrounding Pixo-Linko are dozens of Rellock ships. Rellocks are an arachnid type of life form, ocular sight, multiple appendages, a solid exterior. Very aggressive in a fight and excellent ship builders but are remarkably difficult to kill and are often dark green in color with a strong oceanic scent.

 The relentless bombardment of Pixo-Linko continues as they destroy the last of the remaining cities.

"Mr. Rays can't this ship go any faster? Atlantis!"

"No Lord Marshal, we are stretching the boundaries of the output system already."

"Mr. Wilder what are all the flashes there?" pointing to the dozen or so spots on the spatial monitor.

"They are other ships entering the outer range of the sensors. They are all heading for Pixo-Linko."

"Any idea who is attacking them yet?" He stands over him impatiently.

"Lord Marshal, patients please."
He slumps heavily on Mr. Silber's console. Bumping his recently broken arm, he winces Placing his other hand over his face he begins to sob.

Captain Daxis comes over to his side and kneels down beside him.

"I'm sure she will be alright Lord Marshal. She has spent her whole life in one hiding place or another. She is someplace safe."

"I know Captain. But, it's all my fault she is in danger again."

"No! She chose to return to Pixo-Linko. It is her destiny to change the destiny of her species."

"Only because I convinced her it was the right thing to do. Now I may have killed her same as leaving her on Stallag-24."

"I don't believe that and neither do you!" Izzy stands up and pokes him. "It wasn't until I came aboard this ship that I believed in destiny! I always believed I controlled my fate. I think differently now. And so does everyone else here. Now I understand your fear, your frustration. But you don't know what is going on down on that planet surface. We know she is still alive. Now let's go and find her!"

"Right!" returning to his feet "You are Captain alright."

"And don't you forget it either!" smiling at him now.

Fleet Commander Kemp report!"

"Kemp here Captain."

"The moment we reach launch distance I want everything we have on this ship that flies to begin searching for the Lord Marshals mate.

"And the ships attacking the planet?"

"Re-enforcements are steadily arriving as we speak. We will let them handle the ships. Our priority is Regent Angel.

"Understood Captain; Mr. Hutchinson?"

"Yes Fleet Commander? Is there is something I can do for you?" his, sarcasm evident as he turns towards Miss Kemp.

"Would you be interested in assisting me in arranging the Flight Deck?" She asks with her sweetest voice.

"This has been a most interesting day. Imagine, Maria Kemp, asking me for my help."

286

CHAPTER 51

"Lieutenant, any luck killing that abomination yet?" asked Courpa Delallo.

"No Madame Courpa we are sending out the drones now." his squiggly, cowardly, response berating him.

"I don't want to hear about it by remote! Send in troops!"

"Madame Courpa, we don't have the troops…"

"I said send in the troops!" She shouted as the Rellock soldier cowered before her.

"Yes Madame."

"I don't care if it takes every troop we have. I want that abomination killed before the planet explodes!"

"And what about the Atlantis Madame, it will come to her rescue."

"I'm counting on it lieutenant."
The skies continue to light up from explosions as planet seekers hit the already leveled cities and forests. Pixo-Linko, a once lush, tropical planet is nothing more than ash.

"Angel!" Shouts Gork. "Come this way! Found good hiding spot.

"Coming Gork!" Angel grabbing a small sprite hiding in the ashes near her enters a small cavern in the hill.

"Why are they attacking us again?" She cries out over the explosions.

"Gork! In here!"

"Gork don't hide."

"Are they attacking us because of you?" cried the sprite looking into Angels wide eyes.

"I do believe so young one." covering her with her wings.

"Gork know for sure it not Lord Marshal."

"How can you be so sure?" Angel shouts out.

"Weapons impacts in group of six.

"Rellocks?" Angel stutters.

287

"Support the Stallag Federation since it started."

"So that is what this is all about. But that doesn't make any sense. The Pixie civilization didn't have anything to do with the destruction of the Stallag Stations."

"The Lord Marshal did, you Lord Marshal's mate." What that?" Turning quickly around Gork hears the roar of an engine. Looking out to see what it is.

"Look like an Empire ship." As he is struck from behind by a scimitar weapon of a Rellock soldier

"Oh no!" Angel screams as the Rellock soldiers enter the small hiding place she and the sprite are occupying.

"fn as;ofan;vnona8n9q438vq3pvni {Found you filth!} was the words coming from the translation device around its neck.
Once again Angel finds herself bound and gagged. Being carried to yet another place, perhaps for more interrogations. Just when she thought it was a distant memory. One thing is different now. Now she has a reason to fight. Not just for herself, she knows the Lord Marshal will come for her.

Did he receive the signal? Certainly he will come for her. After all he crossed the stars for her once. Should she try to escape or just wait? This time she is not alone. She has an ally with Gork. He will not allow anyone to harm her. He will die first.

After a seemingly endless trip they are brought to a small room. Once there they are fitted with restraints then suspended from a high ceiling by their hands and waist.

"Lord Marshal, we are in range of Pixo-Linko. They are being attacked by a fleet of Rellock ships."

"Number Mr. Wilder?"

"Twelve to be sure."

"Alert Fleet Commander Kemp to release the fleet."

288

"Fleet Commander Kemp! Deploy the fleet!" Commanded Izzy.

And like a black plague the Atlantis fleet swept through the space and entered the upper atmosphere of Pixo-Linko. The Rellock fighters dropping out of the sky like rain as the Atlantis Renegade I fighters annihilate them.

"Thank you Fleet Commander." replied Izzy.

"Had good help from Mr. Hutchinson too Captain. I couldn't have done it without him" Maria smiling at him as she slumps back into her chair.

Meanwhile, as this is going on comes a fleet of ships from "cracked space". Ship after ship enter the Pixo-Linko space all coming to the call of the Lord Marshal. The Rellock ships begin to falter as the sheer numbers begin to overwhelm them.

"Lord Marshal, should we begin attacking the Rellock ships?" asked Mr. Silber.

"No. Let the others handle them. Focus our attention on the search for Angel and Gork."

"Well, well, well. If it isn't our fraudulent Regent Angel Abbicus" a voice echoing from the darkness.

"Who are you and what do you want with me?" She shouts into the darkness where the voice came from.

"The Lord Marshal has been contacted and is coming for me and you will pay for this!"

"Silence! Abominations like you should have been destroyed at birth you have no right to speak! And I do hope you speak the truth I hope the Lord Marshal is coming, in fact, I'm counting on it!"

"Why have you attacked Pixo-Linko?"

"Isn't it obvious?" asked Mrs. Delallo.

"Isn't what obvious?" shouted Angel pulling at her restraints.

"Don't even try breaking those restraints. They are Rellock webbing. They are unbreakable. Not even your Gork slave could break them."

"He's no slave! And how do you know me, who are you? Show yourself coward!"
Without further prompting Mrs. Delallo steps into the small lighted area.

"Well! What are you and what do you want with us?" Angel demands.
As she approaches Gork he awakens and is just centimeters from her face.

"Ah, the mighty Gork is awake! Allow me to introduce myself. I am Ezra Delallo; Courpa of the Medical Guild, after your Lord Marshal killed my mate."

"Your mate was a traitor and a murderer!" snapped Angel "He got what he deserved!"

"That might be true. But it wasn't for him to decide. Now I will decide whether to kill you or not so he can understand."
Walking closer to Gork are two Rellock soldiers holding scimitars. {A large hand held cannon} she directs the soldiers to take aim at Gork. He just hangs there, staring at Mrs. Delallo. No sense of fear, motionless.

"Let me show you the face of revenge!"
As the weapon fires, a large, flat, projectile exit's the weapon and penetrates the powerful chest of the monster called Gork expelling his entrails through a gaping hole out his back. He droops down and gasps his last breath as his eyes close for the last time. His pain and suffering forever ended.

"No!" Cries out Angel. Her greatest fears all come rushing back. Desperately she searches the dark hall for the sound of her mate, where is he?" She must wait. The nightmare of the Stallag interrogations come back in a wave of fear as she hears nothing but the sound of Gork's blood dripping on the floor below. Her hearts racing with fear she waits.

"And now for you!" turning her attention towards Angel she approaches and directs the other Rellock soldier to take aim.

"An abomination that should never have been born, just look at the trouble you have caused!"

And once again Mrs. Delallo gives the order to pull the trigger. Angel hears the sound of the scimitar, she feels the impact of the weapon. And just like her protector Gork, Angel dies without a sound. Her hearts fall to the floor. Her massive wings collapse, hanging loosely at her sides, her eyes go glossy, and her last breath escapes.

"It's done!" replies Mrs. Delallo "Return to your stations, this isn't finished yet."
Returning to the bridge of the Volstus, Mrs. Delallo takes the Command chair.

"Lieutenant, take us out of here!"

"Impossible, we are surrounded by an armada of Empire ships, and the Atlantis just arrived!"

"So, the Lord Marshal is here is he? Well he's too late! I can't wait to see the expression of grief on his puny, pink face when he learns his, mate is dead."

"He is going to skin you alive Madame Courpa."

"No matter I win!"

"What about the rest of us Madame Courpa? He will likely kill us as well. Where will it end?" asked Lieutenant Nacian Largoza, the Com officer aboard the Volstus.

"Com, send a transmission to the Atlantis tell him I have his precious Angel here."

"Attention rouge ship Atlantis! This is Nacian F. Largoza of the Rellock ship Volstus, we have your Angel."

"Lord Marshal! The Rellock ship Volstus claims to have Angel!"

"What?" shouts the Lord Marshal rushing over to the Com console.

"There is a Rellock ship claiming to have Angel. They are requesting an audience with you."

"Another trap" Replied Izzy

"Are they stating any demands?"

"No."

"Send them a communication. I will be right there."

"Lord Marshal it's a trap!"

291

"Of course it is Captain. If I don't return the Atlantis is yours."

"Lord Marshal! You can't..."

"Angel is over there. I have to."

"Mr. Wilder, get a shuttle ready.

"Mr. Wilder, I don't care what it takes, you and Mr. Silber safeguard that shuttle." Izzy demands.

"It is done."

The Lord Marshal is running through the corridors pushing everyone out of his way as he enters the elevator.

"Lord Marshal." the voice from everywhere.

"Yes Atlantis what is it?"

"I hope your Angel is alright."

"Me too thanks for your concern."

"But, what if she isn't?"

The Lord Marshal leaves the elevator without answering the question which is burning in his heart too.

"Lord Marshal, you know the policy here. No flag officer leaves this ship without armed escort" As Maria stands between him and the shuttle door.

"Miss Kemp Angel is over there!"

"You know it's a trap."

"Yes. And if I don't return..."

"Don't speak of such a thing. You said you were indestructible, prove it!" A small tear in her left eye trickles down across her cheek.

"If I don't return I have appointed you Lord Marshal. It has always been my intention for you to one day replace me. I have been planning it ever since I first encountered you on New Folden City. I know it's a terrible burden to undertake. You have the skills, determination, and the stubbornness not to be manipulated by anyone. You will make a formidable Lord Marshal. My time is about over. I have to go."

Maria steps out of his way and assigns two soldiers to assist him. They board the shuttle and are soon in the Rellock ship.

Once aboard the Rellock ship he heads strait towards what should be the bridge. However, en-route he is intercepted by a small, Rellock child.

"Are you the Lord Marshal?"

"Yes! Where is the bridge?" He Commands.

"I am Sitzig Delallo, Ryvac Delallo was my father, and Ezra Delallo is my mother."

"And what concern of that is mine?"

"You must come with me Lord Marshal" taking his hand pulling him with her vice like claw.

"All this has to stop."

"What must stop?" Scoffing at her.

"All this death, the war, the hate."

"This way please."

Through the dirty, oceanic smell of the hallways the Rellock child leads him to a smaller doorway. Entering the room he is horrified as in the center of the room is Angel. Hanging from her wrists and waist; her hearts lying on the floor in a pool of yellow blood, her chest a gaping hole. Her beautiful wings drooped behind her, lifeless.

He explodes across the room and attempts to life her body from the burden of the restraints. Ezra Delallo presses a console and her lifeless body falls into his arms. Screaming like a scalded cat the Lord Marshal cries out holding his face next to hers he begins crying uncontrollable.

"Lord Marshal. I have heard the whole story from when you first came to Dorius II until this rotation. It took me many cycles to compile all the information but I do believe I understand the whole story."

"So what does it matter now?" His voice trembling as he holds her to him. "Angel, My Angel is gone. It isn't supposed to end like this."

"Things never end the way we want them to. But, they can end. Things have to."

"Things have gotten too far out of control."

"What control?" asked Ezra Delallo. My mother is responsible for this, I must end it, we must end it."

293

"How can it end with atrocities like this! She committed no crime; she had nothing to do with the Stallag Foundations destruction, or your family! It took me centuries to find her, now she is gone. The most precious thing in the universe to me is gone, why should I care now what happens?"

"You loved her?"

"Liked no other."

"And I love my father and mother. But you killed my father and will most likely kill my mother.

"And so I shall kill your mother!"

"And it will never end."

"How will not, killing your mother end anything?" He snaps at her.

"It won't stop anything by itself. But together we can stop the war, here and now! My mother is Courpa of the Medical Guild after you, killed my father! But she has committed a horrific crime against the principals of the Guild and Council laws. Her actions have endangered hundreds, thousands of citizens of the Empire for her own revenge. She has been forced to resign. And in accordance with law, I am now Courpa of the Medical Guild!"

"So."

"I will stop the Rellock soldiers, and recall the warships. Will you?"

"But you are just a child."

"I am Courpa Sitzig Delallo my age is unimportant."

"And what of your mother?"

"She has been taken into custody by my forces. She will stand trial within the Guild and answer for her crimes."

"And the Rellock ships attacking Pixo-Linko?"

"Recalled!"

"Has the fighting stopped then?" stammering as he rises to his feet with Angel across his arms. Sitzig picks up her hearts and places them inside her open chest as a well of tears flow from the eyes of the Lord Marshal. They

294

leave the small room together. Entering the bridge of the Rellock ship the entire Command crew gasp as the Lord Marshal carries the lifeless body of Angel before the view screen.

"Com, open a channel, all frequencies, all ships"

Sitzig, waves an appendage in approval.

"Do you have such capabilities?" He asked subdued.

"Aye Lord Marshal."

"Attention all ships. All fleets. This is the Lord Marshal. Angel is dead. Killed by Ezra Delallo; the ascended Courpa of the Medical Guild, she was killed as revenge for me killing Ryvac Delallo, her mate. It was my fault. This war was my fault. I left my home world centuries before because war took from me all that mattered. And now it has happened again.

"I officially stand down as Lord Marshal. I no longer have the capacity to rule as Lord Marshal. I have been compromised by grief. I will appoint Josh Donovan as Fleet Commander and appoint Master Pilot Maria Kemp to replace me as the new Lord Marshal of the Empire.

"The regulations are written on Genoa. I have failed. And my Angel has paid the price. I can only ask that this be a lesson to us all of the true cost of war. Proof of what happens when corruption and dictatorship collide. As Sitzig Delallo has stated, it must end here. It will end here. Please accept my formal resignation at this date and time effective immediately."

With all eyes on the Lord Marshal, he leaves the bridge of the Ikared. Returning to the shuttle, he returns to Atlantis shuttle docking bay. The doors open and Maria is standing there her eyes flowing with tears.

"Oh No!" She cries out as he approaches. Overcome with despair, Doug Abbicus begins to weep uncontrollably, breaking down on the Flight Deck, everyone surrounding him as he tries to recover. Word spreads quickly through the ship. In stitches the whole of the ship is aware of the death of Angel.

"Miss Kemp." He whispers softly his voice shaking.

"Yes Lord Marshal?"

"Gork's body is still over there. Will you contact Sitzig Delallo and ask for permission to recover him?"

"Of Course Lord Mar…"

"I'm not Lord Marshal anymore. Miss Kemp, you are effective immediately."

"Sir, we should get her into the infirmary as soon as possible." replied Dr. Reinquist.

"I know."

Meanwhile on the bridge of the Atlantis.

"Captain! The Rellock ships are leaving!"

"Just let them go Mr. Silber." replied Izzy "I think there has been enough death."

"What do we do now?" Asked Mr. Rays.

"Back to Dorius II, where it all began."

"It would be a more appropriate place for it to end."

"Why not return to Genoa? It is the location of the Great Council. Why not return there?" asked Mr. Wilder.

"The Great Council has been dissolved remember, and is to be recreated aboard this ship. We will return to New Folden City. Everyone knows the Lord Marshal has a particular attachment to that city. We will return there." Commanded Izzy.

As quickly as the ships appeared around Pixo-Linko they also disappeared. Maria Kemp returns to the Flight Control room as Mr. Hutchinson is busy returning ships to their docking locations.

"Exiting is easy it's putting them all back again that is hard."

"Well Mr. Hutchinson there is nobody better suited for the task than you."

"And you had better remember that, Lord Marshal Kemp."

"Are you still interested in Commanding the Flight Deck on New Folden City? Or can I

296

offer you the position here on Atlantis?"

"I do believe I have discovered my true destiny, I will remain here."

"Has anyone informed the Captain of the Lord…Mr. Abbicus's return?"

"I believe everyone knows."

"I had better go and make sure."

"Is that a good idea?"

"Better from me, than from a Pilot in the corridor."

Entering the bridge with an air of silence Lord Marshal Kemp approaches the Com.

"I suppose you are here to gloat." Izzy snaps as she approaches.

"No Captain. This is not the time for our differences to be an issue Angel is dead. I just wanted to see how everyone is taking the news."

"Horrified is the best description. Any idea what the former, Lord Marshal wants to do?"

"I'm sure he is not in a sound state of mind. Want my advise?"

"NO"

"What are we going to do then?" asked Lord Marshal Kemp.

"We are returning to Dorius II. All the delegates of the Great Council will be asked to reconvene there, seemed appropriate."

"It was rumored around the Great Council before it was disbanded that Angel was to become the first Empress of the Galactic Empire" Replied Mr. Wilder.

"I heard that rumor too. I'm sure the Delegates will want to offer their sympathies."

"So we go back to Dorius II then." And the Atlantis disappears from Pixo-Linko space.

Returning to his quarters Doug Abbicus crawls into his bed and begins to weep. He remains there for the whole return trip to Dorius II unwilling to find the strength to open the door.

"We are approaching Dorius II Captain."

"I've never seen so many ships here before."

Surrounding Dorius II and all the space around it to

297

the next planet are ships from every corner of the Empire. Row after row of Courpa ships, Fleet and passenger class ships stuffed in between the larger ships. Hundreds of unidentified, non- sanctioned ships line the spaces between.

"Are they all ambassadorial ships Captain?"

"Not all. Everyone knows what has happened now." replied Izzy staring out the view screen.

"Mr. Rays." Izzy says quietly as she stares at the incalculable amount of ships. "Find us a place to park."

"I believe we have a reserved place." As the Atlantis makes final approach an escort of Renegade I ships direct them to a close orbit of Dorius II.

"New Folden City this is Communications officer John Wilder of the Empire Flagship Atlantis."

"Greetings and welcome Mr. Wilder welcome home." comes the gentle voice of the Comm officer of New Folden City.

"We were wondering if we would be welcome here after all that has happened."

"The events that have preceded your arrival were not only inevitable but predictable as well. No one person is to be held accountable, or responsible. All will be held responsible once the Great Council has re-convened under the leadership of Lord Marshal Kemp. Until then, all are welcome."

"How long has the Great Council been aware of such things?" asked Captain Daxis.

"The Stallag-21 Facility was an obvious and predictable target. We have been monitoring it for quite some time. We also know it was destroyed by Ezra Delallo and the Medical Guild and not the Former Lord Marshal. All appropriate actions were taken to prevent loss of life."

"Then why wasn't something done to prevent the death of Angel and Gork?" Izzy snapped at Mr. Apgar.

"It was not anticipated that the Courpa Ezra Delallo would capture Angel."

"Is there going to be a formal investigation into who are responsible?"

"On going Miss Daxis Many have been captured, others are being tracked as we speak."

"And the Corporations involved?"

"The Stallag Federation, Mining Guild, and the Medical Guild have all had their charters revoked and several more are under strict scrutiny. They will not be re issued until all corruption has been identified and eradicated."

"I will be answering for my crimes as well." the solemn voice from behind Lord Marshal Kemp is that of Douglass Abbicus. "I too must stand before the Great Council."

"Your presence will be expected, Mr. Abbicus."

Once in orbit the Command crew of the Atlantis return to the bio-dome of New Folden City.

"Home again. Almost" Douglass Abbicus interjects as he enters the huge doors of the center city entrance. To their surprise they are met with thunderous roars of cheers and applause from the city below.

Cautious, and surprised, the former Lord Marshal, Izzabella Daxis, Fleet Commander Hutchinson and Lord Marshal Kemp step out onto the platform overlooking the city.

The streets and ally ways are jammed packed. Peasants beside Royalty, everyone waiting to see what the Former Lord Marshal, and the new Lord Marshal are going to do.

CHAPTER 52
To End A Century

"You all know why I am here! Everyone knows much of what I had to do had to remain a secret. Now you all know why; my intentions were of the noblest, with the events of the various Courpa's, some of you may understand, some may not. No form of Government is without Corruption, no matter what the intent."

"No individual given tremendous power and responsibility is beyond reproach. Sometimes it takes just one person to expose this, even fewer to eradicate it. I can't change what has happened. Many have suffered at my hands. I too turned a blind eye to the corruption in the various Courpa's when it benefited my needs. I believed it was for the betterment of all of us. I was wrong."

"This is why the Great Council was created in the first place; so that no individual would have the power to control the lives of others without consultation, debate, and accountability. However, corruption did happen. And many died. Much of this is my fault. I abolished the previous Great Council and asked that new representatives be chosen by the citizens of each civilization."

"New faces, new minds, new leadership. I built this ship so that the Great Council can travel from one civilization to another so that no Courpa would have a better advantage to influence the Council than any other."

"I have chosen Master Pilot Maria Kemp to replace me as Lord Marshal; Her father, a well known Councilmember, and her mother, a Royal leader of Dorius I, she will serve you well.

"Will the Stallag Foundation, Mining Guild and Medical Guild be dissolved then?" asked a member of the crowd.

"They will be re-established under new Leadership and new Regulations of the Great Council."

"How are we expected to keep the same thing from happening again? You said it happened before, you weren't able to stop it."

"Conflict met with debate, resulting in communication, ending in accountability. We all make mistakes. It's how we learn. It's how we correct those mistakes that help us evolve."

"And those responsible?"

"they must and will be held accountable. And so shall I."

Roars of cheers, and scoffs of denial echo across the bio-dome floor.

"Well Lord Marshal Kemp. I hope you wore your best uniform, time to take Command."

"Why are they cheering?" Asked Izzy confused. With everything you have done."

"Like What?"

"You defied and deceived the Great Council, destroyed two Stallag Facilities, attacked the fleet, destroyed two fleet ships, and dissolved the Great Council that you founded."

"Only one Stallag!"

"You started a revolution on another world; destroyed that world, and instilled a dictator that was a former prisoner, and this was all done under the title of Lord Marshal. And yet here they are all cheering you."

"Not all Captain, being the instrument of change is never an easy task, especially when the change comes to a concept you yourself conceived. But, it is how progress is made."

"So where do we, go from here Lor… What do I call you now anyway?" asked Izzy with her flirtatious eye.

"My name, is Douglass Abbicus, Captain, and where do we go? To the stars Izzy to the stars."